## About the author

Martin Howe is a journalist who has worked for the BBC, Channel 4 and a news agency in Washington DC. Writing literary fiction is his escape from the constraints of factual news. Coming Down is his third novel.

mbhowe.com
Facebook.com/MartinHoweAuthor
Twitter: @_MartinHowe
Instagram: @martin.howe.925

# Also by the author

*White Linen*
*The Man in the Street*

# COMING DOWN

Martin Howe

Copyright © 2021 Martin Howe

The moral right of the author has been asserted.

Apart from any fair dealing for the purposes of research or private study, or criticism or review, as permitted under the Copyright, Designs and Patents Act 1988, this publication may only be reproduced, stored or transmitted, in any form or by any means, with the prior permission in writing of the publishers, or in the case of reprographic reproduction in accordance with the terms of licences issued by the Copyright Licensing Agency. Enquiries concerning reproduction outside those terms should be sent to the publishers.

This is a work of fiction. Names, characters, businesses, places, events and incidents are either the products of the author's imagination or used in a fictitious manner. Any resemblance to actual persons, living or dead, or actual events is purely coincidental.

Matador
9 Priory Business Park,
Wistow Road, Kibworth Beauchamp,
Leicestershire. LE8 0RX
Tel: 0116 279 2299
Email: books@troubador.co.uk
Web: www.troubador.co.uk/matador
Twitter: @matadorbooks

ISBN 978 1800461 369

British Library Cataloguing in Publication Data.
A catalogue record for this book is available from the British Library.

Printed and bound in Great Britain by 4edge Limited
Typeset in 11pt Adobe Jenson Pro by Troubador Publishing Ltd, Leicester, UK

Matador is an imprint of Troubador Publishing Ltd

For Eleanor

**Eternity is not hard to imagine, believe me, just strap on a parachute, hitch a ride on a small plane, mainline smack, wait a beat before edging the rush with a boost of laughing gas ... then bale out.**

Stanley Overton, the Terminal Tour Archive (p. 127), Woadtown Press.
Published: 16/07/2001

## *Sky-divers are addicts — it's official!*

*They can't help themselves, it runs in the family. You may have thought that "Adrenaline Junkie" was just a phrase, but in fact it is very close to being a statement of fact. Sky-diving fanatics have the same genetic make-up as heroin addicts, so say researchers at a leading University in the UK. They have discovered that a gene closely associated with risk-taking behavior was also linked with the abuse of drugs. So susceptibility to addiction could be inherited.*

*Ambrose Wylie, Stenning Gazette, 14/7/02*

4,116 metres

# ST JAMES'S BIBLE

*Revelations 9:1*

And the fifth angel sounded, and I saw a star fall from heaven unto the earth: and to him was given the key of the bottomless pit.

And he opened the bottomless pit; and there arose smoke out of the pit, as the smoke of a great furnace; and the sun and the air were darkened by reason of the smoke of the pit.

*2 Peter 2:4*

For if God spared not the angels that sinned, but cast them down to hell, and delivered them into the chains of darkness, to be reserved unto judgement.

"God…"

The word was sucked from his body in a whirlwind of escaping air. Unable to breathe, he hung above the world in silence. The clatter and roar gone in an instant.

It never made any difference how often you did it – the jump, the leap, the plunge into the void – the feeling was always the same. Flowing, the body fluid, blood rushing, the stomach churning, juices roiling – a desire to open the sluice-gates, release the floodwaters, overtop the banks – saliva streaming from the corner of a gaping mouth, eyes liquid, sweat pooling in hidden folds, slick on surfaces exposed to the whipping gale, the face and hands, a liquid skin. A drop of moisture falling towards the earth. Raining down.

Senses drowned out. All he could recall was the final touch of his foot on the solid steel frame of the Beechcraft King Air 90 aircraft, the mechanical urgency of its engines vibrating through the thin sole of his Van Buren Blue Flash trainers. He was flying, once again he was flying. Physical laws, limitations and constraints, defied. Beliefs suspended. He could do anything. Yet the sensation lingered – the false memory of a limbless accident victim curling non-existent toes to shake off the persistent pins and needles – earthing his body. Bringing him back to his senses. He began to count out of habit.

"One thousand …"

Dropping tens of metres.

He didn't need to follow this exit protocol any more, he was vastly experienced, had logged many hours in the air, but did it anyway. Shouting out numbers, no one would hear.

"Two thousand …".

The sun was shining, there was barely a cloud in the sky, just smudges of chalk dust scattered in the atmosphere way below, blurring his view, tricking the eye. A blanket of haze cushioning all that was harsh and rugged, smoothing the edges, shading lines, comfortably tucking up a slumbering world. The curvature of the earth gave the merest hint of where solid met vapour – a faint line, a slight shift in the spectrum, a barely perceptible change of hue, shades of blue so similar as to be beyond definition – marking where it had to end. The landing.

Bird-like he flapped his arms as he spun slowly, somersaulting through the air. The plane above his head was yellow in silhouette against the blue encircling sky. Wings tipped with black, propeller a silent blur, the open door framing a pale shaven head looking down at him, an arm sinuously waving as if caught in the slipstream. Blinking he watched as it grew smaller and more distant, jerkily diminishing as if being sucked against its will into a heavenly vortex.

"Three thousand …"

The machine's passing left the sky unblemished, a shade of vivid turquoise so profoundly bright that he knew he could never forget it. Had never forgotten it.

Lying on his back in the dunes with Louise, her hand inside his shirt next to his skin, that very same turquoise sky an overbearing canopy, pressing down, hurting his eyes. Her head had been resting on his chest, her wispy blonde hair tickling his throat. She had been reluctant to leave the warmth of Flynn's bar, said it was too cold for the beach, but he had reminded her of the promise she had made the night before on the grassy bank beside the rushing Corrib River in Galway's inner harbour. And she had smiled and followed him outside.

That previous evening, drunk beyond his imagining, they had been discovered in the gloomy shadow of the Spanish Arch, lying together. He had been partially on top of her, his jeans around his thighs, she had been giggling her dress crumpled beneath them, tights and underwear around her ankles. They hadn't cared as the passersby laughed at their disheveled, intertwined bodies, just hugged each other more closely. Euphoric at being with a woman, he buried his head between her breasts and imagined that they were invisible. He couldn't believe that she had helped him through, massaging, cajoling, as keen as he was to make love in the damp evening air.

"Don't worry, I know a lovely place on the strand out in Salthill. We can go there tomorrow and do it all over again, I promise."

There would be no relief from the imprint of that turquoise sky. Its intensity banishing the darkness, every time he closed his eyes. Out of this blue, women would come back to him as he leapt time and again into the void. Blondes mainly and always with staring, azure eyes. There had been so many that he had no fear now. The exhilaration was everything, the thrill of the fall. He was an addict.

He had consumed drugs that came close to achieving that level of euphoria – on the good days, in the summer, in the sunshine – but not often. In his line of business he had the pick of the best – dope from the highlands of California and Lebanon, speed, ecstasy, cocaine – but none had given him the ultimate high, the final escape that he was looking for. Sky-diving, stoned out of your mind, seemed the only true path. Stepping into space over Torres Pines, Dinosaur or Sun Valley, he prayed every time that this would be it – the rapture. He had never given up hope.

From this height, on such an evening, it was possible to believe all was well. He could see forever, sense the totality of existence, feel the passing of time – glimpse the past, interrogate the future, live the present – that's why he loved free falling. There was nothing to stop him, no limit, save the feebleness of his vision, the failure of his imagination. There was a prospect of breaking away, of soaring upwards, of flying, of never coming down. The feeling was there every time he leapt, even if it rarely lasted. How he envied those he had seen at Elsinore diving from planes, circling like wraiths, shadows against the steely azure sky, criss-crossing the face of the sun, haunting the heavens, merely hitching a lift back to earth on the nearest plane when they were done. Or hurtling to earth in some spectacular fashion, performing extraordinary feats on the way down. He had never been good enough, had had to experience the buzz vicariously, using the skills he had to get close to them, his innate affability winning him friends among this enviable elite.

Surfer, Travis Berkovitz, was one he knew well. A maverick stoner attractive to X for his immense capacity to consume stimulants and remain cogent at the centre of the most vicious chemically induced maelstrom. Never deterred by the physically imbalanced consequences of many hung-over dawns he was a resolute companion in the search for the ultimate high. X had known him on and off for years, always linking up with him whenever he was in California. Offering up to Travis what he wanted most, an action facilitator – of drugs, women and adulation. For X it was thrill by association.

A master of waves, both on the ocean and in the air, Travis had dreams of performing the "double": sky-surfing from 3,600 metres then catching a mountainous wave off Laguna Beach, ending his epic journey in the arms of some beautiful bikini-clad girl waiting for him on the warm sands. He talked about it incessantly, insinuating his enthusiasm for the adventure into the consciousness of everyone partying with him. X was convinced and helped him design and build a special hybrid board. It was shorter and narrower than his usual surfboard, but still long enough and robust enough, they hoped, to allow him to pull of some dazzling "airs" as he surfed in; but longer and wider than the traditional sky-board, which had to be compact to prevent a disastrous entanglement with his parachute. This complex feat was not something you could easily practice and so Travis was meticulous in his planning. The Laguna Reefs beach webcam was permanently open on his laptop – the heavy breakers moving jerkily across the screen, streaming white spray, that faded in and out of view with each shot change, hazy phantoms zigzagging across the sand – he pored over the hourly surf reports giving details of the wave faces, the direction and period of the north and south swells, tides, rip currents, wind speed and direction, water temperature and finally cloud cover and the path and angle of the sun. It was weeks – X overstayed his visitor's visa so that he could be there at the end – before all the disparate elements converged into one glorious alignment. A Friday morning in the middle of September – the beaches would still be crowded and he would have his audience.

Travis was in the air within the hour, X was at the beach, video camera in hand, an eager witness to history in the making. It was going to be perfect. Travis launched himself from the plane on the mark at 3,600 metres, scorching across the sky, arms outstretched, board quivering beneath his feet. A shift of his weight and he was upside down surfing back in the opposite direction, then with a flexing of his legs he rotated through 360 degrees, once then twice, gathering speed as he did so until he was spinning rapidly, a mere blur to those watching below. Steadying himself he appeared to soar skywards in a graceful arc before straightening his body, his board pointing earthward, and pirouetting tightly he dropped like an arrow. Erratic movements alerted people to his apparent distress – his violent tugging at the ripcord had failed to deploy his main parachute and he struggled to open his reserve. For seconds he appeared to have recovered, the canopy burgeoning above his head, his descent slowing, then the chute collapsed in on itself, trailing behind Travis like the tail of a demonic Chinese fighting kite, as he twisted violently in the air, hurtling towards the ocean. On the strand a woman screamed. X was stunned. It looked as if his friend's board had become entangled in the lines of his reserve, rendering it useless, and that he would hit the glassy unforgiving surface of the sea head-first at terminal speed. This couldn't happen, but it did. Spume fountained high into the air, clearly visible from the shore, and the foaming waves closed over the distant diminutive figure.

"Fucking hell."

X shouted in disbelief. Then seconds later Travis bobbed to the surface, paddling furiously on his board, catching the next streaming breaker and streaking towards the water's edge hunched, poised and balanced.

Yellow wet suit glistening in the bright sunlight, dripping board under his arm, he sprinted up the beach, grinning inanely.

"Ace don't you think, caving in my fucking chute like that. Had you all going, I bet?"

He yelled, flinging his board on to the sand and embracing X.

"Fucking right, dude, you are the man."

X loved Travis, he was his best friend, yet the rivalry between them was intense, if one-sided. X always suspected he could never match Travis's courage or possess his vision, that he would never be good enough to perform the stunts he did. But this awareness didn't stop him trying and, in the meantime, his close association with this accomplished soloist of the airwaves was electrifying. The day of the "double" subtly changed the relationship, from then on X knew deep down that there was no possibility of transcendence, he would always be in thrall to Travis, unable to break free. The man's unorthodox success meant there was ultimately no chance for him to ever emerge from his shadow. All hope was gone. And this was where the danger lay for X, in the profound ability of life, at its peak, to let him down, to not deliver on the promise. He hadn't given up on the search or extinguished the yearning, but found himself again, as was often the case, experiencing the thrill vicariously.

Getting stoned was how he coped with his conflicted feelings. The night of the double he celebrated with Travis and his entourage at the Hideaway in Aliso Beach just off the Pacific Coast Highway, higher than he had ever been, only smoothing out the edges in the early hours of the morning by fucking scrawny Melissa in the Casino Motel – a room with a view of the pool. She had "flown" twice that day, was SoCal Sky-diving champion in her class, but barely spoke about it, just stared at him blankly with eyes the colour of the Californian sky she was the mistress of. Her nonchalance made him angry, she could fly, vanquish the natural order of things, play God and yet seemed to hold no contempt for mere earth-bound mortals like him. She should have been sleeping with angels and yet here she was with him. Cocaine and tequila, his ticket to fly. Slipping her gaze, he stared down at her naked spread-eagled body, sculpted with muscles clearly defined, sweat glistening on the ridges that circled her limbs and torso, the runnels in shadow. A Californian condor, wings outspread, tattooed on her tanned belly, gliding below a pierced navel, bridged by two interlinked silver rings. Their taste dully metallic on his tongue as he flicked them from side to side, a bitter contrast to the perfumed saltiness of her skin. A heavenly giggle. He would bury himself in her, discover the secret, it was the only way. Kissing her taut stomach, he left a trail of damp smears, snail-like, across her skin, until the moment when he paused for breath and she rapidly turned to lie on her front, her sleek body sliding through his grasp. Without hesitation he clasped her tightly from behind, moulding his body into hers, sensitive to every tremor and flexing of firm muscles. He imagined they were soaring now, her arms and legs outspread, he could almost believe it. A sinner like him would fall in love with an angel if that's what it took to fly.

"Four thousand ..."

# UNOFFICIAL WEST COAST SKY-DIVING HANDBOOK 2015 (UWCSH) (EXTRACT FROM)

### PUBLISHED ANNUALLY BY CAMARILLO BLUFF BOOKWORKS, CAMARILLO, CA.

### 5.2 FREE FALL LOVE MAKING

You've got it Dudes — this is where it gets interesting. The Mile High Club comes down to earth. Believe it, it happens — more often than you think! Beware it's not for the novice. However much you may be hitting on the guy/chick next to you on the way up, you need to have put in the drops to come on the way down. "A" Licence minimum. We all know "Free Fall" is sex, so let's make it real. USPA (United States Parachute Association) and FAA (Federal Aviation Authority) definitely not approved.

Where: anywhere the sun shines, the pilots are cool (most in our experience turn a blind eye), and the fliers welcome a come on. If you ask us SoCal is the place to be. Dudes from down here seem to hold all the UWCSH records (and make up all the rules).

When: whenever the sun is shining, your mom isn't watching and your High School teacher isn't on an AFF course.

How: you'll need that favorite flier of yours to have said yes (there are records for those going solo, but they are unofficial … really. No one here in the office will admit to anything) and the pilot will have to be hip to the action and that's it if it's just recreation you're after, then party on, but if you're seriously after a record you'll need an official UWCSH adjudicator to jump with you. (It's not that difficult to arrange, bro'. Go to the website: www.uwcsh.com/records and sign on. We'll be it touch pronto)

What: time is of the essence. Believe me you cats don't have long. You need to be up for it from the git-go. 12,000 feet is the official record altitude (you've already worked it out — it gives you about a minute. Start practicing now!). A couple of daredevil dudes have managed to do the deed from 10,000 feet. More on them later. There are two official categories: Gold and Silver standard.

Gold: Jump separately, get together, do the deed, land separately. Silver: Get together in the plane, jump a deux, get your rocks off, land separately. What could be easier than that?

(Hey: some dudes are getting into a third category — Free Style (we'll leave it to your imagination) — and want the Handbook to make it official. It's under consideration Guys. Never say never. What more can we do!)

Who: this year's Role of Honor (so far) in chronological order:

Gold: Steve Boseman/Alice Fletcher; Chuck Sanders/Ramona Kilbride; John Swift/Pearce Cassavetes

Silver: Curtis Hyde/Jan Hingis; Hunter Raphael/Stannis; Burt Sharon/Kris Saviour; Prentis Curran/Ziggie Platinides; Roger Miles/Tina Lopez; Rick Saturn/Mel Simone

And finally, the President and First Lady of FFLM — Gold medal holders at 10,000 feet: Randy Levagio/Melissa Witten

## 5.3 SKINNY FREE FALL

A hardcore pursuit. Interested? We can put you in touch with the dedicated few with the overall tans.

## 5.3A A CAUTIONARY TALE

Lionel Sapsted — the ultimate naturist adventurer, who held many of the official nude sky-diving records — high altitude, the octa ruby expert wings award for 18,000 free fall sky-dives, the sexta emerald free fall badge for putting in 300 hours of free fall time, the Eagle Award for taking part in sequential free fall formations on eight-person and larger sky-dives, the Canopy Crest Solo Award for individual sky-divers who have entered eighth or later in a completed eight-canopy or larger and the ultimate prize the Golden Eagle Award for those who have taken part in a 64 person or larger free fall formation — and most of the unofficial ones too. He was jumping with a new lover — Jane Malone — on the day he died. No records were in the offing, they were just enjoying themselves, frolicking naked in the warm thermals over the Californian desert. Hugging, caressing, kissing they fell, their bodies alive. Jane excited, somersaulted away, legs flailing wildly. Her exuberance and inexperience were Lionel's downfall, her knee caught him below the jaw as she spun, knocking him unconscious. Screaming she watched as he dropped away, his body limp, long blond hair obscuring his vacant face. The rushing air revived Lionel and he regained consciousness three hundred feet from the ground, just in time to release his chute, but not to prevent the opening canopy becoming entangled in electricity power lines, stretched between tall metal pylons that disfigured the barren landscape. Lionel was found hanging naked with a massive er****on, 40 feet up in the air, a nylon cord wrapped tightly round his neck.

3,956 metres

## SKY-DIVING MANUAL 2001

Terminal Velocity: in scientific terms terminal velocity is variable and defined as the constant velocity of a falling body when the frictional resistance is equal to the gravitational pull. The higher the altitude, the thinner the air and the reduced friction mean a higher terminal velocity.

Above 12,000 metres terminal velocity is 1,600 kilometres per hour (kph). At 3,600 metres, which is the highest altitude practicable for a parachute jump without supplemental oxygen equipment, terminal velocity is approximately 192 kph. At this speed a person will fall 1,500 metres in 30 seconds. A 3,600 metre jump will allow 60 seconds of free fall, with the parachute being deployed at 600 metres.

Free fall – about 300 metres in the first 10 seconds then 300 metres every 5.5 seconds thereafter.

There was though an inevitability about free falling that meant he had been growing increasingly bored. It had become routine. Maybe he was getting old but he had vowed he wouldn't do it anymore, every time he jumped, he thought this one could be the last.

"Five thousand …"

Rolling over to face the earth he slowly extended his arms and legs and dropped. A falling star hurtling towards the earth at over a hundred and sixty kilometres an hour – doing a metric ton and a half. If there was ever any doubt in his mind it was not when he was poised to leap from the plane, holding the rattling frame of the doorway, the slipstream battering his body, clawing at his clothes, watery eyes staring into the emptiness beneath, but now when it was far too late, the initial thrill having dissipated and he focused for the first time on what he was doing. An object obeying the laws of physics, defying all other natural rules of common sense and survival. No matter how often he jumped there would always come a point when some primitive area of his brain would awake from its slumbers and scream a warning of the elemental danger his body faced. An appeal for self-preservation of such intensity that it could make him nauseous. Stoned or sober he could rarely summon up an adequate response and his fear would subtly charge the cells in his body. Electric, alert to every material and chemical nuance of the air around him, he would plummet through the atmosphere, a beacon radiating a base human energy.

The dreadful rush was one of the fundamental keys to his life. It was central to the community of which he felt a part. That select band that challenged nature and communed with the fallen angels. Conquering terror and banishing emotions that brought mere mortals to their knees. They fed off the triumphs and disasters that befell their peers, growing powerful on a warped legacy of success and misadventure, of broken limbs, crushed heads and smashed bodies, creating a mythology, peopled by characters as phantasmagorical as any classical epic. Fame grew in proportion to their luck, both good and ill. Recklessness, a virtue among the living, was less revered among the shattered dead. If you could dazzle with your antics, taking risks that threatened your very survival, without endangering others and survive time and again, then your lack of discipline, your disregard for the basic rules of safety would be ignored and you would be elevated to the sky-divers' unique pantheon of twisted souls. If you died, your body mangled beyond recognition, bones cracked, organs splattered in the dust, blood seeping into the thirsty ground, then opinions of your lack of care would be rapidly revised, being seen thereafter as retribution for your own stupidity, your reputation only restored if the nature of your death was sufficiently horrific. The true plaudits were reserved for those whose style in the air and on the ground was revered – sensational, daredevil, even psychotic – but who were careful and meticulous in their preparation – proponents of the code that said "pack it yourself, you can't trust any other fucker" – yet who still met with disaster. Shaped amid the smoky haze of driftwood stoked campfires and marijuana, their exploits grew in the retelling into monstrous legends that drifted over the actions of lesser beings, like clouds casting shadows, shading the daring among them from the heat and glare of the sun.

Tugg Curtis was one such heroic character who was revered and often talked about. X had known Tugg since he and Travis had shared a joint with him one night in a club at Riverdale, and watched as he circled the dancefloor drawing women to him, communicating with a kiss, a movement of the body, a caress. Committed to excess in everything, he was wasted to the point of inarticulacy when earthed, but a poet when airborne. He fell from great heights, hallucinating from the lack of oxygen, his parachute mushrooming only feet from the ground. An astounded public looking on in awe. But he reserved his greatest magic for the very few, those privileged to be up there with him, for Tugg could fly, mocking his rival's earthbound proclivities, by, as he said, never needing to come down. He had done it many times, his tall, thin body, unnaturally light, encased in a specially designed suit – white carbon-fibre, high-tensile, multi-weave fabric, with aerodynamic red and blue flashes, flexible air-resistant membranes under his arms and between his legs for extra lift (looking like the webbing on the feet of a duck or as Tugg would proudly proclaim like the skin between the toes of his Tennessee cousins), which allowed him to travel great distances in the air, change speed and direction, in short allow him to glide wherever he wanted – an outfit modelled, as Tugg claimed, on the wardrobe of his hero Elvis Presley during his waning Las Vegas years, his billowing suit from above resembling the bloated figure of the old rock and roller, the taut wings the expansive cloak he famously wore to mask his stumbling entrances on to the stage. Many times, Tugg took to the air with X to the cries of "Elvis lives." Indeed, he seemed immortal, unlike his idol, returning again and again from the riskiest of adventures unscathed, and God-like he came finally to believe in his own indestructability. One night tight in the embrace of two young women, one blonde the other brunette, in the back room of a San Diego bungalow during one of the endless parties that were his life, he came to a decision to take the ultimate flight. His lovemaking, thereafter, was insatiable, he had never enjoyed himself in the same way before. Debra and Candy were amazed, familiar with his dope-induced lethargy, they appreciated his caresses, relished the slow-burning intensity that inexorably led to satisfaction for all. This however was different, intense, focused and rapid, Tugg roaring with triumph, before slumping back onto the cushions piled high in the centre of the room and falling into a deep sleep.

His plan was madness, X told him so, while silently marvelling at his brazen audacity, his brilliance. When, not if, he pulled this off he told his best friend then everyone would be convinced that Elvis was alive and well and living in the skies above the U.S of A. Tugg smiled, as he would believe it too.

It was simple and so obvious, that he was amazed he had not thought of it before. He would jump as he had done on many occasions, soar like an eagle for all mortals to see, then land triumphantly back on the plane that would bring him back to earth and the adulation of the crowd, but this time without the security of a parachute. There were a number of free-flying sky-divers on the circuit, Tugg would be the only free-flier.

"Six thousand."

There was a haze over the distant Ortega mountains to the east, the smog of LA lay like a brown blanket along the northern horizon, while the sun blazed down from a pallid cyan sky baking the parched earth and sending up spiraling dust-laden thermals, ridden by myriads of birds of prey, solitary and in pairs, on the day Tugg "Presley" Curtis made his bid for immortality. Only a select few were gathered at the remote arid landing strip, all trusted friends, all prepared to witness history in the making. In the retelling many more claimed to have been there than actually were, such is the stuff of legends. There was only room for two passengers to go up in the plane with him to observe from above, Candy and Debra had insisted even though they were afraid of heights, so X and the rest had to watch from below. Tugg had been careful about who he had told, he knew people would be out to stop him. There were no FAA officials on this trip. Once he had talked his old friend Brad into piloting the plane, it was just a case of consulting with Janet, an astrologer he knew, to seek out the most auspicious day. As they climaxed together in the dunes close to her beachfront home, her children playing in the sand nearby, she chose the afternoon of June 14th at three fifteen as the best time for him, the conjunction of Uranus and Venus in Tugg's fourth quarter being particularly auspicious for anyone engaged in aerial pursuits.

At two fifty-five on that fateful day, Tugg embraced X, waved goodbye to his friends and walked towards the plane, a Cessna 182, its idling engine sending up clouds of dust that clung to the hair and filled the eyes, ears and mouths of the onlookers. He was wearing a parachute as he said, "to confuse any prying fuckers," but took it off immediately he clambered into the plane, even before they were airborne. His confidence was supreme.

X watched as the tiny aircraft climbed to eight thousand feet and then began circling overhead. At exactly three fifteen a small figure left the plane and began swooping across the sky. There were cheers and whoops of triumph. A joint was passed around. Music blared from a ghetto blaster perched precariously on the roof of a yellow Type 1 Volkswagen Beetle, emblazoned with peace symbols.

"It's his favourite song, man."

To the pounding beat of "Electrobank" by the Chemical Brothers, Tugg and Brad performed their finely choreographed dance high above.

"Tugg's flying, man, he's really flying. It's too much."

X sat down heavily on the gritty runway, dazed, then lay back and stared up at the tiny black dots, floating in the infinite sky. He saw them move together, merging into that final embrace that would consummate Tugg's ultimate achievement. The climax of all climaxes. Overwhelmed he shielded his eyes from the aching glare, absorbed in the melody. There was a gasp.

"Fuck me, no!"

Opening his eyes, he could see, to his horror, two dots again, the smaller one falling away, the larger hanging in the air, static, unmoving.

"Tugg, you fucker. Fly man, fly."

But Tugg's power was finally spent, his ethereal supremacy broken. Gripped by a force he had challenged and overcome many times before, he hurtled towards the earth, spinning out of control. X, to his despair, could clearly see all was lost. Transfixed he watched his friend as he drew nearer, waving and kicking, growing larger, the details clear. His body smashed into the crazed concrete a hundred metres away at three twenty-one, the ground vibrating beneath the feet of the stricken onlookers, the sickening thud drowned out by the incessant popping beat.

It was only later after his funeral, attended by several hundred sky-divers – the wake lasted for days – and his ashes had been released into the rising air currents over his beloved Elsinore, that the story came out about what had really happened in the sky above Temecula.

Tugg had been inspired, executing turns and swoops he had rarely tried before, yet disciplined, staying close to the plane, not taking any unnecessary risks. Scared witless, Candy and Debra found, that faced with such majesty, they were unable to keep a smile from their lips. The agreed signal had been given and Tugg had moved towards them, grinning inanely, history made. Candy held out a hand, helping, congratulatory, concerned. He was almost there, floating beneath the wing, an instant away from touching down, when the plane suddenly pitched violently, a hapless victim of warm turbulent air – one moment Tugg's life-giver the next his nemesis. His forehead smashed into the sharp exposed upper edge of the open door, his expression vacant after the stunning blow, then shocked as the pain enabled a collapse of control. As his body slackened, he was plucked by the slip-stream and swept away, breaking his back across the tail fin, before spinning into the void. Brad struggled to keep control of the damaged aircraft while the others stared aghast at Tugg, who for all the world looked like a bloated rock and roll star gyrating earthwards.

Tugg was a God, revered by all free fallers who lived in terror of meeting his fate. His legendary achievements were instantly inscribed in the canons of sky-diving and posted by the UWCSH on their website, hours after his death. Yet where there were Gods there were also daemons, individuals, who chilled the hearts of the daring, who struck fear into the brave. Mortals who had fallen from great heights and survived. The probability of their good fortune so incalculable that it was outside the realm of comprehension. A massive ratio that by its sheer size seemed to suck the meaning from the word luck, destroying the chances for survival of anyone who came into contact with them. By overcoming such incredible odds, they could only increase the risks for everyone else, for as many sky-divers passionately believed there was only a finite amount of good luck to go around. Even if these fluky outcasts themselves had the courage to return to the air, and there were some, they always jumped alone. Solitary wraiths moving through an insubstantial world devoid of any mathematical form. No calculations could be made, no plans laid, they struggled to extract any meaning from a life punctuated by such an extreme act of serendipity.

Linda Reading fell four thousand feet after her parachute only partially opened and then became entangled with her reserve chute as it unfurled. She suffered broken ribs, a punctured lung, concussion and spent two weeks in intensive care before making a full recovery. She lived alone in North Vancouver, a reclusive figure, for nineteen months before leaping to her death from the Capilano suspension bridge. Brian Symonds jumped from high altitude, only to be caught by a freak thunder storm, he was lashed by icy rain and hail, lightning flared around him, thunder burst his eardrums, the turbulence buffeted his body and a powerful downdraft collapsed his parachute, folding it over him like a sheet, and entangling his legs in the shroud lines. He crashed into a pine forest, his plunging torso stripping the branches from one side of a tall Douglas fir as he decelerated. Dusting himself down he rose from his bed of pine needles with barely a scratch, his only injuries a violent bruise across his chest and bleeding ears. People said it was a miracle and he believed them, leaving his family without any explanation three weeks later and disappearing forever.

Such were the spirits that haunted X, every time he took to the air. The tales multiplied, had a life of their own, gestating in his fertile imagination, they burst forth in drug-induced sessions of parturition, terrifying their creator. He knew it was healthy to face his phobias, be aware of the dangers, calculate the odds, but in his calmer, lucid moments he did wonder. As a sky-diver X aspired to immortality but was not one of those that took unnecessary risks, if he ever joined the pantheon of the greats it would not be because he hadn't taken care of the details.

Adjusting his position, he felt equilibrium restored – the view was breathtaking – arching his back, arms and legs outstretched, a stable spread, which avoided spinning and the entangling of rigging lines. Or was he a falling star hurtling through space. It was impossible to separate the banal from the profound in his mind. Dragged down by the mundane or saved by an obsessive attention to the particular. He'd lived his life by planning for every eventuality and he'd done all right out of it, if he was honest with himself. But there was always that niggling doubt, optimist that he was, that he was worth a whole lot more. In this game you lived by zoning in and he was happy with that. Respect for the unexpected had served him well, it paid to be paranoid, he knew now there was no such word as trust, a lesson he'd learnt the hard way.

The memory of early betrayal still left X cold. His brother, thirteen and two years older than he was, pushing him maliciously in the chest at the top of the stairs of their terraced house in Romford and shouting with glee.

"That'll teach you to follow me around, you little runt."

Feet leaving the ground, body falling back, the sickening emptiness in the stomach, the horrific sight of muddy Converse All Star high top basketball boots drawing into view then passing out of sight above your head, the amazement at the bounce as he landed on his side on one of the lower treads, then the pain striking as he rebounded once again, whirling through the air like a spinning ball. Limbs flailing helplessly, the rug at the bottom of the stairs drawing closer, the crunching impact as his chest grounded, sliding down the last few steps before rolling to a halt, eyes fixed skywards, memory imprinted with images of his descent, replaying over and over in his mind as he passed into unconsciousness.

The sensation of absence, the lack of solidity he'd experienced remained with him, nurturing an insecurity about the insubstantiality of existence. A feeling that recurred whenever he found himself in danger – his first fall vividly flashing back, the airiness, the anticipation of pain, the premonition of disaster. It was all he could think of on the day – a bright, sunbaked June afternoon, a week before his twentieth birthday – when his own chute didn't open. The earth – a green and yellow patchwork of irregular fields, a rash of small sparkling ponds pock-marking the surface, slashed by the twin lanes of a busy motorway – was fast approaching, the ripcord useless in his hands. A novice, reflexes ill-attuned, actions not yet second nature, he desperately tried to recall what he had been taught, but found there was nothing but the stairway of his family home revolving through his mind, obliterating all other thoughts. Vice-like his stomach, gripped by nausea, squeezed the air from his lungs. Gasping, fighting sickness – perversely, he realized afterwards, he had been very anxious not to vomit in mid-air – he waited for the impact, his body spinning slowly inches from the swirling reds and dirty greens of the runner in the dingy hall of his childhood home. His hands saved him, instinctively clawing at his chest, breaking nails and tearing skin, until they chanced upon the reserve chute and pulled it free. A few hundred metres from the ground, he was plucked violently skyward, his descent slowed, but he hit the earth hard, crumpling not bouncing on impact, breaking an ankle, a stiff breeze dragging his rigid body across the field of young wheat, until his chute became entangled in a hawthorn hedge. He lay immobile in a border of strong-smelling rape, self-seeded from the neighbouring field, for over an hour before being rescued

X would never allow anyone else to pack his parachute after that. Even though it had been unclear why his chute had failed – an Inquiry finding that it could have been the packing or it may have been his poor body position at the time of deployment – he was taking no chances. There evolved a familiar ritual before every jump, from which he never deviated. His friends said he was an obsessive, but he knew they had never fallen like he had.

Methodical and precise in his actions he would start his preflight preparations by sweeping the smooth shiny surface of the low wide packing table with a duster, then carefully lay out each piece of his equipment, avoiding overlaps and checking for any damage to the fabric or lines. First to be arrayed was the small round pilot chute, then the bridle and deployment bag, followed by his specially designed all-yellow ram-air canopy, which he laid out in a broad arc with the leading edge uppermost, he would then deliberately straighten out the upper control lines, the cascade lines, the slider, connector link, lower control lines, risers and steering toggles, carefully avoiding any kinks. Finally, he would inspect his reserve chute, checking the packing data card was still in date and the seal intact, that the pin was seated correctly and not bent, the pin cover flap was shut and the closing loops were in good condition. Stepping back, he would view the display with satisfaction. Then he would begin to meticulously stow it all away. The pilot chute would be neatly folded and eased into a tight pouch, he then ran his hand along the smooth connecting bridle up to the point where it met the main chute to check it was sound, pulling it taut as he did so to keep it clear of the main packing operation. Slipping his arm under the fabric of the main canopy he then folded it into a series of S-shapes, before sliding it into its bag, which he fastened securely with a pin attached mid-way along the bridle, the various lines were then all looped in order and stowed outside of the bag. The packed chute and the reserve were then attached to the main harness, with the pilot pouch stowed on top. A purposeful glance ensured that the straps were routed correctly and not twisted and that all loose ends were tucked away. Wiping his goggles with a cloth he would again step back and muse on the jump ahead.

 He found he was easily able to factor in the mundane data of wind speed and direction, the altitude of the sun and other key bits of meteorological information without besmirching in his mind the quintessential spirituality of what he was about to do. A calm abstraction at his core would remain unbroached. The stark black and white images, he had seen on television as a boy, of Shinto ceremonies performed by Japanese kamikaze pilots before their missions on desolate runways hacked out of the tropical jungles of remote Pacific islands, seemed to encapsulate the essence of his endeavours with a sufficient degree of black humour to satisfy his moods.

A grey Cookie Openface helmet with a customized red flash was loosely placed on his head, chin-strap hanging free and he was ready, hoisting the pack on to one shoulder and striding out across the airfield. Stowing the equipment was always the final performance before taking to the air, as he was not prepared to leave his kit unattended, even for a minute. Paranoia was a way of life for him and he had grown accustomed to it over the years.

This day was like many others, he felt there was something else he should have done, that there was an item missing, a gap, a hole at the centre, it was a momentary feeling, passing from his consciousness as quickly as it entered, but it terrified him, concentrating his anxieties about falling into one intense jolt of fear. The sin of omission for such a perfectionist was one that deserved to be punished, but not now. Feeling the first stirrings of a plea for absolution before the exhilaration took over, he would never admit to offering up anything as bald as a prayer, just the hint of an appeal to some greater agency that had him ensnared in its overpowering grip. This force was vanquished by a hardened resolve committed to life and the avoidance of an horrific death. Again, self-preservation stepped in to unlock the mental paralysis that would lead only to inaction and certain disaster.

Drool dribbled free from the corner of his mouth, spinning off into the void, its shimmering form coalescing into a perfect sphere as it dropped, cooling before evaporating, its constituent molecules swept away into the natural cauldron. He shook his head to clear his senses. Blood drained from his face, the warm rushing air stretching and smoothing the pale skin, his two-day stubble – each individual hair erect – a dark green-tinged patchy shadow in the otherwise vivid brightness of the sun seared aura that clung to his body, thinning brown hair dragged flat against the uneven surface of his cranium and dry cracked lips pared back to reveal teeth clenched in a cadaverous grin. He stared at the earth through glazed openwide orbs, the eyeballs flattened and forced back in their sockets, as if an unyielding pressure was seeking to take his sight, like the thumbs of a medieval torturer, his retinae pin-pricks in the bright all-pervading light. Man's ultimate fate foreshadowed in the finely delineated detail of his skull etched against the pale shimmering blue.

The straps of his backpack were tight across his shoulders, restraining his billowing clothing, the skin beneath chaffing slightly as his body rocked and twisted in the buffeting gusts. He should have worn a thicker jacket, his Versace blue and pink shadow check blazer over a Muji white vest together with beige Hedi Slimane trousers had seemed a good idea when he considered the day of business ahead, standing in front of his full-length mirror in the bedroom of Ramona's apartment in Docklands. But now they were plainly inadequate. If he hadn't been in such a hurry and had known how things would turn out he would have worn something more suitable – his acid green Sanjo Ninyanomaka cargo trousers perhaps, a red embroidered Harry Nugent cowboy shirt and his black embossed customized Sabretooth leather bomber jacket, featuring on its lower left sleeve, picked out in fine silver studs, a skull silhouetted in profile with flames flaring from eyes and mouth and trailing fire far behind like the tail of a comet, which, a fact known only to a few women – currently the count stood at sixteen, which was X's lucky number – and one man, replicated the tattoo on his upper inner left thigh. But that was how his life was these days – expectations were always exceeded by events. He could only admit honestly to being happy about one thing he was wearing today and that was his pair of Van Buren Blue Flash trainers, with the yellow laces.

These things were important, the clothes he was wearing affected his mood, could build him up, bolstering an errant ego at those critical moments when business outcomes depended on life and death decisions, or bring him down, undercutting a robust constitution to the point of emotional collapse. Now he felt awkward and the most rational line of thinking could not persuade him otherwise. It was a curse. He had wondered if it was simply down to the risks he took and the fact that he was concerned about being found dead inappropriately dressed, the rationale of his mother and her mantra "always wear clean underwear, you never know when you'll be hit by a bus." But in the end had decided this was too complicated an explanation and resigned himself to the fact that even as an intelligent man he simply couldn't get beyond believing appearances were everything. "I can pull off anything if I'm wearing clothes worth a couple of grand," was his mantra. Women, friends, business rivals fell under his sartorial sway with a regularity that defied the vagaries of mere chance. He had every reason to believe the fortune he spent on his brightly coloured, finely tailored clothes, was a sound investment.

His mood soured. Thoughts of mid-air collisions, explosions, being shot-down, bailing out in flames, chutes failing to open, knotted lines, hitting a tree, branches ripping, hanging entangled, landing heavily, crushing a body on the ground, splashing down, pulled under by his parachute, drowning, all flared through his mind. Unease flooded his body. Pooling in his stomach, the aqueous sensation surged like a powerful natural spring, bubbling upwards, slopping over, seeping outwards, liquefying limbs, drenching tissue, oozing through gaping pores, dampening wind-blasted skin, staining fabric, chilling as it dried in the airy rush.

## A SUMMARY EXTRACT FROM: AFTER THE FALL - IMPACT INJURIES AND THE ASSESSMENT OF PROBABLE CAUSES OF DEATH.

Brent W. Hudson PHD, Professor of Investigative Pathology,
Valdaro School of Criminology, University of Muskegon, Mich.
The Pathologist and Violent Death - Vol 24 - No 4 - March 01

... The vital factors determining the extent and nature of injuries in a fall victim are the length of the descent and the nature and form of the impact substratum, the positioning of the body in falls from heights of greater than 20 meters has been found to be non-critical (5). Causes of death should be looked for in one of four impact-related areas or combinations thereof:

1. Crush injuries to vital organs, particularly the brain, heart, lungs, liver and spleen. Munro D, Samuels P and Wislon X (3) have effectively demonstrated times of death for degrees of stricture of the cardiac and pulmonary systems.

2. Ruptures in essential body membranes, for example the chest cavity, diaphragm and stomach wall. Traumatic diaphragmatic herniation is a likely outcome and as a result (Desmond C, Ferrers P (7)) a useful diagnostic tool for confirming cause of death.

3. Tearing of musculoskeletal tissue, and

4. THE MULTIPLE FRACTURING OF THE VERTEBRA AND OTHER BONES (IMPALEMENT AND SEVERANCE INJURIES ARE INCLUDED IN THIS CATEGORY). HARRIS B ET AL (9) AT THE UNIVERSITY OF BAHRAIN'S INSTITUTE OF CLINICAL PATHOLOGY HAVE FIRMLY ESTABLISHED THE LINK BETWEEN MORTALITY AND PUNCTURE INJURIES IN HIGH-PRESSURE IMPACTS THRU AN EXTENSIVE ANALYSIS OF WORLDWIDE DATA ON MILITARY PARACHUTE DEATHS AS PART OF A US DEFENSE DEPARTMENT PROGRAM TO DEVELOP PROTECTIVE CLOTHING FOR AIRBORNE UNITS.

AN INVESTIGATION OF THE PATHOLOGY OF SUICIDE DEATHS BY JUMPING IN THE US OVER THE LAST TEN YEARS BY VANDERBOTEN V (4) HAS SHOWN QUITE CONCLUSIVELY THAT RUPTURES OF THE MAIN BODY CAVITY ARE FAR MORE PREVALENT IN WATER-BORNE IMPACTS THAN THOSE ON HARD SURFACES AND THE CONSEQUENT SUDDEN MASSIVE HEMORRHAGE IS ALMOST CERTAINLY THE MAIN CAUSE OF MORTALITY IN THESE CASES, SUPPLANTING PREVIOUS BEST PRACTICE THAT THE MAJORITY OF SUCH DEATHS WERE CAUSED BY DROWNING. TERRESTRIAL IMPACTS HAVE A FAR GREATER INCIDENCE OF VITAL ORGAN CRUSH INJURIES AND IT IS CONJECTURED THAT THESE, PARTICULARLY TO THE BRAIN, ARE THE PRIMARY CAUSE OF DEATH, ALTHOUGH AS ALREADY NOTED THERE ARE THOSE AUTHORITIES (9,13,17) WHO MAKE A FORCEFUL CASE FOR SEVERE BLOOD LOSS RESULTING FROM EXTENSIVE INTERNAL LACERATIONS, PUNCTURING AND VESSEL AND MUSCULAR SEVERANCE CAUSED BY SPLINTERED SKELETAL TISSUE.

3,672 metres

vertigo n. (pl. ~ s) – an illusion or subjective sensation of movement, especially of rotation, either of one's self or of one's surroundings; any form of giddiness or dizziness; condition with sensation of whirling and tendency to lose balance; commonly associated with a fear of heights; so vertiginous.

There came a time early in every jump – the initial euphoria waning, the practicalities of leaving the plane dealt with – when he felt the sickness inside. An instinct for self-preservation asserting itself against the sheer selfish hedonism of his intellect. A brief sensation of reasonableness insinuating its way into his consciousness and screaming a warning: beware, danger, careful how you go. An aura of concern he associated with his first sexual forays, a nervy recklessness tinged with caution, the essential human attributes, he now knew, of a predator in his prime.

The girl, she was that but seemed much older, even though he knew she was in the same year as him but at a different school, lay face down on the carpet her legs stretching towards him as he knelt on the floor at her feet. She was naked except for a pair of white knickers, the rectangular St Michael's label protruding above the frilled waistband, which provocatively she had left on as she'd undressed demurely facing away from him in the dim flickering green light of the Lava lamplit bedroom. The floorboards throbbed beneath his knees to the unrelenting bass line from the Happy Mondays' 'Wrote for Luck', a masterpiece he never tired of listening to. The organ and jangling guitar duetting over the intoxicating beat, spurred him on, the familiar boosting his courage as he surveyed uncharted territory. Someone at the party below must have turned up the volume, because he swore he could hear nothing when the two of them had slipped giggling, hand in hand, into the room. They had locked the door but he was nervous, his body twisted in anticipation of discovery. He felt giddy, as she stripped off her clothes, unable to stand. Kneeling he felt a little better and watched closely as she stepped out of her denim skirt, kicked off her shoes and rolled down her tights. He noticed she had a pronounced dimple in the side of her upper left thigh and wanted to touch it more than anything, but didn't dare. Closing his eyes space began to spin, not unpleasantly at first, but as the volume gathered speed, he felt dangerously nauseous and forced his eyes open, just in time to appreciate, for the first time in his life, the shadowy gap at the top of the girl's thighs, as she lay prostrate on the floor in front of him, her pale thin body illuminated by the warm sickly glow of the slowly pulsing lamp. Staring at her long black hair draped over her right shoulder he pondered whether to take his clothes off as well, she had promised to do "it" to him after he had done "it" to her but he wasn't sure if he liked the idea. Sober he would have laughed at the absurdity of seeing a naked female body for the first time and hesitating, but drunk he found it hard to decipher what was going on. Painfully aroused, but uncertain, he waited.

She raised herself up on one elbow and turned her head, hair fell across her face, she flicked it away with manicured fingers, the nails polished black, beneath her raised arm he caught a glimpse of a breast, the nub of nipple erect. Noticing she smiled.

"It's always cooler with no clothes on, come on take yours off. You didn't forget the bottle, did you?"

Unbuttoning his shirt with trembling hands he shook his head. The tightness in his gut eased, the pressure of not knowing lifted. Flushed in her unflinching gaze, he threw the blue cheesecloth aside and began unzipping his Levi's, acutely conscious of the bulge in his pants, he sat back awkwardly seeking shadowy cover. Easing the tight, clinging denim over his buttocks he stretched out his legs on either side of hers, his gaze fixed on the line at the top of her left thigh – exposed now where her cotton pants had ridden up on one side as she undressed – where the tanned skin of her leg ended and the hidden pale white skin began. Absorbed in a sexual reverie, exciting in its unfamiliarity, he slid his jeans down to his ankles, realizing too late that he was still wearing his desert boots. The tight roll of denim was stretched across the back of her knees, resting gently on her skin, if he tried to stand, she would be painfully pinned to the floor. Hazily he pondered the problem then impulsively acted, flinging himself back while simultaneously raising his legs into the air and swinging them to one side. They crashed into the bedside table to his right, splintering the thin wood and smashing the glass of a framed photograph of two children with ice-creams standing on a fence. At the same time the back of his head struck the polished black wooden floorboards with a crack.

Stunned he stared up at a patch of glaring white cotton and the paler female form beyond diminishing into the hazy half-light of the high-ceilinged room.

"What did you do that for?"

The girl was kneeling over him laughing, her knees tucked neatly into his arm-pits, her arms resting on either side of his head. Her long dark hair cascaded forward, sweeping her breasts as her body shook.

"You're an idiot. You really are."

She paused, looking around.

"Whose room is this anyway, do you know?"

He wanted to answer, impress her, participate, but found he was unable to articulate the most basic sounds. His lips were moving but the link with the communication centre in his brain had been severed, all his sensory and intellectual capacity given over to suppressing the painful throbbing in his head and the nausea welling again in his stomach. The seductive image floating enticingly inches from his face was a revelation, any appreciation of beauty had long escaped him, preferring as he did to celebrate action rather than spend time in the contemplation of nature's wonders, but all would now change, he swore to himself, over and over again.

"You obviously don't know."

Mouth silently opening and closing, his ravished eyes blinked rapidly.

"Are you alright?"

Her voice contained a hint of irritation melded with the obligatory concern. He nodded.

"Good. Here I'll help you."

She sat back her full weight pressing down for a moment on his belly. He groaned. She then stood up, turned around, straddled him again, this time facing his feet, her toes tickled him under the arms as she leant forward and began untying the laces on his desert boots. Desire, until now familiar only as a strong urge to acquire and possess, transformed itself in that instant into an overwhelming need to give himself to another. The picture before him of her buttocks clearly delineated by tightly stretched, semi-transparent white cotton, the crack between the cheeks just visible where the taut lace band dipped slightly in the middle of her back, made her irresistible. He was entangled in a nexus of lust and longing. The confidence she exuded in her own nakedness, her assured demeanour, oozing experience, placed the girl out of reach. He was not bold enough to make the first move.

But then he had more pressing worries. The frayed double knots of his boots were proving resistant to her fumbling fingers and she wriggled in frustration. He was acutely aware of the heavy pressure of her body on his groin, moving from side to side, back and forth. The pleasure was intense, but muted almost immediately by concerns about whether she would notice his stifled climax. Initially he was reassured by the semi-darkness and her apparent fixation with his footwear, but as the warm damp feeling spread outwards, he knew she couldn't fail to sense his embarrassment.

"Do you ever take these things off? This is bloody ridiculous."

Speechless he waited for the inevitable response – the disgust, turning to ridicule and finally laughter that would haunt him over the weeks and months ahead. She knew so many people that he knew his life would be unbearable.

"At last. You should get some new laces."

First one boot then the other was yanked off and thrown across the room, then shuffling forward she pulled off his jeans, coins and a key-ring clattering noisily to the floor. He tried to sit, but head spinning gave up and lay back to watch as she stretched cat-like in front of him.

"Are you still up for this?" she asked in a husky voice tinged with tones far more seductive than he had been expecting. A backward glance over her shoulder reassured him further and he knew the question demanded an audible answer. Playing for time he levered himself up on to his elbows, focused on the shadowy concavity at the bottom of her spine, inhaled deeply and hesitated for what seemed like an age before the sobering influence of self-interest finally forced a croaked assent from his lips.

"Good," the final letter of the word merging into a high-pitched squeal of joy, which surprised X, "I'm glad you said that."

Snatching up the bottle of red wine they'd brought with them from the makeshift bar in the kitchen downstairs she drank deeply, drops of claret spilling onto her chin and splattering over her breasts. Holding the bottle out towards him she wiped her mouth with the back of her hand and smiled. He shook his head. He had drunk too much already. The turbulence in his gut was becoming more intrusive, as his libido temporarily waned. The last thing he wanted was to be sick in front of her.

Placing the bottle carefully on the floor she gyrated slowly across the room, grabbed a cushion from the armchair in the corner of the room and skipped back, slipping it beneath her hips as she resumed her position face down on the Persian rug, legs slightly apart.

There was a scream from below, followed by a loud crash, then laughter. The beguiling instrumental break at the beginning of "Waterfall", one of X's best loved tracks by his favourite band of the moment – The Stone Roses – could be heard, building towards its crescendo of crashing chords and surging buzz-saw guitar, as the volume crept up on the stereo. Smiling at the thought of his friends playing air guitar, mouthing the lyrics and swaying as one to the increasingly frantic rhythm, X relaxed for the first time, the tension in the pit of his stomach easing. He sat up, crossed his legs, and gently placed his hand on one of the girl's ankles, an action which elicited a contented sigh and a flicker of a smile that attractively creased the side of her face. Cocooned together in a warm, dimly-lit other world of shifting images and muffled sounds, eyes closed, they drifted off into an intoxicated reverie of shared musical appreciation, their bodies imperceptibly moving to the infectious beat. An instant of mutual contentment that would be X's sweetest memory of the evening, an early demonstration that lust could manifest itself in quieter, less physical ways than he had, up to that point in his life, ever imagined. A mood that bolstered confidence and gave succour to ill-formed schemes for making love to women. Everything was possible.

The illusion was abruptly shattered by angry shouting from outside the house and the frenzied repeated trilling of the front doorbell. Startled, X stiffened. Conjured-up images of irate adults, spitting furious words and threatening violence, failed as a spur to action and the near-naked couple remained frozen in a tableau to debauched youth, senses primed, straining to hear what was going on.

Immobility heightened awareness of illogical neuroses and anxiety, a state of mind that rarely afflicted X when sober, gripped him. He hoped fervently that someone had cleared up the mess in the front room. Dim memories came back to him of a full glass of cider emptying itself into the blazing fire, the red-hot coals erupting before his eyes, a plume of steam and black ash rising from the hearth and swirling across the room, coating the groping couples sprawled over the cream soft furnishings and the pale grey carpet in a thin layer of dark sticky residue, the noxious fumes choking the few swaying dancers still on their feet. The word "wanker" ringing in his ears, X had sloped into the kitchen in search of another drink and if he was lucky another joint, only to find the girl who would thrillingly re-direct his evening from a drunken descent towards insensibility into a thrilling trek across the nursery slopes of sexual discovery, corrupting him forever. No names were exchanged, anonymity cloaking their adventure in mystery, providing safety.

Raised voices in the hallway, the words indistinct, led to an abrupt end to the music. The tense silence, accentuated by the rapid pumping of their hearts and the shortness of their breathing, was brief. An animated conversation burst forth directly below them, a deeper male voice dominating, barely letting the others speak. X, perspiring now, his skin rough and bumpy, erect hairs bristling, listened attentively. Suddenly he heard a melody, unmistakably that of "Light My Fire", by The Doors, quieter than before, but clearly audible. The front door slammed shut, footsteps moved away down the gravel drive, for several beats the company in the hall was silent, then there was laughter, stifled but euphoric. A signal for the paused party to resume, but at a lower intensity, the host aware for the first time of the world outside watching and listening.

"Oh my God, that was close."

The girl sighed as she turned over onto her back and grinned. X smiled warily, his gaze shifting from her face, to the dark mass of pubic hair, which he'd noticed prickling the taut white cotton surface of her underwear, stray curling strands protruding over the top of the elasticated waist band, and then back again.

"Do you still want to?"

Tongue-tied, X nodded.

"Good, so do I."

Relief at their shared ambition induced the pair to move. The girl rolled back on to her front, sliding the wine bottle across the wooden floor towards X. It almost toppled on the uneven boards and he lunged forward to catch it, suddenly aware once again of the fluid seething in his stomach. The nervousness returned – an involuntary quiver flowing outwards to the extremities, an imperceptible tremble shorting across a taut chest, a slight paralysis of the limbs, an inability to act decisively.

The girl tensed then relaxed her buttocks in anticipation, the white cotton rippling sluggishly. After adjusting the position of the cushion beneath her hips, she lay still.

Willing himself to perform, he forced his reluctant body up from the floor, silently repeating to himself that there was nothing more he wanted than to see her naked. Shuffling forward, the emerald room spinning erratically before him, he manoeuvred into a position where he was standing above the girl, with his feet carefully placed on either side of her knees. She looked unworldly, exposed, as he stared down at her prone figure, his body gently swaying.

He was miles above the ground, watching her fall comatose towards the earth, an angel cast out of heaven, wings torn off in the turbulent jet-stream of God's wrath. Fleetingly omnipotent it was suddenly blindingly obvious – his fate rested with hers. She would be his saviour, if he could only rescue her, be her life-saver. Sickeningly he swooped, dropping like a stone.

She sighed, a plea fluttering fitfully in the charged air.

Slumping to his knees, their bodies merged, cool skin dissolving beneath his warm touch, enveloped by her smoky scent. A pile-up of souls. She was his.

The girl shifted beneath him, turning her head from one side to the other, eyes closed.

There she was. Unblemished, glowing viridescent in the tinted, unfocussed, half-light. His mouth was dry and he couldn't swallow. The bitter after-taste of red wine and scrumpy lingered, settling uneasily. A fortifying swig from their bottle and he was ready. Deliberately he reached forward and slipped the fingers of both hands beneath the elasticated top of her pants and firmly gripped the soft pliant cotton. He had been expecting resistance, the material providing some protection, a last defensive redoubt against the intruder, but there was none, and it stretched effortlessly beneath his gentle pressure.

He could hear her breathing now short and rapid, almost panting.

The garment slid easily over her buttocks, exposing the pale freckled skin, then tightening, it snagged on her hips, taut and immovable. Words again failed him and he hesitated, the courage to manhandle her body, lifting her up to complete this first basic task, eluded him.

Pause, a beat, another then she flexed, rippling, her midriff edging up towards him, freeing her trapped underwear, which in an instant lay twisted and limp-hooped around her upper thighs.

Needy, barely comprehending, X ogled. Sights exposed, overwhelming in their unfamiliarity, fuelled a hunger that snatched glimpses at the pages of Playboy magazine had not primed him for. This sudden appreciation of the delicious potential of a woman's body awakened in him the first glimmers of understanding of the freedom that giving in to base urges would bring in his quest for gratification. It would become the credo of his life.

Nonchalantly, she announced, "there's a pen in the pocket of my skirt," and an arm lazily pointed towards the bed. As directed, he blinked into the shadows, glancing around myopically until he dimly made out the darker outline of what he took to be a pile of her clothes. It seemed a long way away.

"Go on then. Go and get it."

Her voice gruff and muffled, excited him. As he unsteadily got to his feet, easing the pressure on her thighs, she moved her legs, parting them to the limit of possible movement, her rolled underwear again taut against her skin. He stood transfixed.

There was a thud on the bedroom door and the brass handle rattled, followed by giggles and a rapid whispered conversation. X crouched, his arms self-consciously covering his groin; the girl tensed, listening.

"Anybody in there?"

The slurred intonation and breathy enthusiasm of the disembodied female voice, together with her persistent staccato hammering on the door irritated X. He sensed the collapse of intimacy as his antipathy towards the intruders rapidly insinuated its way into his consciousness. The focus subtly shifted. Concentrating on the scuffling on the landing he forgot about the naked woman at his feet, lying motionless an index finger pressed tightly to her lips, a beatific smile imprinted on her glistening face. Distracted now by the infectious driving base line of the Doors, "Break On Through (to the other side)", he straightened up, giddy, annoyed, but uncertain what to do.

"Hello, Earth calling ..."

The protracted inhalation of breath was audible in the bedroom, the extended pause, then the relaxed attenuating exhalation, interrupted the flow of the sniggering male voice, which only picked up again once a fit of inane chortling had been suppressed.

"… calling the mother ship. Are you receiving us?"

His companion squealed with glee, there was a burst of irregular knocking, then the door shook noisily on its hinges as the couple, clasped in each other's arms and charting a psychotropic wavelength uniquely and hilariously their own, crashed heavily against it as they tumbled to the ground.

"This is the mother ship calling earth. We're busy, now bog off."

X was startled at the loudness and barking tone of the girl's voice. Its vehemence easing his displeasure at the intrusion and he loudly croaked his agreement.

"Tossers!"

"We love you too, man."

Faint groans could be heard, followed by stifled laughter. Shadows flitted across the bright scrap of light filtering beneath the door. Then silence.

"They've gone," her words slurred, "and they won't be coming back."

X said nothing, heart thumping, he watched as she rolled over, sat up, leant towards him, her breasts bulging outwards as they pressed against her raised thighs, reached forward to slip her pants over her ankles and tossed them into the gloom. The luxuriant black triangle of her pubic hair, a fuzzy image briefly glimpsed, but fixed, an erotic snapshot he would treasure.

Temporarily at a loss, his ardour diminishing, X swayed to the music, mouthing along with Jim Morrison, indistinct, but strangely apt words. Break on through he must, but he was lost, his strength ebbing away, a calming somnolence seeping over him. Movement at his feet gave him a bearing as the girl stretched out and settled once again onto her front. He had been carrying out a mission, searching for he knew not what, his mind filled with visions and sounds that distracted him, his memory failing. There was a need for urgency he sensed that, but her pale body was beguiling – her naked form a novelty to be devoured piece by piece, refined, embellished and then reproduced, ready for consumption whenever required – and he felt composed. He set about his task with relish. From where he was standing, he could easily chart her contours, trace the outlines, map out who she was, banish the stranger.

His delight began to disconcertingly fade, as the small details coalesced not into an object of lust but a disturbing picture of distress and discomfort, a premonition of decay. The long black hair, he had so admired in the kitchen, now seemed washed out and brittle, splayed untidily across her back, while her neck rested at an awkward angle tilting her head upwards away from her shoulders so that he could just make out her white teeth through parted lips, and with her eyes and nose in shadow could distinctly follow the profile of her skull. Thin limbs protruded from an emaciated body that barely narrowed at the waist, shoulder blades and hip-bones jutted out prominently, stretching the blanched plastic skin, her ribs clearly etched into the translucence. The voluptuous buttocks, he had so admired seconds before, now seemed diminished, a sunken depression on her left side dominant, its hidden depths a dark blemish. His girl was no longer an angel, but a figure broken by a fall. A black and white photograph of a suicide victim illustrating an article in a Sunday colour supplement, titled – Empire State Building, New York, 18th June 1937.

Agitated, X couldn't believe his eyes. He felt queasy at the loss, yet intrigued by his shifts in mood, experiencing for the first time that warped natural progression – beauty, degeneration, decay, renewal – that would form the narrative structure to many of his more profound hallucinatory episodes, and he wondered what would happen next. Would the flesh of his body waste away? Slipping from the bones, crumbling along with hers, their dust mingling, together in death, if not in life. Charged by the enticing thought of a coupling throughout eternity he glanced down at his own body for confirmation of his imminent exit from this world, only to be forcefully reminded of his own rude health. It all seemed faintly ridiculous.

"What are you waiting for?" the voice was hushed, sleepy.

There was no sensible answer.

"The pen? In my skirt?"

It was a relief to be back. He had no idea how much time had elapsed since he'd set out – it seemed like an age – but his companion appeared blissfully unaware of his absence. Stumbling across the room he found her clothes heaped one on top of the other and crowned by her denim skirt, which had fallen there retaining the perfect shape of her body as she stepped out of it. Rummaging through the pockets he felt the erotic spark rekindle and he imagined he could still feel her warmth in the unforgiving fabric. Finding the pen – a simple biro – beneath a discarded tissue he grasped it and held it aloft in triumph.

The girl giggled.

Buoyed with a renewed confidence he stepped up to the prone figure and gently parted her thighs with his foot, then knelt down between her legs. The skin was cool to the touch. Anticipating his uncertainty, the girl issued clear instructions, as if reading from a manual.

"Remove the pen top."

Silence. X realized she was waiting for a signal he had completed the first part of his task. He squeezed her left buttock.

"Unscrew the end."

Her tone jollier than before.

Pressure on the right buttock.

"Take out the ink cartridge."

A kiss on her lower back.

"Lick the rounded end."

Another kiss.

"Take a swig of wine … and away you go."

X had always been unsure about what he was about to do, ever since it had been suggested to him in a whisper in the kitchen, and he felt no better about it now, but whereas he had hoped as they had slowly climbed the stairs hand in hand that other things might happen to distract her, he finally knew as he reached for the wine bottle that he had no choice but to follow through.

Mouth full, the bitter acidity of the red wine irritating an ulcer beneath his tongue, he leant forward the pen clasped in his left hand and parted her cheeks with the thumb and forefinger of his right. Without hesitation he eased the tapered end of the pen into the tight brown crinkled button of her anus and pushed gently downwards, her muscles twitching slightly under the pressure. He then placed his mouth over the open end of the pen casing, dribbled wine slowly into the plastic shell until it was full to the brim, and blew, a faint spray dotted the stubble on his chin, forcing the intoxicating liquid deep inside her. A gasp followed by a long, relaxed exhalation of breath. She had experienced it all before.

"It's the most sensitive part of your body, loads of nerve endings close to the surface" she had muttered urgently into his ear, her warm breath raising hairs on the back of his neck. She had squeezed his hand as she spoke, and pressed heavily against his chest, forcing him to lean back across the black granite kitchen worktop. He had been unable to refuse her.

Not moving he refilled the pen and blew again, this time swallowing the dregs. As he shuddered at the harsh aftertaste, her trunk flexed luxuriantly like a cat rising from repose, buttocks clenching forcefully, plucking the pen from his lips.

"Once more, then it's your turn," she purred.

Reaching for the bottle, X ignored the ludicrous presence of the plastic tube sticking into the air inches from his face, and kept his gaze fixed on the girl's genitalia, absorbing the detail, marvelling at the delicious physical intricacies, appreciating the voluptuousness of the folds and creases, the sheer all-consuming desirability of the blood-pink reality.

The passing familiarity gleaned from hurried glances at glossy airbrushed colour photographs had ill-prepared him for the powerful feelings engendered by close proximity to such a beautiful object. The need he felt to share his lustful urges with this girl was overwhelming, as well as surprising to someone who up to this point had been selfishly committed to achieving his own personal goal of self-satisfaction.

"I never sleep with anyone on a first date," she had murmured, almost as an aside, "If that's what that look of yours suggests you're thinking."

He supposed it probably did, although between absorbing what she had just asked him to do and coming to terms with the fact that an attractive girl, long an object of distant yearning, was propositioning him at a party, he lacked the surplus mental capacity to clearly decipher what any of his actions meant. A bleary smile was offered as reassurance and she softened.

"You never know though, maybe some other time."

Spurred on by a vainglorious optimism, he drunkenly believed that by doing everything she asked then this vague promise might firm up, the timescale would be miraculously truncated and he would lose his virginity this very night in a memorable haze. However, to his annoyance an insurmountable obstacle stood in the way of him taking advantage of her present trusting openness and that was an unshakeable belief that she had meant what she said. A resolute and powerful character – everything she did exuded firmness of intent – who clearly signalled that she would not tolerate any countermoves in her game plan, however subtle or well-intentioned. Strategy in the end played a part, inebriated as he was, X could still think ahead to that beguiling "some other time" and deduce that it might be sooner rather than later if he did as she wished. Part of him thought "bugger that," feeling a girl of her experience wouldn't really mind, but he wasn't yet brave enough to just fall on top of her, handicapped as he was by a degree of anatomical uncertainty that restricted his knowledge of the physical act to the barest outline. A lack of understanding that if exposed, he felt sure, would prove embarrassing. Resignedly he swigged again from the bottle, before re-establishing a remote connection with the subject of his aching adoration.

The music abruptly ended downstairs, then blared out again, the same Doors compilation album but a different song, one that X didn't initially recognize. Musing as the wine drained from his mouth, he slid his moistened lips down the plastic tubing until he could feel the fine down that covered her buttocks and sense the heat emanating from her body.

"Ship of Fools."

The title came to him at the same moment she spoke out.

"Come on it's your turn."

He pulled back as she began to move beneath him, peeling herself up from the floor and gymnastically swinging one of her legs over in front of his face so that she ended up sitting facing his kneeling figure.

"Let me see."

He felt the cool draft of air flowing across his skin as she slipped down his Y-fronts. There was no awkwardness, just an enduring sensation of longing lustful yearning. Smoothly efficient she pulled him forward so that he lay across her lap, then calmly pressured the remaining wine into X. The bottle, discarded and empty, rolled noisily across the wooden boards until it came to a stop with a loud chink against the leg of the iron bedstead.

Apprehension subsiding as the stinging eased, X felt tranquil for the first time that evening. A delicious numbness permeated his being, suppressing all feelings, banishing nausea and accentuating his senses – he could smell the beeswax on the floor, organically sweet, musty and warm, hear the music, still the Doors, with note-perfect clarity, feel the pulsing vibrant vitality of the girl's skin, where it pressed supportively against his midriff and see bright colours of such swirling vividness, that he moved his hand to shade his eyes, even though they were already tightly closed. An immaculate experience, which was profoundly transcendent for a young man versed only in the blissful excesses of marijuana, beer and cider. A yearning had been fulfilled. With no desires left, barely able to distinguish who he was and with yellow light flaring around him, an emotional X believed for an achingly brief moment that he had attained the perfect state of enlightenment.

His grounding when it came was a surprise and a crashing disappointment. Pushing hands set him moving and he rolled over her legs onto the cold floor. He felt as if he was falling and the nausea returned in waves of sensation that broke unpleasantly against the foundations of his crumbling consciousness, before foaming over the low protective wall of his addled perception. Grace, he was discovering, was an ephemeral state, one you could grasp for but rarely hold on to.

"How was that? Amazing isn't it?"

Expecting no reply, she began crawling on her hands and knees across the floor towards her heap of clothes.

"I must get my tin."

Confused and unable to focus X tracked her pale form as she scrabbled around, scattering garments, moving crab-like back and forth across the room, before finally stopping in front of him and slapping down a small dented red tin with a triumphant whoop. Scratched gold lettering on the sides, abraded but still legible as OXO, gave this obviously treasured object an aura of mundane ordinariness that amused a perplexed X. Unused to such erratic mood swings and bereft of appropriate emotional responses he simply stared wide-eyed at her delicate fingers as they struggled to open up the tight-fitting lid. An age passed, her movements in slow motion, rings of plaited gold and silver threads moving erratically in front of him, then finally, with a sigh, the release, the rough pitted underside of the lid revealed, a wafting aroma of marijuana and a glimpse of three neat tightly rolled joints, placed twisted end to twisted end on a bed of shredded shag tobacco.

"This'll mellow us out."

A red and yellow box of Swan Vesta matches appeared next to the tin, its abrasive exterior strips pristine except for a single pink gash along one side. Shivering the girl carefully aligned the two containers then rose unsteadily to her feet, reached across and dragged the coverlet from the bed, draping it around her shoulders. Standing there with tousled hair silhouetted halo-like in the lava green glow from the lamp on the chest of drawers she looked like a holy figure to X, who was unable to take his eyes off her, preparing to officiate at a holy rite in front of the small altar she had so reverentially constructed on the floor between them.

Seated again cross-legged, wrapped in her velvet shroud, she fumbled in the tin for a joint then raised it to her lips.

"One I prepared earlier," she giggled.

A match flared and in the silence between album tracks, X could hear the faint crackle of burning paper and tobacco overlaid by the soft insistent draw of breath. The air fizzed with the heady aroma of hemp-laced incense. The future perfect.

Relaxing, the heavy cover slipped from her shoulders, baring her breasts. X watched. Each time she drew on the joint the lower half of her face – narrow mouth with full lips, small round nose and finely sculpted chin – glowed in the dim light. Seeping smoke curled across her skin caressing features, filtering through dangling hair before drifting upwards into invisibility. With a slight shake of her head she passed the joint over to him, then covered herself. X rose groggily onto one elbow to accept it

"Which end does this one go into?"

He thought for a moment that he had not spoken the words only imagined them, then she laughed. A vaguely mocking explosion of emotion that X uneasily registered could be directed at him rather than being, as he hoped, an amused response to his feeble attempt at humour. Adding to his embarrassment was the sudden realization that these were the first words he had said to her in a long while and even in his inebriated state he knew it was crude and out of place in such a sanctified atmosphere. He inhaled. The smoke scorched his throat and the tiny roach burnt his lips. He coughed and as the puff diffused throughout his body he knew he was going to be sick.

His recollection of the evening, filtered through the blinding pain of the worst hangover of his life, was partial. The erotic charge remained and he bolstered himself against the dismal feeling of having blown it romantically and sexually with the knowledge that he now had in his possession a pleasure trove of explicit memories. The girl's name worryingly escaped him, but images of her would be enough for the time being.

To his amazement she called him after school on the following Tuesday to pass on the news that her parents were out ten-pin bowling on Saturday night and did he want to come round to her house? They spent the evening in her stark minimalist bedroom, bare white walls and green-painted floorboards, smoking, drinking red wine and playing on her futon, adding to his personal, private stash of remembered sensual delights but not to his carnal knowledge. The musical cocoon – Stone Roses and Happy Mondays – that bound and protected them, nurturing their fixations and obsessions was torn apart when Ali – her name had surprised him with its unfamiliarity when he had glimpsed it on an envelope protruding from a scuffed leather duffle bag dumped in the middle of the room – suddenly stood up, switched off the CD player and with a yell ran naked from the room.

"I've got a treat for you."

Flushing water broke the silence. A door creaked as the gurgling in the pipes subsided and X stretched out, seeking the cool extremities of the double duvet. The awkwardness he had felt at exposing his body to the gaze of another had gone and he was finding he got a perverse pleasure from showing off his erection, the persistence and rigour of which amazed him. Ali, herself completely unabashed at her own nakedness, had shown no particular interest in his physique, commenting only once that his skin was very pale. They had barely touched despite the intimacy of their games and he couldn't bear the thought of her once again eluding him. His ambition had soared as the evening progressed and he longed to slide his hands over her body, feel her breasts, slip his probing fingers between her legs, and kiss her passionately before making love to her. He vowed to try as soon as she returned. Footsteps drew near and he quickly pushed back the covers.

"Listen to this."

Squatting in front of her stereo, Ali inserted a CD and turned up the volume. An unfamiliar up-tempo country beat – guitars, piano and thin percussion – blared out.

"What's this hippy shit?"

"You don't mean that, this is the Dead, man."

Ali stood in front of X, smiling. One side of her body gleamed in the soft light of a tall lamp standing in the corner of the room, its orange glow diffusing through the hazy gauze of a silk scarf draped over the shade, the other a dark shadow accentuating the curve of her waist, hips and thighs.

"Dead right."

"I like them … Look out of any window, any morning, any evening, any day. Maybe the sun is shining …"

Ali swayed as she sang along, adding her voice to the ragged chorus. X listened mesmerized by the deep, melodious sounds she was making, so different to her spoken words, and yearned for her even more.

"… birds are singing, rain is falling from a heavy sky … What do you want me to do for you …"

"Fuck me," X muttered.

Ali appeared not to hear.

"I can't believe you know all the words."

She stopped singing and looked down at him aghast.

"It's the Dead, man. The Grateful Dead. I've been listening to them all my life."

"Never heard of them."

"That's un-cool man, dead un-cool."

Laughing she jumped onto the futon and pummelled his chest.

"My eldest sister's a real Deadhead, she plays them all the time."

"That's no bloody excuse…"

X grabbed her arms and tried to roll over on top of her, but she resisted.

"… they're still shit."

"Don't say that."

"Why not if they are?"

Forced to lie back X struggled to drag her over him, but she fought back using her legs to push his body away.

"Let go and I'll tell you."

After a final straining effort failed to bring them closer together, he released her with a sigh.

"Go on then."

"You've got such a closed mind! If that's what you really think I'll not invite you to come and see them with me."

Her voice, a breathless whisper, excited X.

"They're still going?"

"Duhhh!"

She pulled the duvet over them, casting what X imagined to be a wistful glance at his taut groin.

"Wembley Arena, next Thursday. Last night of their tour."

"A school day?"

"A school day."

His parents would not be happy and from what he'd heard – jangling, freeform jamming with a cowboy vibe – he wouldn't be either. He wasn't keen on the band, and it would probably cost him dear. His less than generous weekly allowance would only stretch so far. But how could he say no and stay cool? The old anxiety returned, a disconcerting uneasiness in the pit of his stomach, and he was only vaguely reassured by Ali's smile.

"Yes, OK."

Her powers of beguilement reaffirmed Ali snuggled down beneath the covers and to X's pleasurable relief brushed one of her arms against his leg.

"Don't sound so excited, will you?"

"No, no I want to go, really."

"Good."

She rested a hand on his right thigh and squeezed gently. He sighed involuntarily. No explanation was necessary, Ali knew, but in her mood of soporific intoxication she needed to draw him ever further in to her dreamy world.

"My sister, Ramona, she's the eldest … she's a drug dealer and is taking some clients to the gig … "

X smiled. Ali waited for a reaction, but there was nothing further.

"… A spot of corporate entertaining."

X opened his eyes and could just make her out staring obliquely at him from the shadows of the duvet.

"There are two spare tickets."

X laughed.

"Right."

"She's ten years older than me and a bit of an old hippy. That's why she likes this stuff… Some of it's not bad, I suppose."

Her hand was slowly creeping up his leg, nails digging painfully into his flesh.

"Yeah," X swallowed hard, "they're growing on me too."

"There'll be anything you want … "

"Yeah?"

Her fingers were now combing through his pubic hair, tugging playfully.

"Acid, E, coke, even H. As much as you want … all on the house."

"Wow."

Incredulity, tinged with amazement, was obvious in his voice.

"The band play for hours and you can get really out of your head, all courtesy of my sister. What more could you want? It'll be great, believe me…"

"I do."

"Oh no you don't. If you did, you'd show a bit more enthusiasm."

Her hand grasped his penis. His body stiffened expectantly.

"I did some E when I saw the Happy Mondays with Ramona last month, it was amazing."

X was no longer listening.

Free falling there was always a moment when your perception of the airy world around you would irrevocably change. An exhilarating – or terrifying – fraction of a second, that would demonstrate the awful speed of your descent. A fleeting shadow across the retina, a flash as your body passed unfeeling through a wafer-thin pane of insubstantiality, visible from above as a faint silken sheen misting the landscape, but masked from below by the incredible blue vastness of the sky. X had seen the phenomenon before, indeed had heard it explained away as being simply the boundary between two bodies of air slightly differing in temperature, an optical illusion hiding a physical deception, but had never been so overawed by its beauty.

Diving through, eyes wide, X glimpsed along this ethereal plane, sensing the immense curvature of the earth, appreciating the infinite magnitude of the barrier through which he was passing, knowing the exact instant when he slipped beneath this sacred cloth blanketing the planet. An instinctive uninformed believer in the divinity of existence he imagined the subtle fabric to be woven from motes of dust floating in the bright beam of hallowed light escaping through the narrow gap beneath the gates of heaven. Unheard his celebratory laughter rang out in the thin air as he resolved that before long, he would again trip along this magic carpet high above the globe.

The wet concrete vastness of the car park, glistening in the harsh neon glow of the security lighting, stretched away to the sheer walls of the hangar-like Wembley Arena shrouded in shifting clouds of drizzle. Crowds of people, coats flapping, heads bowed against the wind and rain, hurried past. Stragglers rushed to catch up, briefly individuals – open parka revealing a garishly tinted tie-dye shirt, long hair tucked beneath a knitted hat of many colours, multi-hued jumpers in vivid blues, reds and yellows, a long flowing floral dress covered with a thick striped poncho, patched denim jackets, sleeves fraying, soaked head scarves holding hair hanging lankly – before merging into the anonymous mass. X stared out at the bustle through the steamed up side window of Ramona's Jaguar XJS V12 HE, his excitement tempered by nervousness. Ali, squeezed in beside him on the cramped back seat, was leaning forward attentive to the discussion going on in the front. She was smoking a joint, the sweet pungent smell filling the air. Ramona, who had driven them and three of her "clients", as she called them, at reckless speed around the North Circular, had open on her lap a small pink vanity case.

"Well then guys what's it to be – acid or Es? My treat."

X, already intoxicated, prayed she wasn't expecting an answer from him, he felt ill-qualified to express an opinion having experienced neither. He was hoping, somewhat apprehensively, that Ali, someone he was still uncertain he could trust implicitly, would guide him safely through this initiation.

"Rick, you're the only true Deadhead here?"

The leather-clad man shifted next to Ali.

"Acid, nothing else will do man."

"Hell, Rick you're so fucking predictable."

The woman's voice was slurred and she stumbled over her words.

"Tear me off a tab too Ramona, there's a love."

The couple flailed playfully at each other, Ali ducked out of their way, crushing X against the side panel.

"Steady on you lot."

Ramona waited for them to settle before carefully handing them a small piece of blotting paper.

"Josh?"

"Brownies for me."

"And you two love-birds?"

"Fuck off Ramona. The same."

Ali's voice was hard and unyielding to any suggestion that she was in a relationship.

"I don't know about him."

She elbowed X.

"The same for me as well, thanks."

X hoped nobody picked up on his unease.

Amused Ramona reached into her case and lifted out a small sealed plastic bag, opened it and poured a number of tablets into her hand. She passed them to Josh, a shaven-headed man in a black suit seated beside her in the front seat, emptied the bag, swallowed three herself, passed the rest to Ali, then turned up the volume of the car stereo.

"I love this one."

She lolled back in the leather bucket seat, her head falling against the headrest, dark feathery strands of hair coiling free. Jangling distorted guitars blasted from speakers front and rear, a song X didn't recognize, but as the pounding bass pulsed through his body, he had an intense craving to suck on one of Ramona's curls as they bounced in front of him, forcing his tongue through the eye of the loose ringlet.

"Fuck I haven't heard this for a while," Josh swallowed his tablets, washing them down with a swig from a tarnished silver hip-flask, "Give me a fucking clue."

"Groovy man," Ramona lit another joint and inhaled deeply, "Flaming groovy."

Josh stared blankly, his brow furrowed. Fuzzy guitars screeched out their infectious rhythm over a chorus of shouted voices, before one tore free shredding the air with a blistering solo that left X breathless, his head throbbing.

"It's on the tip of my fucking tongue, come on," Josh gestured with his hands.

"Slow Death by the Flaming Groovies," her words were clipped, spoken through clenched teeth, as the smoke held deep in her lungs permeated her body.

"Fuck me it's not is it? Where did you get it from? They must all be dead by now."

Josh chuckled merrily, a boyish sound at odds with his scarred, hard-man appearance.

"The Groovies dead, never!"

Ramona exhaled slowly, the smoke billowing upwards, before massing in thickening clouds in the padded roof space above her head.

"It's a compilation, one of my little boys put it together for me. All the hits."

"Right," Josh again laughed happily.

There was a sudden thud on the door and the occupants of the car tensed.

"Shit."

"Who's that?"

Ramona, soberly in command, closed her vanity case and slipped it under the front seat, waved away the haze of smoke wafting in front of her face and wiped at the steamed up side-window. X did the same and saw a brightly coloured skull grinning at him, a wreath of thorny red roses jauntily sitting on its cracked white dome, the whole sexless grotesque woven around by indecipherable psychedelic lettering. Tattooed hands cupped against the gusting wind fumbled with a roll-up, as match after match flared fiercely then died.

"It's only some stoned Deadhead," the relief was evident in her voice as Ramona eased back into her seat, "trying to fire up a joint, in the shelter of my car."

Rick giggled. Ramona tapped on the window. Startled the man leapt back then turned, leant forward and peered myopically through the smeared glass.

"He's out of his box, can't see a fucking thing. Go on bugger off."

Josh flicked a V-sign at the bearded figure, who muttered inaudibly, straightened up and staggered off into the streaming crowd, his oversize Grateful Dead tee shirt ballooning in the rush of air.

Heart thumping, X turned to face Ali – the persistent tugging on his sleeve was beginning to annoy him – and morosely snapped, "What?" just as the stereo fell silent. Her offering was rapidly withdrawn, fingers snapping tightly shut over the two pink tablets nestling in her hand, long purple nails digging into the fleshy cushion of her palm.

"Suit yourself, if you don't want them."

The tone was cold, her irritation at his indiscretion clear, a hint if he had cared to notice it that their relationship had already passed its passionate cusp. His response, instant yet abject, succeeded in restoring some momentum to their individual destinies together ensuring, for that evening at least, they could run along parallel trajectories, but the balance in their partnership was forever skewed against him.

"Sorry Ali, I was miles away ..."

The smoky air reverberated to the clash of a cymbal and thump of bass drum, then immediately pulsed to a body-moving reggae beat and lilting Jamaican voice.

"Hey Jim, Jim just a minute you all..."

Engrossed for a second by the intriguing lyrics, X faltered.

" ... Hey Jim, how'd you spell New York?"

The tug on the sleeve, harder this time, her fingers pinching his skin through the thin cotton.

"Ali sorry. I love this. Who is it?"

"I don't bloody know, Ramona's always listening to all kinds of shit. You'll have to ask her. Now do you want these or not?"

Her hand opened slowly to reveal the tablets. X uncertain, rested his head on her shoulder.

"Brownies?" he whispered.

Ali looked mystified and X feared she hadn't heard him over the deafening music.

"What are they?" he mouthed.

Flexing her shoulder, forcing his head to lift, she spat out her reply.

"E's stupid."

Smiling nervously, he reached over and picked one up. Nondescript, small, triangular in shape and imprinted with the image of a butterfly, it weighed heavily. He felt sick, the air for the first time tasted acrid and bitter, the atmosphere stifling. Without hesitation he popped it into his mouth and washed it down with a swig of beer. Ali followed suit, drinking from the same can, and smiling for the first time.

"Come on sis, let's go."

Ramona turned grinning and waved her joint in the air.

"When this is done, love, when this is done."

Smoke curled from her nostrils and the corners of her partially open mouth and in the yellow filtered light X noticed to his surprise that she was good-looking. It was as if Ali had been taken as the base template on to which had been crafted innumerable refinements – a delicacy of features, finer lines to the eyebrows and cheek bones, a shimmering skin taut and unblemished, the slight creases around the penetrating green eyes giving depth, an added maturity, the asymmetry of the narrow slightly hooked nose accentuated by the glinting diamond stud in her left nostril, a startling contrast to the array of dull gun-metal jewellery gracing her pierced ears. The revelation seemed, in his heightened state of excitation, to be a profound one and from then on Ramona became X's Warrior Queen – the tip of her tongue moistening full red lips subjugating her vassal – Ali a mere handmaiden.

The thrill of anticipation racked X as he walked across the damp tarmac towards the auditorium. Trailing the others as they hurried forward in a huddle, hunched against the rain which was now falling in heavy sheets, he sensed the tingling of the chemicals in his stomach as the small pill dissolved, releasing its powerful intoxicants into his bloodstream. In his mind the delicate pale pink butterfly unfurled its wings to reveal fine hues of green and blue, then startling swirls of yellow and purple, before being swept away in the ruby-red torrent. He was aware of his body's dynamics like never before, the beating of his heart, the pulsing of his veins and arteries, the dull throbbing in his head, temples distending, pressure building behind transfixed eyes, his loud rapid inhalations and exhalations, clearly audible over the heavy slap of his footsteps on the wet ground.

Around him people gathered, closing in, nudging and pushing, relentlessly moving ahead. The mass carried him along, the scent of begonias and patchouli threading the air. A sense of isolation, of being alone in the crowd, took hold and he noticed strangers glancing at him, heard whispered words and instantly sensing their disapproval, sought out the mocking laughter in their babbling voices. Sounds rang in his ears, their meaning unclear, a bearded man his damp greying hair tied back, pointed in his direction the wide-open sleeve of his striped over-shirt flapping in the wind. X stared back, the chemical battery assailing him mentally, had a physical manifestation that was singling him out, making him visible, a beacon of un-cool in this sea of retro-chic hippiedom. His amusement at his own powers of social commentary was bittersweet as the phrases reverberated across a blank mind, the wonderful incisiveness of his thinking exposing a complete inability to orientate himself and act. He knew he was losing control and felt for the first time a twinge of regret at his own recklessness. The seething multitude offered no sanctuary and he retreated inwards seeking solace in vacuity.

Shuffling forward in a queue that stretched along one side of the high, corrugated metal wall of the venue, he suddenly remembered the others and wondered where they were, a vague anxiety creeping over him as he pondered the fact that one of them had his ticket. Genie-like Ali emerged out of the crowd, her earnest face scanning the line of concertgoers. Smiling, X waited, his ebullience restored, their eyes met, a flicker of exasperation before Ali acknowledged him.

"Here you are."

She slid in beside him, her shoulders brushing his.

"I knew you'd find me."

"You're lucky I did, Ramona was all set for going in without you. She's a hard bitch at the best of times, but gets even worse when she's with those tossers."

X kissed the top of her head and placed his arm around her.

"This is amazing."

"What is?"

"You know," he squeezed her shoulders and leant over to murmur in her ear, "the E."

Ali drew back and looked at him mystified.

"What do mean?"

"You know."

"I don't."

"I'm feeling different," Ali's puzzled expression forced him to expound further, his voice dropping to a whisper, "you know things have started to happen and people have been looking strangely at me."

Bemused, she giggled, uncertain as to whether she found his naivety amusing or an annoyance. At her age she was beginning to question whether physical attraction alone was enough to outweigh the crass immaturity that seemed to blight so many of her male contemporaries. X had seemed different, tall, good-looking and coolly fashionable, with his gelled blond hair – number three cut at the sides – blue eyes and athletic body, quiet, not as cocky as some boys she had known, yet amusing, tactile and attentive and very importantly for her prepared to experiment and take risks, in short have a good time, but looking at him now she thought she could have got it wrong. He appeared diminished, almost childlike, clinging to her, imagining he was stoned. The simple calculation that she didn't want to be left on her own with her sister and clients convinced her to humour him, but she vowed it was for the last time.

"You're just paranoid," she pushed him gently on the chest, "it takes at least half an hour to kick in and you only popped it five minutes ago so nothing can be happening."

X smiled meekly. Logically she was right, but he knew something was going on. He'd never felt like this before, even though he was calmer now, the transformation was underway.

"You'll know when it kicks in, believe me. You'll get that loved-up feeling, everyone's your friend, and you'll want to dance man, dance like never before. Just give it a chance."

X nodded.

"I just hope this Dead lot are up to it."

Ramona smiled as she passed over a plastic pint glass brimming with foam.

"You look like a lager man to me. Come on we're over here."

Liquid slopped over X's hand and shirt as he sat down in his seat in the front row of the stalls. Exasperated, he gulped at the cold beer, swallowing hard, then gazed at the vast deserted stage that stretched away from him at eye-level. To left and right amplifiers and monitors, glowing lights flickering red and green, were piled one on top of the other standing sentinel either side of the two vast drum kits sitting next to each other on a raised platform immediately ahead of him. Intricate twisted assemblages of glinting metal forged against a framework of huge brass gongs and assorted hanging percussion instruments, pale skulls bedecked with wreaths of flowers grinned out from the two huge bass drums, three microphones rearing above them, their bulbous heads pointing searchingly downwards like malevolent cranes. Mountainous banks of speakers towered above the stage from the wings, precarious building block constructions that mysteriously leant out over the heads of the audience, their summits invisible in the vastness of the gloomy roof space. In comparison the array of sleek keyboards on the right raised on slight wooden legs seemed incongruously puny and inconsequential. The whole installation was bathed in an aura of pink and purple light, which was reflected in the upturned faces of the audience in the seats around him, and seemed to float above the bare wooden boards on a huge Eastern carpet of arabesque reds and golds. The crackling hum of an immense electrical potential charged the atmosphere and X, tuning intuitively into the powerful pulse, began to move his body. The rhythm so compelling his limbs gathered their own natural momentum as the tension built – feet tapping, head nodding, hands slapping thighs, shoulders shaking – feeding off the static in the air, his frenetic motion adding to the ambient force in a symbiosis of flowing energy.

Ramona and Ali exchanged wry smiles.

"Isn't he sweet."

"Embarrassing more like."

Ali turned her head to look back at the gathering crowd, ignoring X, while Ramona drew heavily on a joint, leant back in her seat and, slowly exhaling, gazed at his body through a veil of gently rising smoke. His movement, fluid and twisting, exerted an addictive appeal, but what interested her more was his obvious sensitivity to the subtle chemical and physical changes bearing in upon him. She was certain that he was instinctively tapping into a base flow only he could yet feel, but that others, herself included, would soon be charting. Such qualities of unselfconscious leadership were rare in her experience and his youth offered up the wonderful opportunity to influence and manipulate.

A roar rippled across the vast auditorium, ebbing and flowing as waves of sound rose from the cheering fans to violently merge with echoes ricocheting off the unforgiving metal walls. An agitated maelstrom of sound overwhelming everyone in a deluge of anticipation. The diffuse shouts, cries, whoops slowly coalescing into a coherent rhythmic clapping and stamping that shook the fabric of the huge building. X's excitement was palpable, infant-like in the simple unalloyed thrill of the moment.

He rose to his feet with the others as the band ambled on to the stage, six of them led by an overweight man with a shock of grey hair, neatly trimmed beard and glasses. A diffident wave before taking up their instruments elicited howls of approbation as X hesitated, missing a beat, his expectations of a visual riot of colourful, dissolute excess rudely overturned. The musicians were all somberly dressed in unfashionable loose-fitting Tee shirts, baggy jeans and worn trainers. The inspiration for the brilliant psychedelic mayhem of the Deadheads in the audience was not apparent in the appearance of their revered idols. Their cumulative ages, he calculated, must be in the hundreds, and he sensed an abandonment of energy, a world suddenly rotating in slow motion. For the first time he could smell the sweet fragrance of marijuana and hear the words being spoken around him, he was deflating, sinking to the ground.

Discordant notes from on high lifted him, a cacophony of plucked strings and feedback then with a deafening thump of the drums and a blinding explosion of purple, green and red light, the band took flight urged on by a wave of sound from the auditorium that all but drowned out the opening bars. Searchlights stabbed the darkness through rents in a black canvas, crisscrossing the stage and flitting across the sea of heads and waving arms pushing ceaselessly towards the front as the band surged on with jangling bursts of high energy music – twin guitars duelling over sliding drum rhythms intermeshing with the serpentine bass line then breaking free, the plonking run of a honky-tonk piano, then a scorching guitar solo accompanied by shrill whistles and cries, all swept over by a great wash of groaning organ.

X, buoyed up on the rising swell, began to dance, quickly carving out a compact space between his seat and the safety barrier and patrolled it efficiently, establishing his territory. Mind clear, limbs lithe, he ceased to think, his body, acting on instinct, began responding in surprising ways, achieving a synthesis of mood and mobility that was revelatory. Tripping after that deceptive lick, reaching out to hook that elusive note became possibilities, catching them a profound thrill, a yearning instantly satisfied, the reward a renewed rush of energy, building, reinforcing and so the cycle ran on, never-ending ecstasy. Whatever the tune, melody, tempo the songs all melded beautifully with the musical orchestration running through his head and he danced in time with eyes closed. Cheering and clapping madly with the others between numbers, but forever moving, he hugged Ali and Ramona and embraced pliant strangers. A plastic bottle thrust into his hands slaked a craving – the streaming water absorbed thirstily by a parched body, doused in sweat – the tepid liquid tasting like nectar. The contents of the bottle then upended, water pouring from soaking hair and dripping from his ears and nose, a rainbow of droplets spraying everywhere as he shook his head in pure joy.

The interval came and went. The second set more informally structured was an inspiration with the band letting go, jamming freely, easing into extended periods of musical experimentation seamlessly interpreting each others aspirations, thinking, swings of mood. The music a harmonious medley of colours, luscious reds and oranges, screaming yellows, peaceful greens, a throbbing vibrant blue, swirling indigos and violets. The scent of roses and newly cut hay filled the air. All senses finely attuned to the continuous flow.

High above the stage and caught in the spotlight a proscenium arch of multi-coloured balloons, trailing silken ribbons, began to crumble. Its rigid structure sagging as its supports were cut away, an individual red balloon breaking free and floating away, the rest colliding and spinning as they tumbled earthwards in a gaudy shower.

"That was fucking amazing, thank you," his lips slid across Ali's damp cheek as she slipped from the back seat of the car into the chill dankness of the early morning.

"Bye."

The door slammed shut. X flopped back on to the empty expanse of leather, shivering in the blast of cold air, his sodden clothes cooling rapidly, but still deliriously happy. Ramona peered over at him from the front seat.

"You had a good time then?" her voice was huskily alluring.

"Yes, I did," his sore throat made conversation difficult, "Ace."

Eyes open briefly he smiled at her, then closed them again barely registering that she had moved, and was now looming above him as she slid through the gap between the front seats and joined him in the back. Peering through a ragged smudge in the steamed up side window she checked to see that Ali had disappeared inside the house before she began to undo the belt of her jeans and unzip her fly. X jerked awake as she slid a lit joint between his lips and tugged off his trousers and underpants.

"One more little treat before I take you home."

X always wished he could remember more of the details of what happened. The basic facts that he had made love for the first time with an experienced, attractive, older woman in the back of a vintage Jaguar after a blissfully stoned evening he had no problem recalling, but as he was to learn, from Ramona amongst many others, there was much more to be noted than the simple details of who, when and where. He also knew that she had changed his life when at last she looked down at him and breathlessly said, "I have a job for you if you're interested."

He had been but was beginning to feel slightly unwell.

## *Stenning Gazette – 30 April 2004*

*An edited extract from "Lucky B...s"
by Seymour Gretsch, Features Editor.*

... "Lady luck is smiling on him," is a phrase bandied around all too frequently by those of us who do not really understand the meaning of the word chance or have never had the good lady shower her favors on us. Let's face it some people are lucky, others make their own good fortune ... all true to a point ... the toss of a coin comes up heads, the boss remembers the hilarious hours spent with you in the bar, it all works out for the best. Life goes on, your winning streak may last, but more likely it won't. But some people are really lucky b...ds and what I want to know is how you go on living after something like that?

I got to thinking about life's lottery after I heard about Shameka Peterson and Joe Masorka, two New York office workers on their way home after a hard day's work, who stepped into an elevator on the 44th floor of the Empire State Building and then plunged over 400 feet in four seconds, juddering to a halt on the fourth floor. Lucky or what?

"I thought I was going to die," said Joe surprisingly calm for one so accurate in their assessment of their situation, after clambering along a beam to an adjoining car and hauling himself out of the elevator shaft. "It was like a bungee jump," was all a phlegmatic Shameka said after the ordeal.

And there are many more living amongst us. Scott Durant aged 11 was on vacation at the beach with his parents when a gust of gale-force wind caught him and blew him over one of England's highest cliffs at Boulby in Yorkshire. He fell 450 feet, was knocked unconscious, but suffered only minor cuts and bruises and three broken teeth.

An 8-year-old boy survived an eighteen-story fall from the Sheung Shui apartment block in Hong Kong after hitting four clothes-lines on the way down and landed on a canopy just above the first floor. He broke an arm and a leg. There is a similar tale from Georgia where a 13-year-old boy was playing on the roof of a nine-story building when he tripped and fell over the edge. Clothes-lines again saved him and he only broke his leg. My favorite though is the 17-month-old baby girl who fell off the Capilano suspension bridge in British Columbia plunging 230 feet before landing bruised on a narrow ledge three feet from the icy fast-flowing Capilano river.

And it's not just kids.

Daniel Hudson, 34, plummeted 1,000 feet down Scotland's highest mountain, Ben Nevis, breaking only his arm and bruising his face. He described himself as "the luckiest man alive." Possibly.

A middle-aged Ohio woman parking her car in a multi-story in Pittsburgh, plunged through the barrier and fell seven stories after the brakes of her Buick Century failed. The sedan landed on the driver's side collapsing the roof and narrowly missing a man walking past and a car entering the parking lot. Minor injuries were all that the woman suffered.

A British air force officer on an adventure training course in the Scottish Highlands tripped on a crampon and fell 1,300 feet down a ravine. She survived and suffered serious head and back injuries, but at least eight other climbers had died in similar falls in the same place.

Miraculous. It makes you think.

I could go on but for some reason I'm starting to feel ill-starred. I don't want to use up what may be a limited personal supply of good fortune. Touch wood, fingers crossed, black cats permitting I'll be speaking to you next month. Be lucky.


*Postscript: Stenning Gazette – 7 May 2004*
*Mervin Samuels, editor writes: Seymour Gretsch our distinguished and long-serving features editor died last week in a tragic accident on Bowden Street. He was returning home from the office late at night and tripped and fell, catching his head on the curb. He was killed instantly. Seymour was a perspicacious, prescient and trend-setting journalist ...*

3,558 metres

## ST JAMES' BIBLE – THE FALL FROM GRACE OR THE FALL OF MAN.

*Genesis 2:16/17*
And the Lord God commanded the man, saying, of every tree of the garden thou mayest freely eat; But of the tree of knowledge of good and evil, thou shalt not eat of it: for in the day that thou eatest thereof thou shalt surely die.

*Genesis 3:6*
And when the woman saw that the tree was good for food and that it was pleasant to the eyes, and a tree to be desired to make one wise, she took of the fruit thereof, and did eat; and gave also to her husband with her and he did eat.

The air was clearer now and perceptibly cooler, refreshing skimming across a moist skin. There was a scent of brine, the salt a faint burn on the tongue, and a sting to the eyes. The view was invigorating, the definition stunning – physical features aeons old and broiled for geological ages. Twisted and thrusting, their contorted skeletons laid bare, bones exposed by the wind and rain, the harsh detail picked out by unforgiving shadows. The dark broken-teeth silhouette of a distant mountain range loomed over the vast expanse of a sun-lit alluvial valley – a muted palette of drifting sands, russet grits, pale crushed silica, grey quartzite and rust-coloured shales – slashed by the meandering torrent of the San Joaquin River. Rapids speckled its course, shimmering their frothing defiance into the pressing sunlight. The undulating plain, spotted with patches of lush green, rolled down towards the rugged coastline, the grasslands parting around the isolated conical remnant of an ancient volcano, its summit flecked with wisps of cloud, until the land rose sharply forced against a ridge of granite that ran along the terraced coast as high cliffs – a natural bulwark against the relentless onslaught of Pacific breakers, whose destructive efforts could be seen as a thin smudge of white rimming the edge of the great turquoise eye of the ocean. The churning textured surface, patterned and alive, daubed with subtle shaded gradations of blue and green, cut by a foaming scar of broken water crashing against the rocky foundations of a hidden offshore reef, that ran in parallel to the scrap of beach. Man's efforts – a fishing boat steaming a resolute course, highways, settlements, farms, the white plume of smoke rising from a distant fire – were puny but clearly visible. Encroaching, they lay purposeful patterns across the natural flux.

 Falling towards such beauty, gracefully, was a responsibility, X acknowledged. He turned his head from side to side, moving his fingers, dispelling the faint ache of nascent cramp, adjusting his flight posture, his angle of re-entry. Perfection was in the positioning. It was all a matter of fine-tuning.

The waiting around was what got to him the most – derelict, ravaged landscapes; scraps of stunted greenery clinging to life on piles of smashed rubble or else running riot in an excess of tangled, impenetrable thorny growth; broken shells of buildings with splintered wooden frames and shattered windows, water dripping from cracked pipes, pooling in dirty dark festering puddles; wind-blown, stained, concrete multi-stories, like this one, all deserted and devoid of any trace of a sensitive humanity. Lou Reed had got it right when he sang, "the first thing you learn is you've always got to wait."

In the year he'd been doing this job, working for Ramona, "waiting for the man" had been refined into an art form. He'd read more books over the last twelve months – much to the amusement of Alfie sitting beside him, who did nothing but chain-smoke Marlboro's and crack his knuckles – than he ever had in the rest of his life. He'd listened to more Radio One, as well, Alfie would let him play nothing else – "I'll have none of that fucking hyped-up shit you like" – and he was the muscle. Ramona showed little sympathy, laughing brightly and telling him he had to learn the business from the bottom up, sugaring the pill with shameless flattery – anyway he was the only one she could trust for the really big deals – and an energetic 'knee-trembler' in the alcove at the back of her office, the door unlocked, blinds half-drawn. That was what irritated him, it was a business they were engaged in after all. In what other line of work would associates treat you like this? Gratuitously wasting your time without a fucking by your leave. If the money and perks weren't so good, he'd have moved on.

The view from the car-park was stunning. The sky a burning iridescent canvas of glowing orange, screaming candy-floss pink and flaring reds edged in puce, the purples melding into the star-studded darkness of the encroaching night. The flashing lights of a jet airliner high above, hurtling towards the inferno, was the only movement. In the distance, the glinting jewel-studded tower blocks clawed skyward – their highly patterned, brightly toned cladding still visible in the dusky haze, myriad lives framed in gleaming regimented rows – six of them in two lines of three marching across the urban landscape, their footprints black open expanses stamped out of the maze of Victorian terraces, long demolished. The old street layout illuminated only in the lines of street lamps that ended abruptly at the edge of the sombre grass wasteland, the phantom lights criss-crossing the gloom.

Leaning on the grimy concrete parapet, X looked down on the quiet access road that ran beside the car park, the surface still wet from the early evening rain. Four girls hurried past, their chattering voices surfing the waves of stillness; a house door slammed, and X tuned in to the sounds of the autumn evening. The background roar of the traffic, distant but ever-present, the occasional car horn discordant and angry, clattering high heels fading away, a dog barking followed by a yell, the car-radio quietly droning on, the beat persistent and rhythmic. There was a chill in the air, the moist freshness of the downpour still suppressing the fumes of the polluted city air, X turned up the collar of his thigh-length leather jacket and crossed his arms.

"God, how much longer?"

The twin beams of the headlights moved slowly along the damp road, clearly visible long before the car, a black BMW 3 series convertible, came into view from beneath the tall plane trees. It was followed closely by another lighter shaded BMW coupe. Both halted for a moment at the car-park entrance directly below X, then moved slowly up the ramp and disappeared from sight.

"Shit."

Alfie appeared to be asleep, his eyes closed, feet up on the dashboard. The radio seemed louder. X rushed round to the door and flung it open. Alfie slumped sideways then, jerking awake, thrust a pistol into X's face.

"Don't fucking do that."

"How many did Ramona say we should be expecting?"

"Just that arsehole, Jake. Why what's fucking happening?"

"He doesn't drive a Beamer?"

"Oh, for fuck's sake. No. He snorts all his money up his nose."

Alfie pushed violently against the door, rocking X backwards, and then hauled himself awkwardly to his feet.

"He's grassed us up then."

"What the fuck?"

"And whoever it is the bastards have come mob-handed."

"Fuck."

"They won't know we know, so let's get out of here. You drive."

"Hold on."

Alfie tossed the pistol to X, slid round the car and opened the boot. Lifting the liner mat he pulled a package out of the spare tyre-well, tore off the brown paper wrapping, letting it drop to the ground, then slipped the sawn-off shotgun into the large customized inside pocket of his black overcoat.

"Come on Alfie, for Christ sake."

"Hold your fucking horses, I'm coming."

The large man dropped heavily into the driver's seat and fumbled with the keys in the ignition as twin headlight beams shone brightly from the darkness of the down ramp, followed closely by their mirror on the up ramp. The sound of two cars revving hard, treads squealing, shredded the night.

"Fuck."

"Shit."

"Leave this to me."

"Oh, fucking yeah."

The engine burst into life and Alfie reversed the car in a broad arc, flicking the headlights on to full beam and illuminating two figures in dark overcoats stepping out of the BMW and moving towards the concrete pillars framing the exit from the level, Uzi submachine-guns in their hands. Looking in the mirror Alfie could see the shadowy silhouettes of two or three men approaching from the other ramp.

"We're fucked mate!"

He slid the shotgun from his pocket and placed it across his knees.

"Don't start anything Alfie."

"Yeah right."

"Let's see what they want."

"They want our fucking bollocks, that's what they want."

One of the men motioned for them to switch off the engine.

"Peter Foster, I should have known. Ramona will be pissed."

"We'll be more than pissed, unless we fucking do something."

"Do what he wants."

"What?"

X noticed Alfie was sweating heavily, moisture beading on his upper lip and furrowed forehead.

"We're not going anywhere are we, for fucks sake? They're tooled up for a bloody war."

"I could get a couple of the fuckers."

"Don't be an arsehole. We'll give them the stash and pay back later, Ramona'll not ..."

"Fuck Ramona."

The tap-tapping of metal on the car's rear window silenced their exchange and both turned to see the muzzle of an Uzi resting against the glass and pointing straight at them. Barely moving X allowed the pistol to slip from his grasp and slide down the side of the front seat, and Alfie reached forward to turn off the engine, as he did so gently pushing the shotgun off his lap onto the floor.

"You two lover boys, out you get. Gently does it."

"Peter ..."

X extended his hand, but it was ignored.

"Mr Foster to you, pretty boy, Mr Foster. Show a bit of respect."

Two of the men opened the door for Alfie and dragged him struggling from the car. Before he could gain his footing he was hit hard in the solar plexus and sank to the ground fighting for breath.

"Tell your boy to take it easy."

X glanced across at Alfie intending to signal reassurance, but he was oblivious, his eyes blinded by rage, his face contorted with pain. A gun barrel pressed against his temple kept him on his knees.

"That's the business. Now you won't try anything stupid, will you?"

X shook his head, concerned for the first time for his own safety. Peter Foster was not known to be a hard case and this show of force was out of character, his preferred mode of operation was negotiation, cutting a deal rather than shooting it out. Ramona had been rubbing along with him for a number of years with the minimum of trouble. A real "pussy" was how she described him, "not like some of the other bastard polecats I come across." Someone was obviously squeezing him.

"Good, then we can have a proper little chat."

A short man, the heavy coat draped over his shoulders reaching almost to the ground, he appeared ill at ease, playing nervously as he spoke with the large gold signet ring on his right hand, turning it through ninety degrees with each beat of the conversation. He was wanly smiling and the rotundity of his face, accentuated by the close-cropped cut of his thinning brown hair, seemed vaguely absurd and non-threatening, his waxy skin was shiny and moist, hooded eyes glowing red in the reflected light of the dying sun, his left eyelid twitching erratically. His expression was bland, yet his body language – chin raised, back erect, frame drawn up to full height, chest inflated, shoulders squared, feet squarely placed – exuded a powerful air of violence suppressed.

"How's Ramona? Still giving you the 'special treatment' I'm told."

"She's fine."

"Glad to hear it. Now I know she has a soft spot for you …"

"Boss."

One of Peter Foster's henchmen was holding up the shotgun and pistol.

"Found these in their car, under the front seats."

"Tut tut, now what would you be wanting those for?"

"To sort out fuckers like you."

Alfie was defiant, a heavy blow to the side of the head silenced him. Blood began oozing from the deep cut and trickling down the side of his face.

"Keep him quiet and search him," the harsh sound of authority displaced Peter Foster's previously solicitous tone, "you're not carrying anything else, are you?"

"No."

"Good, wise lad."

His words were still softly spoken, but the modulation of his voice had imperceptibly changed and was now venomous.

"Check him out as well. You can never be too careful."

Rough hands pawed X's body, disturbing the line of his clothes, delving into pockets, patting, ruffling his hair. The man, vaguely familiar, grinned at him and tweaked his ear as he finished his search.

"He's clean boss.'"

"Where's the stash?"

"What stash?"

"Don't be a prat."

Peter Foster motioned to one of his men, who took a step forward, "You make a habit of standing around in shitholes like this for nothing, do you?"

"It's barely a stash, just a small delivery."

"Come on, old Jake's one of your main buyers. He doesn't fuck around for small deliveries."

"Where's Jake?"

"He's busy."

The menacing upward curl of his lip, the furrowing of his brow, the weak smile suggested pleasure at X's growing appreciation of his predicament, the anxiety encroaching on his face – the blinking of the eyes, the hand nervously touching sagging lips, the short rapid intakes of breath.

"Otherwise engaged is what you'd say. Anyway, It's no concern of yours."

"He's working for you?"

"More resting. Putting his feet up."

He looked around seeking affirmation and his men duly smiled in acknowledgement.

"Ramona won't be happy."

"When is she ever happy?" he paused, "except of course when she's giving you or some other little boy a good seeing-to."

Alfie groaned.

"Keep him quiet."

There was the innocuous sound of a smack then an animal bellow of pain.

"Quiet I said, for God's sake Chris. I'm trying to hold a conversation over here."

Silence followed the crack of metal on bone.

"She's not meant to be happy, that's the whole idea. Now where is it?"

X nodded at the car.

"Where in the car?"

Obfuscation was pointless, he knew that, but he hesitated, a nagging concern about Ramona's unpredictability giving him reason to pause. Was there a deal to be done here? There was obviously someone else behind all this, Ramona's renowned brutality when crossed would normally have deterred a small-time operator like Peter Foster.

"Ramona would be interested in talking to you about this, I can guarantee that."

"You can guarantee what?"

"If you're being squeezed, we can work something out."

"You think I'm being squeezed, do you?"

"Why would you ..."

"Shut the fuck up. I don't work for anyone else."

"So why?"

There was renewed menace in his voice when he spoke, moving in close – X could smell whisky on his breath – to make his point.

"Listen you little shit, I'm doing this because I want to for my own business reasons. It's about time Ramona and her pack of runts were taken down. She's been fucking a few important people off lately, so, I'll be doing everyone a favour."

He grasped the collar of X's Saint Laurent bomber jacket and twisted, tightening it around his neck.

"Tell me where the fuck the package is or I'll hand you over to Ted there, he's much more of a bastard than me."

X stared blankly, further exasperating Peter Foster.

"Sort him out will yer, he's doing my head in."

He was thrust backwards into the arms of a tall man, who grunted as he grasped X firmly around the waist and lifted him off his feet, swinging him violently against the front of the car, denting the bonnet. Shocked and winded, X struggled for air, his feet barely touching the ground. His cheek pressed hard against the smooth metal could feel the residual heat from the engine, a fleeting reassurance. A shadow approached and grabbed his arms, dragging them forward, then his jacket was hauled up over his head – blocking out the light – and gathered tightly around his outstretched limbs, immobilizing him. There was a disconcerting silence, then X felt a hand fumbling with the belt of his trousers. He struggled vainly, the pressure on his back and arms increasing as the barrel of a gun, unmistakable even through layers of cloth, was jammed painfully against his temple.

"Keep fucking still, nothing would give me more pleasure than to blow your shitty little brains out."

Acquiescent in the stifling darkness, senses alert to the slightest change in the static of his surroundings, X experienced a collapse of faith, a sudden breakdown in his natural ebullience, that was close to fear. A small part of him clung optimistically to the belief that this was a bluff, resolvable through reason, the larger part knew that in the short term the balance had shifted irrevocably and that violence, even death, was highly likely. A cool calculation that momentarily stilled the terror, but failed to stop his reflexes tripping over into panic – racing heartbeat, short rapid intakes of breath, blood draining from the extremities, fine perspiration, muscle tremors.

"Mr. Foster, we can talk about this."

It was difficult to speak – his voice muffled, mouth and throat desiccated by intruding folds of fabric, soaking up saliva – and he was uncertain if he could be heard.

"Let's talk."

His Ermenegildo Zegna belt was pulled forcefully from around his waist, the Z buckle catching slightly as it passed through each of the half a dozen belt loops on the waistband of his Acne Studios face-patch jeans.

"What are you squealing about?"

"We can work something out."

X was breathless, the pressure on his chest was unrelenting and increasing, his words husky and indistinct.

"We can," the voice was close, "but there's only one thing I want to talk about."

"Let me …," swallowing was difficult, " … up. I can hardly breathe."

"Piss off."

The gun barrel was twisted against the side of his head, a motion that screwed the metal painfully into the soft tissue of his temple, the thin woollen jacket no protection. X grunted, unable to articulate a word.

"I've had a fucking enough of this."

There comes a time when you believe, for a second, that you are flying – soaring skyward and not hurtling towards the earth at immense speed – the chemistry of exhilaration warping the electrical signals discharged by the senses; your eyes, wide-open staring at the ground below, absorbing the bigger picture, poring over the detail, that now appears to be growing more distant, silence falls and the wind on your face and hands eases, all contributing to this twisted understanding of your capabilities. The gravitational imperative becomes just one of many possibilities.

X held his breath. He had experienced it once before, the absolute stillness that descends in the closing seconds of a man's life, the cessation of breathing, the stiffening of the body – a rigidity prefiguring the rigour of death that was soon to follow – as the certainty of his execution takes hold, all vestiges of hope gone. It was what he remembered from that cold autumn afternoon in a drab basement flat in Leyton, not the contrasting spasm of violence that followed as the informer's head exploded messily, spraying all in the room with blood and brain tissue, lifeless twisting body thudding to the floor. To have himself reached that point where his end was approaching was something he had never considered, even as a boy reading about death row inmates in Louisiana or Texas, he had extracted pleasure from imagining he only had hours to live, but had never mused on those final moments as the poised needle targeted the pulsing vein, believing as he did, with a naïve belief in his own immortality, in the last minute reprieve. Foolish, but such optimism, he realized, had been an asset in his line of business, putting off until now – the full stop at the end of his life – any consideration of the imminent agony, the fall into nothing.

A silent world of darkness and solitude, heralded the faint glimmer of an idea, not yet positive enough to constitute hope, that Peter Foster may have seen sense, thought better of his decision to steal from Ramona and abandoned his mission and gone, leaving him alive. X daren't move. Then the crushing disappointment as the grip on his arms tightened and the pressure on the gun barrel intensified. Unseen he screwed up his face, eyes tightly shut, lips tensed across clamped teeth, in a willful attempt to ward off the worst physical effects of the anticipated blast.

His expectations were confounded when suddenly a hand fumbled with the button at the top of his flies, attempting to release it, a task hampered by X's prone position and his rapid breathing – his protruding belly tight against the taut fabric.

"Lift the little fucker up, I can't get the bloody things undone."

His feet left the ground, his waistband burst apart and the zip on his jeans was roughly pulled open, he was then lowered back onto the car bonnet. X's arms ached as the loosened garment slid around his knees and the evening air chilled the exposed flesh of his buttocks and thighs. Skin bristling, he shivered involuntarily. Puzzlement turned to a horrible understanding as his underpants were roughly dragged down and he waited for the insertion of a cold metal muzzle between his cheeks.

The thought was appalling and he began to shake, his febrile imagination charting the passage of the bullet as it scorched through his body, ripping apart his abdomen, slicing through the soft tissue of his lungs and exploding his heart, before burning upwards along the oesophagus into the skull cavity, whisking his brain to a soup before bursting forth through the cap of his cranium in a fountain of splintered bone, tissue and fluids. His blood-stiffened blond hair standing upright in a crown around the shattered crater, investing his corpse with a final grotesque dignity. The agony of such a prolonged violation infinitely more horrible to contemplate than the clinical dispatch of a shot to the head.

It was very cold, his perspiration evaporating efficiently from his exposed skin, chilling his blood. He was conscious of his genitals pressed hard against the car radiator, yet exposed. There had been no movement, only the constant muzzle pressure at his temple, and he began anxiously to contemplate their vulnerability.

He heard a distant rustle – almost like the burr of a zip – then felt the presence of a person moving in close, another appalling reality struck him and he began to struggle, twisting his body and kicking out with his jean-tethered feet, but to no avail. A heavy blow across the shoulders forced him back on to the bonnet, while a couple of painful taps from the gun barrel to the side of his head subdued him. Stunned, the loathsome certainty grew of his imminent humiliation, his anger tempering fear, the thought of revenge re-vivifying a desire for life that had all but ebbed away.

The stage was set, the actors well-rehearsed in their parts. The chief protagonist, Peter Foster, about to exert his dominance, yet seeding doubts that would lead inescapably to his own destruction; the antagonist X, a victim who will gain strength rising up from the base depths of his present subjugation; the support, Alfie, soon to play a small but vital role in the drama and the bit players, Ted and the others, crucial but silent witnesses to the developing plot. Each act of the tragedy would be rendered according to the well-thumbed script.

The hairs on the calves of X's bare legs stood erect as someone stepped onto his gathered trousers, clamping his feet in position. A hand grasped his left shoulder. The person was near, the proximity repulsive yet the warmth of such intimacy obscenely welcome against the cold. Penetration was accompanied by a gasp and the crushing weight of the man's torso, heavy across his chest, forcing the air from his lungs – biting hard on the damp cloth of his jacket, breathing was difficult. A sensation of cramping restrictedness, beyond anything he had felt before, scorched his nervous system, his discomfort only diminishing in intensity as a rhythm was established. Immobile, resistance was impossible his body shifting up and down on the smooth metal surface, his knees knocking in time against the hard edge of the car bumper.

Next to his ear the breathing increased in intensity, only the masking jacket protecting him from the moist heat of the man's passion. Nothing was as sweet as the faint mutterings filtering through, the words inaudible, but enough to identify his rapist – Peter Foster. Lifting the cloak of collective responsibility and focusing the icy beam of retribution on just one man, strengthened X's ability to cope with the burning indignity. His rage a shield, burnished by every humiliating spasm and thrust, protected him from the uncertainty, the return of fear, insulated him from the corrosive effect of his inability to read what Peter Foster would do next. Survival now became the key, the ability to pay back this man his sole purpose, the slab of cocaine, hidden in the windscreen washer reservoir beneath the bonnet, just inches from his head, merely a tainted payment for safe passage to that vengeful future.

A frenzy of thrusting, the rapid intakes of air rattling in the lungs, marked the steep climb to the summit. A moaning climax, suppressed then clipped, a late acknowledgement of the silent darkly clad witnesses. The first seconds of post-coital calm were marked by heavy pressure from the heaving stomach of an unfit man across the small of X's back, his breathing rapid and deep – a moment of harsh contemplation before the sudden, rough withdrawal.

Was this a lesson or a final humiliation? X, discarded, the focus of attention shifted briefly elsewhere, had no idea and was scared of the answer. The crude logic dictated that if X was allowed to live, then Peter Foster was himself a dead man. But he was such a thick fucker, who knew what, sated, he would do next.

The uncertainty was compounded by a chorus of incomprehensible grunts and shuffling sounds. A turbulent aura of violent exertion – waves of vibrant compression breaking across his bare skin, a caress prickling goose-bumps into existence – conjured up the abhorrent thought that he was about to be raped again, gangbanged, many times over, locked in a repetitious cycle of desecration. Resistance was impossible, the physical binds if anything stronger than before, grips tightened, the pressure ratcheted upwards. Awareness a curse, hampering preparation for mental abasement and a breakdown of all barriers, willpower redirected into an act of epic endurance beyond previous reckoning. Vows of reciprocal violence now seemed lame, the equivalence paltry and unrewarding, strength fading, their effectiveness as a shield crumbling in the face of overarching power. Animal, inarticulate sounds close behind screamed defiance. Familiar yet distorted, a death rattle or futile act of opposition, X knew only one thing, that it was Alfie. Dull, inarticulate, violent, reliable Alfie, nothing would have sickened him more than the rape. Dread of the same happening to him would drive him wild and insane with the horror.

Heavy thuds, resonant of a sound X had heard only hours earlier as he had passed the "Groom and Horses," of full barrels of beer landing heavily on the mat at the bottom of the steep ramp down to the cellar, resounded around the echoing cavern of the multi-story, as blows struck a body. The grunts of physical exertion of cellar man, assailant and victim all sounding forth in a raucous anthem to the virtues of hard graft and the contract that bound them all, the simple exchange of rewards for the sweat of your labour.

The harsh scraping sound of a bulky object being dragged across rough concrete was accompanied by desperate animated scuffling, then Peter Foster, his voice high-pitched, excited, called out.

"Do it, for fuck's sake."

X flinched. An icy panic obliterated thought, his body stiffened.

A cool spray of saliva and blood exiting under pressure from between Alfie's cracked teeth and lips, spritzed the bare skin of X's buttocks and thighs, then he could feel the contrasting humid warmth of his short rapid breaths as he was manhandled ever closer. There was an anguished snort of disgust as Alfie's face was forced between X's buttocks. He struggled for air and in his fury inadvertently bit X, who screamed.

Peter Foster was amused.

"You two can go on having fun or you can give me what I came for, your choice."

Alfie head was hauled back. He stared up at them, eyes swollen and bloodshot, his face dirty.

"Fuck off."

"Man, you're a slow fucking learner, bury him."

Alfie's breathing weakened, wet sucking wheezes punctuated by long silences, the twitching of his body grew more spasmodic. X fought the persistent pain, able only to focus on keeping quiet. Alfie and the stash, meant nothing in this struggle, his survival did but so did the outcome of the reckless game of dare they were playing. It mattered, X realized, that they went to the bitter limit, win or lose. There were rules that everyone in the car park understood. Peter Foster had played a unique hand, but it was not yet the winning one, that would depend on the cards, if any, he had up his sleeve.

"Your boy here is finding it hard to fucking breath. He may not care, but what about you sonny, had any thoughts about helping us out?"

X was prodded in the side of the head with a gun.

"I've just about had enough of you two. Ten seconds then you'll be joining boyo here."

Again, the metal barrel pressed painfully against his temple. Bluffing or not Peter Foster was making his final play, the trump card. X had no option but to concede.

"In the windscreen washer water-bottle."

X's voice was muffled, deliberately softly spoken.

"You trying to tell me something?"

The gun jabbed at his skull, a repetitious tapping, an exponential agony, blurring all thought, dimming perception of his shady, enclosed world.

"In the engine compartment," the words slurred into existence, "in the washer bottle."

"Say again and speak up."

There was humour in the voice, the blows ceased.

"In the windscreen washer bottle, under the …"

Grasped roughly Alfie and X were pushed off the bonnet on to the cold cement floor, where panting for air they weakly struggled to disentangle their entwined bodies. His face free Alfie began to retch, exuding noisy gurgles as liquid bile and phlegm bubbled in his chest and throat. The belching diverted Peter Foster.

"Shut the fuck up or you'll have me puking up over you."

There was laughter then the bonnet was opened and Peter Foster moved round the side of the car trampling over splayed limbs, kicking out at their battered torsos. Bloody vomit spilled silently from Alfie's mouth, staining the concrete, a pale semi-opaque liquid seeping away in rivulets channelled along the faint runnels that patterned the car-park floor.

"Ugh, you filthy bastard, if you've got any of that muck on my brogues I'll do …"

The threat hung potently in the air.

"Boss."

"What you got? A couple of kilos?"

"Easy, boss, easy."

The brick-sized block of white powder encased in clear plastic and sealed with grey duct tape was tossed casually over the engine to Peter Foster, who caught it smirking.

"At last, now we can go and get something to fucking eat."

He lobbed the cocaine to one of his men and stepped away. X blearily watched them go, the jacket had slipped from his head and he peered up from between the wheels of his BMW. Highly polished black shoes several pairs, came together then moved apart, their soles scuffling on the rough surface, above an animated chatter. Doors slammed, engines flared into life, squealing tyres faded away into a silence punctuated by Alfie's rasping, viscous, whisper repeating, "Say nothing about this, for fuck's sake, say nothing," over and over again.

There was a ship, a mote on the distant horizon, its smokestack smudging the bright off-white glare at the edge of existence. Steaming along the disappearing curve of the earth, dropping out of his world.

The indentation in the pale creamy skin, black hairs clustering, the thick purple vein pulsating below, was shallow. A hollow in partial shadow, harmless, yet of infinite potential. A clearing in a blighted forest, doomed to burn. The smooth plastic syringe, pregnant with menace, trembled in his hand. He was poised, resolute, pin-point accuracy assured and time passed exquisitely. Not since infancy had he been so aware of the elasticity of existence, yet so unsure of his ability to order consecutively the stages in his life. Never before had he knowingly ticked away the seconds remaining before an eclipse. Played God.

Staring back with harried eyes, a penumbra of bloodshot white encircling dark full irises, his prisoner strained at silk bindings. The brass bed, gleaming, reflected the man's nakedness in the highly polished upright bars of its headboard, smears of distorted anatomy, segmenting the whole frame. The bare walls, undistinguished paint shades bathed in the glow of a side lamp draped in red chiffon, the stark setting for the few ordered gewgaws – hairbrush, comb, cuff links, signet ring – laid out on the solitary bedside table in orderly homage to an uncluttered life. The fragrant scent of Acqua di Parma talcum powder clung in the nostrils, overpowering, as they – X and Ramona – had entered the bedroom, the two bodies on the sagging mattress silently disentangling, leaving the spread-eagled man bound hand and foot to the metal bedstead, the fine white powder liberally dusting his toned torso, which was darkening here and there in perspiring patches. The rank potency of his betrayal momentarily silenced any protest in the seconds before the application across his mouth of two-inch wide black gaffer tape foreclosed that option forever. The lover, hired for the occasion, dressed quickly and slipped silently from the room. Such a compliant sexual partner had not been difficult to procure for Peter Foster, his promiscuity notorious and undiscriminating, inducing a reckless disregard for his own safety that belied the paranoia that permeated all other fields of his existence. This lack of caution together with a need to fence off a private space in an otherwise crowded life meant that he had dismissed his bodyguards for the evening.

Ramona, incandescent at the assault on her men and the theft of her property, had sponsored the plan, her need for containment as urgent as X's demand for secrecy. Whispers of humiliation and despoilment were not good for business, even if in such a predominantly male world the rumours stretched the bounds of credibility, but the rapid execution of the guilty, for crimes unspecified, would stand as a warning to anyone wishing to exploit any perceived weakness. She was adamant that the response should be immediate and disproportionate and saw her involvement in its enforcement as vital in helping to rub out a potential stain of defilement that could besmirch her whole organization. Alfie – shamefaced, uncommunicative, unreliable – was sent to Spain to work out his frustrations at a safe distance as a bouncer in one of Ramona's clubs on the Costa del Sol. X had tried to speak to him before he left, desperate for one vital piece of information, but his partner in humiliation was monosyllabic and could barely look at him. Their shared experience an insurmountable barrier to all further discourse.

"Alfie, I need to know something."

The statement lingered unanswered as the two men, who had known each other for years working for Ramona, edgily sat together, steeped in the dingy patterned afternoon light of a deserted pub on the Balls Pond Road. X had drained his pint before continuing, while Alfie stared blankly at the ornate coloured mirrors that adorned the wall of the alcove, his glass untouched, a cigarette, smoke rising in a vertical column as it burned down to the filter, in his hand.

"Alfie, I've got to ask you."

A flicker of the eyes was the only acknowledgement that he was listening. The smouldering column of ash dropped onto the stained wooden tabletop, dissipating rapidly in a puddle of lager. X nudged at it with a beer mat, spreading the glistening liquid over the smooth veined surface.

"It's important."

Alfie's bulky body hunched inside a tight-fitting black Harrington jacket appeared to inflate, stretching taut the rucked cotton, pulling the seams close to bursting point, before he rose up in his seat, turned to face X and shouted out.

"None of it's fucking important. What's done is done."

X was taken aback, it was unlike Alfie to be verbally violent, usually articulating his true feelings only with his fists. The barman looked up from his paper, stared at the pair, then returned to his reading relieved they appeared to be behaving themselves.

"It's not over, Alfie."

"It is for me."

"Come on, we'll get the bastard and you're off to get some sun."

"Yeah, an' I won't be coming back, not if I have anything to fucking do with it."

"Help me out now Alfie, one last time."

He looked away from X, his head turning into a shaft of dusty sunlight that infused his blond close-cropped hair with a radiant glow that offset the grim set of his face.

"Look, I'm not going to fucking beg."

Silence. X's question when it came was, he knew, an exercise in futility, the final act of a dying relationship.

"Did he use a Durex, Alfie? Did he?"

Anger and disgust flooded across Alfie's rotund flushed face.

"I've got to know, it's killing me. Did the bastard use a Johnny?"

Alfie hauled himself to his feet and turned to leave.

"For God's sake, Alfie."

He waved a hand dismissively and left. The pub door swung shut. There was no answer. The terror was real, breathing difficult. X gripped the table with both hands, fighting back nausea. His dislike of violence was nothing compared to this feeling. Force was sometimes a business necessity but its use was mediated by an instinct for survival, a concern to avoid injury, and the knowledge of his own innate ability to look after himself. Now his life was threatened and there was nothing he could do about it. The suffering was a presage of his death. His mortality leering at him over a beer stained table, a full pint raised in salutation. Cheers.

Gulping mouthfuls of air, he whispered an abject prayer, vowing that if he survived, he would change the way he lived, become a different person. He meant it, the foreboding was real.

Ramona had been solicitous through her anger, cradling his head, caressing his back, assuaging his fears with reassuring words and a practical attention to the necessary details of arranging an HIV test. It was chilling and he sobbed quietly between her small breasts when she finally voiced the terrifying acronym. Conjuring up the appalling image of a man free falling from a sunny, cloudless sky, his chute wrapped inelegantly around his twisting body. His survival was down to luck – an unassailable alliance between nature and physics, coming together to gamble with his life. X was pessimistic about the odds, preferring always to work at reducing risks, and this unspecified threat terrified him. Powerlessness was an unfamiliar feeling that he hated, corroding a character built on a supreme confidence in its own abilities. Ramona offered him a way forward and he followed, ashen-spirited and dead of heart. Revenge a short-term palliative, an explosion of cathartic energy, that would shore him up for the agonizing wait.

The trio were alone in the bedroom – a triptych of angels, avenging, fallen and death, an altarpiece in the church of human endeavour – Ramona resplendent in fur coat, headscarf and high heels standing sentinel at the foot of the bed, X, the lean executioner, leather-clad, the tools of his trade laid out neatly beside him, towering above the condemned, Peter Foster, a sullied star, puffy boggle-eyes. The house was completely silent.

There was nothing to say, as all present understood, in their own way, the motivations that had brought them to this final scene. Yet X standing, syringe in hand, wanted to ask the question, needed Peter Foster to tell all, make penance, perform a final decent act. Ramona, aghast when he had told her earlier as they sat in heavy traffic, had tried to dissuade him, arguing persuasively that giving the bastard a final chance to torment him even as he went to his death, was a power reversal neither of them should tolerate.

"He's a fucking weasel, you couldn't believe anything he said. What good would that be. Final satisfaction for him, that's all."

She had patted the black leather shaving-case that sat between them on the car seat and whispered, "Give it to him straight, no chat, and we'll be gone, that's a good boy."

The temptation to behave recklessly, satisfy yourself, disregard good counsel, betray was acute. The urge overcome only by an act of extreme, intellectual suppression. A crime of passion, X grimly reflected, this was not to be, just a moment of achingly refined pleasure.

Applying gentle pressure deepened the indentation in the pale creamy skin of the man's upper thigh, shadows gathering, a vein alive just below the surface. The centre of attention, X exchanged glances with his cohorts, all eyes fixed on his. Affirmation plus negation, an unequal equation, working itself out to less than zero for Peter Foster. Steepening the angle of the hypodermic syringe, the liquid crystal shimmering delicately off-yellow, the needle pierced the skin, slipping deep into the fleshy muscle, an involuntary spasm as X squeezed. Pleading eyes rolled round to stare at his hands as they delivered the infant cocktail, thrusting a steady stream of liquid brimstone into his assailant. A burning inflammation instantly gathering, clutching at the capillary of its own destruction, sucking the last drop dry. Pulling free of this monstrous grip left a fiery purple bruise as the only mark of assault on the dying man, topped with a glistening pearl-sized drop of ruby-red blood.

A moment of contemplation, the aesthetic rigour of packing away the deadly equipment was calming, then the prison shadows on the wall flickering, the bars shaking, as his victim, hands and feet tied to the bedstead, bounced up and down on the soft feather-filled mattress, the regular love-making creak of well-used springs, a thumping backbeat to his thrashing death throes. The only sound he made, escaping under pressure from behind his gag, was an incoherent whistling. Eyes rolled back, white and inhuman, he desperately articulated his last breaths. His shrivelled penis flicking back and forth in its trimmed, perfumed nest, with the diminishing motion of a waning pendulum.

The final spasm of life was dramatic, an arcing of the body, a tautness of the skin across his hairless chest, clearly defining muscle and rib cage, head thrust forward, eyes briefly focused, then the deflation, the torso, dead-weight, falling back, air hissing from liquid-filled lungs through obstructed nose and mouth. Puckered and yellowing the overwhelming scent of talcum powder, clouding the dank air of the bedroom, barely masked the bitter-sweet stench of corruption.

Ramona touched X on the shoulder, affectionate yet commanding, the gentle pressure easing him away.

"Let's go. Out the back way."

He resisted, flooded with a murderous energy that urged one final act of desecration. A violent outburst that would leave an indelible mark on the cooling body, may even make some vestigial impression on the fading electrical signals shorting out in the dying brain. Drowning in a chemical soup, that anaesthetized as it killed, seemed barely adequate, only the agony of physical destruction – the carving of the flesh, the spilling of vital juices, the seeping of the blood – could compensate for the pain he was suffering.

"Sorry Ramona."

He slipped from her grasp, fumbled with the blade of his Swiss Army knife and then plunged it deep into Peter Foster's abdomen. It entered easily. Blood oozed through his fisted fingers.

"Oh God! That's enough, come away now." Ramona's voice uncensorious, exuded understanding, "Leave it. Let's get out of here."

Stepping back and staring at the bright red handle with its silver cross standing proud in its puddle of coagulating blood, X acknowledged for the first time that it was over between him and Peter Foster. He could deal with his legacy dispassionately, any damage done was part of his future now, not the past, which lay punctured and bleeding before him. He knew this was not the way to do business, this had been, may even still turn out to be, too close a call. Scared witless was not a state of being he empathized with and Ramona would just have to listen.

"Don't forget it," she nodded over at the corpse, "Let's not make it easy for them."

For the first time X felt faintly squeamish, his precious knife had a new owner, donated in a fit of overwrought pique, but now appropriated by the simple fact of possession, removing it would be to commit yet another offence. Metal and plastic in a symbiosis of death with body fluids, muscle and sinew. Remove one from the other would be to destroy a long-established, natural order.

"Come on. There's taking satisfaction and there's pratting around. Carl will be getting edgy."

Resistance, the suction of moist flesh, an audible slurping as the blade slid free. Gelatinous red, coalescing on the stainless surface, an aberration that had to be cleansed, wiped away, taking with it the miasma of the charnel-house.

"Wash it in the bathroom, it's over there."

Indecision countered by practical advice, undermining his reluctance to move. Led by the hand into the steamy room, used towels piled haphazardly on the tiled floor – dark slate with a grey slightly translucent grout – puddles of cool water on the uneven surface, the walls spattered with silver droplets, he washed the knife in the refreshing stream, splashing his face and arms.

"Mop up won't you, there's a love."

Ramona hitched up her skirt and sat down heavily on the lavatory beside him.

"Wouldn't want to leave anything as fucking obvious as a clue, would we?"

She laughed, a cruel cackle, sobering in its malice.

"Don't want anyone pinning this on us, do we?"

X looked at her and smiled. He was feeling better, the clarity of perspective returning. The haze lifting. He folded the blade back, appreciated the satisfying heft of the knife in his palm before slipping it into his jacket pocket. Nineteen minutes and forty-five seconds was what it had taken to extinguish a life – he halted the stopwatch racing on his wrist and as the luminous numbers stilled noted with satisfaction that a nightcap in the club was possible if they got a move on – less than they had anticipated.

"I need a drink."

"What's new? Pass me that will you."

X handed over a damp roll of toilet paper.

"I haven't seen Ali recently."

"She's in Oz, having the time of her life, apparently. Why d'you think of her?"

"I do quite often."

"Not a lot of point in doing that – don't know when she'll be coming back."

"I know that, but it's thwarted passion, I guess."

"Sounds a bit fucking romantic for you?"

"You know, certain women …"

"You calling my sister a certain woman?"

"No, I liked her. Simpler times."

"You're going soft. I never took you for a sentimental twat."

"Fuck off."

Ramona stood and hitched up her pantyhose.

"You were all over each other for a while, what more can you want?"

"I never, you know …"

The sound of flushing water was loud in the silent house and they both glanced at the door into the darkened bedroom, listening attentively.

"You never what? Told her you loved her?"

Ramona looked after all her young men, X knew that, him in particular, and succeeded in making them all think they were special, but she could be a right cunt sometimes.

"I never fucked her."

His tone of voice angrier than he'd intended.

"Good God," she was laughing at him, "that's got to be a record for Ali. She's a lovely girl, but she's not slow in coming forward."

"We did just about everything bloody else."

"Interesting! Tell me more."

"Oh, fuck off, will you."

He couldn't understand why he'd never made love to Ali, why with all the vintage claret and cocaine they'd ingested, he'd never possessed the thing he wanted the most. She'd just drifted away, slipping out of his reach, no doubt blowing other minds.

"Come on," a mock seductive edge to Ramona's voice, placatory, "at least you've had me, one half of the set."

Ramona peeled off one of the cream surgical gloves she was wearing and touched him gently on the cheek.

"Let's go, enough of this old-time, reminiscing bollocks."

X smiled then, surprising himself, he blurted out with unintended intensity.

"This is scaring me shitless Ramona. I can't stand the hanging around, all this bloody waiting."

"I know, but we've got the bastard and he looks fucking well to me. A surprisingly fit body. No obvious sign he was wasting away."

Ramona adjusted her skirt as X absorbed the comforting logic that lay behind one of the oldest jokes he knew – the one about the deceased at a wake looking well after a recent seaside holiday. His father had told variations on the theme all through his childhood never tiring of mining a tradition of black music-hall humour that was ancient even for his generation. The comfort of the familiar, the soothing balm of repetition forging the cumulative defence of generations, shoring up the present against the terrors of an uncertain future.

"I can't go out on the streets for you anymore, Ramona," he hesitated expecting a reaction, but there was none, "It's not the violence, I'm always up for that, but this has really done for me."

Ramona stood passively in the bathroom doorway and waved at him to come forward.

"We'll sort something out, you chickenshit."

She then grasped him firmly by the arm and with an open mouth kissed him, her tongue searching out his. X felt an intense loyalty to this older woman that went far beyond the ties of master and worker. The erotic charge she gave to many of their transactions was always a jolt and wanting to please her, he responded, their tongues duelling.

Slightly breathless she whispered, "I'll see you right. You're my best boy, you know that, don't you?"

X nodded.

"I've got a plan," he remarked emphatically.

"Fuck me, you're a quick worker."

All traces of the steaming vessel were erased, the horizon now clear. He was alone. Plummeting earthward, a prosaic fact of nature, in a sublime world.

Ramona shaved her pubic hair, shaping, crafting, cajoling and often dyeing the wayward fuzz into intimate statements of tender artistry, surprising for one so tempered in her business dealings. A personal human topiary exhibited only to the select few, a restricted public that belied her voracious reputation. Despite the close carnal familiarity of their working relations X had seen her naked only infrequently – the more numerous moments of grabbed intercourse often just partially clothed instances of disheveled passion – and was always surprised at the inventiveness of her designs. Each one a fleeting object of desire: moustaches – from the minimalism of the "Charlie Chaplin", through the "stiff upper lip" bristles of the small brush, to the leanness of the "Zapata" and the "Fu Manchu", and ultimately the bushiness of the handlebar; beards of varying degrees of luxuriousness and hue – a particular favourite the goatee; rectilinear flags of recognizable pattern and national rectitude merging into patches of expressionist daubing, different tints and textures close cropped, shaved and luxuriant, wispy – all perfumed cushions of erotic amusement.

Tonight, a glimpse into the slashed centre of a blood-red heart – inches away – the point tapering away between Ramona's thighs. It was shocking, triggering a surge of excitement, outside of X's usual experience of the sensual. The depth of his feelings struggled in his muddled mind for articulate expression – the very word love sat uncomfortably with his perception of Ramona, yet seemed right somehow – and he hesitated before slipping the tip of his tongue into the slight runnel that traversed her sculpted body between firm thigh and taut stomach – muscles clearly defined, a grid of light and shade – a channel for perspiration. The salty flow was bitter on his flickering tongue as it sensuously slithered downwards, supping on a heady, sharply perfumed cocktail, urged on by gentle pressure from Ramona whose hands gripped his head firmly, fingers caressing, guiding him to a heart-stopping halt.

Slipping, sliding, slumping, subsiding, sinking, spinning. Down, dropping, descending, diving, declining, destruction. Tumbling, toppling, tripping. Crashing always the fear.

X was awakened by a glint, sunlit, painfully piercing his eyelids, shard-like, after kissing the mottled surface of the antique mirror, its Baroque gold leaf peeling, that hung on Ramona's bedroom wall. The space saturated in a hazy orange light, appeared alive, its boundaries moving gently in and out, the lulling breath of air seductively calm and barely audible. Rolling onto his back, he stretched mildly aching limbs, spreading himself across the capacious mattress, pulling tousled fragrant sheets across his chest, the humid heat of bodies wafting. It had been an age since he had indulged in such post-coital napping, waking up in bed with a woman. The impotent terror of AIDS had emasculated him, turned him into a hermit – lying crucified, sweating and alone, limbs spread, filling the vast expanse of his bed with the reek of defeat. Now with that morning's news of his "all-clear" echoing in his mind he lay, his body touching Ramona's curled, slumbering form, back arched and naked, the covering of soft blonde hair bristling in the mild chill of the late afternoon.

The reprieve. Elation, pure and unconstrained. A tattoo adorning a body. Pigments vivid. Crystal clear. Flowering at the base of her spine. Nothing had ever tasted or smelled so sweet. A delicate head of pink petals nodding to its fall. Extending a finger and tracing its form, stirred longing. A shimmer of life. An existence retrieved. She flexed and rolled over, their limbs entangling. The breathless expectation of a snuffing out, abating, he sucked in air, moisture, warmth. Absorbing. Growing under the tender caresses of a passionate embrace, his blood again the elixir, he was finally reborn seeking between her legs, a force for regeneration not extinction.

Dozing ruminations upon past affairs, often routine and short-lived, were startling in their conclusion: that he'd never made love before. He'd fucked, shagged, rogered, bonked, laid – depending upon who he was telling the tale too – more than a dozen women, but Ramona was the only one he cared about. Ill-prepared to combat such overtly sentimental feelings, X sank into a cloying reverie of misplaced domesticity that contrasted starkly with the reality of his and Ramona's lives.

"Coke fuelled insanity, babes, that's what that is," Ramona laughed, "Can you see me in my pinny? Changing nappies?"

X raised his eyebrows, unaware he'd said anything.

"You've got to be joking, babes. Here, have another line. Then you'll talk sense."

Plumping up the pillows she hauled herself out of the tousled bed clothes and reached across, her breasts brushing X's face, and lifted an ornate oval tray from the bedside table, its fine braided silver rim glinting in the sunlight that was now streaming into the room. She placed it carefully on her lap. Four smudged lines of cocaine radiated out from a small crumbling white powder pyramid at the centre of the tray.

"Something I prepared earlier," she giggled, "You know you'd better stop going on about all this lovey-dovey nonsense, it's doing my head in."

She busied herself tidying up the grainy traces on the tray with a single-edged razor blade.

"Not what I'd have expected from you, at all."
"But I love you, Ramona."
"For fuck's sake."
"I really do."

The whining affectation in X's voice convinced Ramona he was joking, but for a moment she'd been uncertain. In her time she'd heard much passionate drug-crazed nonsense – espousals of eternal love, abject promises of perpetual subjugation, proposals of both self and mutual harm, personal desires articulated that even she had blanched at – so much so that you were never certain with some of them, especially the young ones, whether they believed what they were saying or not. She had higher hopes of this particular lover.

"If I wasn't holding this precious cargo, I'd give you one."

X slid his hand up between her legs.

"Stop it! You'll have the whole lot over. Then I'll be really pissed."

"Don't you believe in true love then?"

"Much overrated it seems to me."

Ramona bent forward – hair tousled, skin radiant – and inhaled a line of cocaine through a rolled up £20 note. Blinking she sat up smiling, her eyes liquid.

"Never had much use for it myself," she said before sniffing several times and slumping back on to the pillows, "… and you shouldn't too."

"So, you never wanted to be loved by anyone then? Commit to just one person?"

"Give over. You sound like my mother, an' you know how much I like her," her smile deepened, "Now look what you've gone and done, conjured up that old battle-axe."

Tentatively touching her breasts, her arms crossing, she shivered, then called out.

"Begone witch, you foul woman … bitch from hell."

Stumbling over her words, their slurred edge adding a sensuous veneer to her naturally husky tone, did nothing to dampen the intense feelings engendered in X. He wanted to climb on top of her, grasp her firmly and merge their bodies. A blending of identities that seemed infinitely desirable, but Ramona was pre-occupied.

"The cow. You know I hate her, don't you?"

"Dead bloody right I do," he sighed, squeezing the firm muscles of her inner thigh, then gently pulling on the sheet, drawing the tray closer to him and exposing first her tanned belly then her fuzzy carmine heart.

X sat up and the familiar ritual began. The slight discomfort of the crisp rolled note against the sensitive skin of his nostril, then the ticklish stimulation of the lining of his inner nose as he inhaled, fighting the reflex to sneeze, followed by the crackle behind his eyes, spreading to his temples, before the spray burst open in his brain, showering multicoloured chaff everywhere. Heart beating rapidly, buoyed up with exhilaration, he felt unstoppable.

"I need to tell you about my big idea."

"There'll be plenty of time for that after …"

Ramona snorted her second line of coke and gestured for X to follow. He obeyed happily. She tenderly licked the white dusty residue from his upper lip with the tip of her tongue before pushing him back onto the bed and climbing on top of him.

"… this."

"It's a fuck of a long way down."

Jake, X's best friend during his early twenties, they had fallen out over a woman, had said that to him the only time they had sky-dived together and, as always, he was right.

"Sherbet dip, sherbet dip, dip, dip, dip."

Ramona's gurgling awoke X. She was lying beside him on her back, naked, with eyes closed, waving her arms purposefully in the air, conducting a phantom orchestra that only she could hear.

"Don't you just love it?"

"Almost as much as you."

"Dip, dip, sherbet dip."

"I need a drink, how about you?"

"Dip. dip, dop,dop, dop ..."

"Ramona ... drinkies?"

He grasped one of her waving hands and she smiled and nodded.

"Sherbet dip. It's been such a long time ... ," her words tailed off, her drifting arms subsiding slowly onto the bedclothes, "... we must get ..."

Sitting on the edge of the bed, X stretched and blearily surveyed the sun-bleached expanse – the bed, centrally placed, appeared marooned in a choppy golden sea, waves of light rippling off the highly polished floorboards – searching for something to wear. Ramona's clothes were widely scattered – silk underwear, Marc T-shirt turned inside out, tights balled beneath the window, Diesel jeans hanging from the bed-post, his were nowhere to be seen. Fragmentary details of his fevered disrobing on the leather sofa downstairs seeped pleasantly back into his consciousness, the spiralling excitement as his arms became entangled in his Holliday and Brown shirt, rendering him defenceless against Ramona's onslaught, black Watanabe denims and Dior briefs hauled off unceremoniously, his Balenciaga sneakers tossed aside, toppling a vase of lilies, the discoloured water a darkening stain on the pale floor. His nakedness visible to the outside world, as his lover chased him past the ceiling to floor windows of her converted warehouse overlooking the Thames, wet footprints on the floor charting the complex choreography of their dance.

Ramona had intercepted him in front of an open hatchway – the ancient block and tackle still intact, dangling from an elaborate iron structure of struts and stanchions that appeared symbiotically rooted to the side of the building, a century of rust having leached into the porous brickwork staining the wall a darker red – and wrestled him into submission. The pleasure of his capture compounded by a view of two women office-workers sunning themselves on a riverside bench, their skirts hitched up, legs stretched out in front of them, oblivious to the rapturous voyeur leering at them from three storeys up.

The white Marc T-shirt was all there was to hand, tight-fitting and smelling pungently of Ramona, he pulled it on and stood up, genitals bared. The rushing swirl of blood to his head made him dizzy and he staggered towards the open stairway, reaching out tentatively for the burnished iron balustrade. A sudden movement outside one of the windows distracted him, and for a moment his instinct for danger flared, registering an imprecise threat, an indistinct perception that all was not right, before fading, the nascent throbbing in his temples and the dryness in the back of his throat spurring him on down the cold metal steps.

Through the expansive glass frontage he could see a stretch of the river, a mere trickle at low tide – the organic salty reek of the exposed foreshore ever-present – a man with a metal detector tracked methodically across the muddy brick-strewn waste, a jet-black cormorant sitting sentry-like on a slimy decaying brown-green wooden post, eying him nervously as he approached. A cyclist in orange and black Lycra riding a mountain bike sped past on the opposite bank, while raucous seabirds wheeled overhead. An object – dark, ragged – fell from the sky spinning slowly across X's field of view before landing heavily, the impact opening up a crater, bud-like, in the thick silt, petals of mud flowering before folding back on themselves. A flock of gulls descended, the black and white melee, a brief orgy of violence before the victor rose, angrily pursued, the dripping prize clasped in his beak.

Stepping onto rough-hewn floorboards – their aged smoothness sensuous on the soles of his feet – X moved towards the open-plan kitchen. There was an appealing quality to life around Ramona, that in his day-to-day existence had so far evaded him. It was almost magical in its ability to alter his perception of the world, adding a level of sophistication to his already finely tuned concern with appearances. The venality of his commonplace actions seemed somehow purer in this rarefied atmosphere.

"Sentimental bollocks," he could hear her voice now, "flattering, but bollocks none the less." She was relentless, never letting up. What she didn't seem to understand was that it surprised him too.

Beneath, the chill of glass-smooth tiles was a shock – the metallic mesh pattern mirroring the spectral pastels of the rainbow, fading one into the other across the vast sweep of the kitchen – red to orange, yellow, green, blue, indigo and violet. He skipped rapidly up to the large double-width stainless steel American-style fridge that was humming quietly against the far wall and opened one of the doors. Washed by the eerie yellow light and shivering in the cool blast he reached into the cavernous interior for a bottle of Krug champagne. It stood with its twin beside bottles of Courvoisier brandy, De Souza gold tequila, Badoit mineral water, a half empty four-pint carton of skimmed milk, a green box of organic free-range eggs, medium-size, a large untouched bar of white Swiss chocolate, and three vials of clear liquid standing upright in a white polystyrene container.

A sudden avalanche of cubes in the ice maker compartment startled him and he slammed the door, stepping back to search for glasses. There was only one large gleaming cupboard – original, solid pine, stripped bare and stained with a high-gloss varnish – built into the wall on his right. To reach it X had to pass a row of small sash-windows that looked out on to the narrow cobbled close and the building site opposite – a development of executive flats that Ramona had some interest in – he checked that his electric-blue Mercedes CLK was still parked below, and desultorily surveyed the deserted street. A secluded world enclosed at one end by overgrown, rubbish blighted plots flanking the river and at the other by a narrow arch in the high brick walls through which the road made a sharp right-angle turn out onto the Broadway. An air of dereliction still lingered in spite of the construction work and affluent new residents. The dark towering warehouses permanently shading the damp, mossy cobbles imparted a dank "Dickensian charm" that seemed to please Ramona. She was nourished by a strange juxtaposition of the ultra-modern and traditional, thriving on ambiguities and visual contradictions – the old and worn next to the pristine – the appeal of which X often found hard to understand.

He stood for a moment. He had to be particularly circumspect presenting his new business ideas to Ramona, you never knew on which side she would fall. Her lines of reasoning were often irrational, in X's view, but, as always, he believed that operational interest and profit would ultimately prevail with her. His was a good plan and he was strangely excited at the prospect of unveiling it – tired, as he was, of working the streets, more respectful now of the risks to his own personal safety.

"Glasses, where were the glasses?"

He opened the cupboard door to the overpowering smell of fresh paint. The cabinet was almost bare. Plates and mugs – no more than two of each – were stacked haphazardly on the bottom shelf. Two champagne flutes stood alone on the third, the rest were empty. He reached up. There was a sudden loud crash and a whoosh of air – like the exhalation of a winded man – that swept across his exposed back and legs, prickling the skin. Glasses trembled, chinking together, crockery rattled as he dropped to the floor and ducked behind the solid wooden sink unit in the centre of the kitchen. There was movement up above – running feet – Ramona's bare legs appeared at the top of the stairs, then halted. He watched as, gun in hand, she tightened the cord on her dressing gown, then crouched down and peered cautiously towards the front door. There was a powerful smell of burning petrol and the room filled rapidly with an acrid smog, obscuring his view.

Struggling for breath he rummaged through the cutlery drawer, which was almost empty, then spotted the knife-block standing feet away across the polished granite surface, it yielded a Sabatier carving knife, its sharp blade scraping satisfactorily across the ridged skin of his thumb.

"Watch the windows, I'll check the door."

The excited quiver in Ramona's breathless voice was unmistakable. "The fuckers may try something else."

She sounded sober and nearby.

The sun cresting the roof of the warehouse opposite, streamed blinding light into the apartment, teasing disorientating patterns from the curling smoke. The atmosphere was toxic, the harsh fumes, physical and particulate, burned his lips, and tore at his throat and lungs, tightening his chest, inducing a hacking cough. Sinking down, his back hard against the wooden unit, the air became more benign, X's vision cleared, his breathing calmed and the pain eased slightly. There was little noise, just wheezing inside his head, the pounding beat of his heart, and a constant scuffling, swirling here and there. He could taste the chemical residue from the night before – red wine, whiskey, champagne, cocaine – smell the overpowering scent of Ramona, feel the throbbing in his temples, the dissolution of his spirit, sense the sickening perspiration chilling across his skin, crackling nerve endings. Powerless – an eruption – he vomited violently, a viscous torrent splaying out across the polychromatic tiles, at the periphery slowing rapidly on the cool grouted surface.

"Fuck."

There was momentary relief, becalming, restful, before a panicked concern swept it away. He picked up the spattered knife and, crouching, moved towards the front door. The underside of the flickering smoke clouds glowed orange and he could smell burning. Ramona, a shadowy figure, loomed ahead wrestling with a bright red fire extinguisher – a beacon in the gloom – that hissed suddenly into life. A fragmented shower of expanding white spume arced impotently through the air, before being directed at the heart of the blaze. The flames died in seconds, releasing from their foaming core a final belch of acrid black fumes, that forced Ramona and X to step back, overcome.

Bent double they supported each other, swaying unsteadily, hawking up gobbets of phlegm as they gasped for air. Spitting and coughing they traced a faltering dance across the floor, away from the noxious smouldering mess in the doorway, before staggering blindly into the heavy black leather sofa in the centre of the room and collapsing onto its voluminous cushions in a tangled heap. Sucking in air they clung to each other, as the atmosphere gradually cleared. Relieved X buried his head between Ramona's sweaty soot-covered breasts, smudging his own grimy features. They hugged then suddenly Ramona stiffened and pushed X away.

"Did I fucking call them? Shit!"

X stared blankly.

"I can't bloody remember. It'll be a bit late now though, they'll be long gone, the bastards."

She pulled her dressing-gown over her bare shoulders and shuddered.

"Can you see my mobile anywhere?"

X reared up and looked around through unfocussed, streaming eyes. Defeated, he shook his head.

"I may as well get Bernie onto this right away, all the fucking good it'll do."

Ramona's quavering inflection was settling, her efficient, clipped tone of speech returning.

"Have a look over there will you. I must find it."

"I can't see a thing. I'm as blind as a fucking bat. Something's really shagging my eyes."

"I picked it up, I know I bloody did."

She slipped the revolver into a pocket in her gown and got unsteadily to her feet. The robe gaped open, the heavy weapon dragging it askew. Blearily X leant forward and kissed her pubic hair, the soapy tang a revitalizing antidote to the stench of burning.

"You randy fucker, can't you think of anything else."

There was an urgency in her voice that demanded compliance.

"I need to get hold of the boys, so piss off back to bed will you, 'n take that champagne with you, while I sort this balls-up."

Free falling solo was, for X, invariably spiritual, a confrontation with the infinite, facing up to his own possible extinction alone. In company there were always distractions, inducing inarticulacy in the presence of his "God" – an ill-defined deity who scarcely troubled him on the ground, but belief in him often exerted a profound hold on his feelings at great heights – the unequal relationship inevitably enforcing the need to communicate on more prosaic subjects. Yet X always believed sharing a common experience, particularly one so exhilaratingly transcendent, transformed the bonds between people forever, building a unique community of the fallen.

Free falling with Ramona, the only time she'd been talked into coming on a jump with him, had tipped the fine balance that existed between them in his favour. For a fleeting interlude he had been more than an employee, greater than a lover, he had been in charge. It had taken him most of the night to persuade her, stoking her courage with cocaine, each line chased down with a brain-numbingly strong margarita, physically wrestling with her until subjugated she finally agreed; yet she still protested as they drove through deserted West London in the eerie dawn light heading for Ringwood Aerodrome in Oxfordshire, a private airfield run by an acquaintance of X and a regular haunt of his, where no questions would be asked about the condition or capability of prospective sky divers. Ramona had been terrified and taciturn, as the small plane climbed steeply through the misty early morning air. Ashen pale clinging to the wing-struts, buffeted by the back-draft, mouthing a refusal. Hysterical, as X grasped her waist and dived into the void, plucking her from safety. Ecstatic as they fell, hand in hand – the vice of her grip, guarantor of the total trust he had promised – fear dispelled by the exhilaration of the plunge. Euphoric, as their canopies opened, plucking them skyward before spiralling gracefully towards the earth though dank, swirling banks of cloud, rays of sunlight piercing the dew-laden air, picking out scraps of humanity. Triumphant, the chill clouding their breath as they embraced standing knee-deep in the sodden grass of the landing zone.

Ramona had paid X more attention after that, fuelling

a passion that demanded they spend more time together. Unexpected, dangerous couplings in public places remained the cornerstone of the affair, but Ramona was now prepared to cast caution aside and appear with him in company, at least the company of their innermost circle, which meant they could spend an evening together in the twitchy presence of her ever-watchful bodyguards and even occasionally the whole night. For X, infatuation required, for Ramona an unsettling defensive breach, but a necessary sop to the stultifying loneliness that was beginning to scare her more than the very real threats to her safety. It had been a memorable drop.

The bed sheets were cool, soothing the after-burn, the champagne ice-cold, and as the pain in his forehead eased, X dozed.

The mellow afternoon glow of pale amber washed with hints of flax, the light of distant bonfires cast against leaden skies, the acrid aroma of wood-smoke heavy in the damp air. Jumping from the knotty branches of a spreading apple tree into heaps of brown curling leaves, shaking the last black wizened fruit from the bows, rotten bombs exploding on impact into a slather of mushy pulp, splattering the stained earth. Again. Climbing higher, falling further, the heavy jarring impact barely cushioned, teeth clenched, limbs flailing, rolling over and over in the damp decay, youthful body indestructible.

Muffled voices whispered below, heavy male tones, punctuated by the counterpoint of Ramona's strident interjections, exerting control. X stirred, body numb, sensitive only to the warm cocoon enveloping him, alert, yet devoid of thought, relishing the clarity of an empty mind. Ramona was very experienced at "Disaster Recovery", that much was certain, and was reassuringly ruthless in carrying it through. There was no need for him to be concerned.

Perched on the yielding, uppermost limbs of the ancient apple tree, casting a low shadow across the orchard, the winged beast watched the young boy, alone, gleefully screaming as he flew, chuckling as he landed, helplessly tumbling through the heaped leaf-mould, burying his face deep in the teeming fermentation, never looking up.

There were creatures of the air. Multifarious, devious, unpredictable, they haunted X, appearing at any time, out of nowhere. Harrying him in the air and on the ground, in his dreams and when awake, stoned or sober, there was no escape. A malignant demonology, depressingly familiar in the traditional forms of their manifestation. Only occasionally was X ever truly terrified.

A door slammed downstairs, the reverberation segueing into the trilling of a mobile phone, answered in an instant.

"Smoke the fucking pub … no problem."

Ramona's voice was clear and disconcertingly close. X raised his head. She was standing silhouetted at the top of the stairs, the light shining through the thin silk of her dressing-gown, her legs, cut off at the knee, were clearly defined.

"I can't let them keep getting away with this, Bernie, you fucking know that."

She sat down on the top step. X could make out the precise form of her breasts.

"I know. I bloody know. You've got a point Bernie, but do this for me will you?"

She laughed wearily.

"It's a total pisser, I know. Every time I take a few fucking hours off. Let me know. Cheers Bernie."

The phone snapped shut. She stood again, deep in thought, then smiled.

"You're right, you're always fucking right," she shivered and pulled the gown close around her, "Is that why I keep shagging you, I wonder?"

X was confused, concerned that he had been absent for a significant section of their recent discourse. Time mislaid: seconds, minutes, hours deconstructed then only partially reconstructed, time warped, it was happening more and more often. Ramona sauntered towards him.

"Any of that bubbly left or have you drunk it all?"

Her mood, cheery and light-hearted, reassured X and he nodded at the bedside table to his left. She poured herself a glass and slipped into the bed beside him. Expectant, X waited for elaboration, but when none came he worried that he may have missed out again on key elements of the syntax of their conversation. It was rare for Ramona to pay anyone a compliment and for him to have passed out at the critical moment was unfortunate. The only saving grace was that she had to be as pissed as he was, so he took the risk and asked her.

"Why am I always right?"

"You know about what you were saying before."

X stared blankly, thinking hard. Ramona appeared oblivious to his incapacity.

"About changing the way we do business, changing the way we work. Our modus operandi."

His ability to think impaired and with mental powers stretched taut across the vast dome of his skull – he could feel the strings vibrating as if plucked – conversation was difficult. Necessity forced a damping down, a stillness. Connections began to be made in X's mind, links established, backwards, a picking up of a line of thought. Ramona stared at him, demanding some response.

"I have a plan."

"I know you have."

"A good one."

"It had better be."

X was still having difficulty remembering, fighting against an overwhelming need to curl up and go to sleep. It had been an excellent plan.

There was a large bird, far below him, off to his left. Soaring, without movement, banking gracefully, feathers rippling in the unpredictable vortices of gyrating air. A black silhouette against the brown landscape, a refined emblem of threat, preying on the mind, invincible in its domain, unafraid. Man, a mere curiosity, hurtling past. Vision clearing, liquid pressured from his oozing eyes, X noticed others all around – eagles and buzzards – effortlessly riding the warm draughts, billowing up from the baking earth. The prevailing offshore wind was pushing the heated cones out to sea, where they slowly cooled, changing character, losing their energy. The thermals, once barely visible, shimmered into view, a hazy sheen of fine dust, a tangible presence on the skin, the subtle changes in temperature only apparent to the attuned. A quality appreciated by wing-less intruders, predators and eaters of carrion.

"Come on, tell me!"

Ramona nudged X.

"How can you sleep after all this? I'm buzzing."

Mind muddy, X stirred, behind heavy eyelids the room was swimming and his empty stomach was gripped by the faint cramp of nausea. He groaned. Ramona laughed and sipped her champagne.

"How stoned are you?"

X grinned, saliva dribbling from the corner of his mouth.

"You need a pick-me-up, my son."

Ramona drained her glass and placed it carelessly on the edge of the table, where it teetered precariously, as she twisted out of her dressing-gown. From the corner of her eye she noticed the glass toppling and lunged unsuccessfully to catch it – the cut-crystal flute spinning free of her grasp to smash on the floor, shards skittering in all directions across the burnished boards – dragging the covers from the bed, exposing crumpled sheets and X's naked body, curled like a foetus at their centre. He shivered violently in the sudden chill, groaning inarticulately.

"Bugger, that was one of my nicest pieces. A family heirloom given to me by my granny if you want to know. Not that you'd care, you piss-head."

Ramona pulled the bedclothes from the floor, shattered fragments raining down, and wrapped herself in the duvet. X stirred.

"There's no bloody plan is there?"

She grabbed him by the balls, her long fingernails catching in his pubic hair, ripping. The sharp stinging pain, brought him round.

"You're going to own up."

"It's coming back to me," he slurred.

"Bollocks, it's all just your usual bullshit isn't it? Go on tell me if it isn't."

X squirmed and attempted to turn away, Ramona tightened her grip.

"What was it you like to call yourself?"

She forced him onto his back.

"Blue-sky thinker wasn't it?"

Blearily X nodded, she had his attention, but the pressure was an uncomfortable distraction and he was incapable of focused thought.

"Pretentious wanker, that's what you are. Full of shit!"

With relish she mangled his genitals, covering his mouth with her hand to stifle his moans. Thrashing around, arms beating the mattress he held on, fighting the intense compression, until the pain became unbearable and he reared up and grabbed Ramona, knocking her off balance and forcing her onto her side, the bedding tangled around her.

"Let go and I'll fucking tell you," he hissed through gritted teeth. The squeezing eased, but he was not free.

"Tell me first."

She laughed, her breathing rapid and heavy, eyes glinting. He bore down upon her and she collapsed onto her back.

"Let go."

"No."

He kissed her on the lips, there was a fleeting response, before she turned away.

"You've got to tell me."

X relaxed, easing himself alongside her.

"OK, but not so bloody tight."

Ramona released her grip slightly, but maintained a firm hold, offering no opportunity to escape.

"This better be good or someone gets it."

X cleared his throat.

"How many times has this happened?"

Ramona frowned, her quizzical look, stripping away the years, gave her the appearance of a puzzled young girl.

"What?"

"The firebombing, what else?"

"God knows … two or three times. Why do you think the front door's one lifted from a fucking bank? The only problem with it is the sodding letter-box. That's why I've got that special petrol-absorbent, flame-retardant mat?"

X laughed.

"I always wondered why you had such a bloody big, ugly mat. It was never really you."

"Shut up, a girl has got to do what a girl's got to do. Get on with it."

"That's it exactly. You need a lower profile, you personally, not the business. We all do for Christ's sake. It's getting too bloody dangerous. I should know."

"So?"

"The information super-highway!"

Ramona's frown deepened.

"We need to get on it."

He kissed her furrowed brow.

"Why?"

"It's the mid-nineties after all. It's time!"

"So?"

"We set up a site online advertising our wares, people log on and browse, order up what they want, all transactions take place anonymously and we can run it from some third world country. Distribution would be much as now, stock would be stored in our warehouses, but deliveries would be made in the mail or if it's urgent we could courier it. Cutting out a whole tier of untrustworthy fuckers, streamlining the operation and putting you in deep cover. We could even run a bespoke service for our high-roller clients, you know assured deliveries within a certain time to your own address or to a designated pick-up point, personal contact service, guarantees of quality, instant no questions asked replacement or substitution if there is a problem. The key is, as now, to keep everyone happy with us. Get good reviews about our operation and post them on the site and, discretely on other social media, to encourage new customers…"

Ramona frowned.

"I can see you thinking what about all the mean fuckers out there that we have to deal with and the bad reviews some of them are bound to write. Well there shouldn't be too many of those but if there are, there are ways of dealing with awkward customers as you well know. I could go on…"

Excited, his head clearing, he looked around, his throat was dry and he needed something to drink.

"Oh yes and you can hide these things, protect them with passwords, that sort of thing, keep moving them around if need be. There are secret parts of the net we can hide in. The "Dark Web", as it's known, which could have been tailor-made for the likes of you and me. Difficult to find for all, except those clever wankers in the know. And there aren't too many of those around, lucky for us. All we have to do is keep our regulars informed, word of mouth will see to the casual punters and we'll stay three steps ahead of the 'authorities' easy."

"Fuck me," she said quietly and let go of his genitals.

# One Way Superhighway – a journey to the dead end of the Net.

Mikey J. Kramer and Ern B. Emmental from Intersect Networks writing in Burbl ezine (the hacker's premier site for Internet gossip!)
12.12.96

N N N N Nineteen!

Paul Hardcastle eat your heart out!!!!!!

A magic number – 19

Q. But why????

A. You can find anything on the internet in just nineteen clicks

– established nettie wisdom: the wonders of the world at your fingertips. More than enough info to give you the buzz.

the hit, man!!!!

but it's NOT true, a recent study shows. (don't you hate them)

No more Super Highway, more a One-Way Street

With more than a few wrong turnings thrown in, leading to a multitude of dead-ends –

Web-sites that go nowhere, link to nothing, a graveyard of aspirations and hopes, of creativity and wasted genius.

B___L__K_ I cry. Most are crap and deserve it. Some don't. Herein lies the opportunity –

the HiDDen Web – It RocKs!

a shady place of mystery – a cult location deserving of reverence and adoration

A realm for the in-Crowd, the cognoscenti, those with the knowledge

Entry only for those who can follow the signposts, have THE map, and know the passwords.

we all know who we are!!!!!

Q. How come you ask????

A. It's all in the wiring!

The net is not uniform – it has a heart (and a soul man, don't you dig it)

At this pulsating core the web pages are linked to each other (heavily connected) deep thoughts ...

Let's get tekkie for a moment and throw out some stats (we know some of you out there luv 'em)

researchers estimate only 30% of all web pages (that is all) make up this core and it is mainly these that the Altavista's, WebCrawler's and Yahoo's of this world rummage through. You only have to Ask! Beyond are the sites that are increasingly sad and lonely –

More figs – 24% of sites have links that lead to the heart, a further 24% can be reached by following links from the centre. The final 22% are completely cut-off ... going nowhere (as far as the straight dudes know)

the HiDDen Web – the dark side

it's yours for the discovering

Happy Trails !!

2,753 metres

Extract from "The Little Boy's Room through Intimacy to Tying the Knot with the Ball and Chain – The Role of Euphemism in the Evolution of the English Language – Prof. Samuel B. Evans. Principle Press, 2003."

Chap 3. Falling from Grace

Falling is a primal fear. The outcome is clear and immutable, possibly the only human condition where this can be said to be true. The way ahead, the view, if you pardon the pun, is uncluttered, the danger transparent, one's ability to influence the situation non-existent, the position hopeless. Your escape from death or serious injury depends solely on serendipity. A challenge surely to your intelligence and to your humanity? The suicidal choose this path with relief and are, within their universe, behaving rationally. Those who opt to step into the void for enjoyment or thrills are acting irrationally. For the rest of us the very thought of falling, the mere mention of the word causes a frisson, it touches that primordial nerve of self-preservation that pulses in all of us beneath the thin veneer of civilization that s our sole protection against such atavistic terrors. Falling is, I would argue, one of the most basic fears and therefore applying the theory detailed in Chapter 2. where action, in this case an aversion to death, leads to a strong reaction, it is, I believe, one of the richest seams for the mining of euphemism. Suppression of fear results in the growth of a rich culture of obfuscation, where truth is hidden behind a smoke-screen of emblematic words or phrases.

As you will see almost all the euphemistic uses of the word "fall" suggest both a clarity of vision about and a negative connotation to the outcome. The others all point to an irreversible change in situation that is often double-edged. Usage and context are obviously the key.

The many multifarious meanings of FALL:

1. The Fall; falling from Grace; fallen angel
2. fallen woman; lose chastity; copulate with a man extra-maritally; fall for – fall in love with. "It is their husbands' fault, if wives do fall" – Othello
3. fallen on – become pregnant; fall for a child; fall in the family way; fall to pieces – give birth; fall through – miscarry
4. fall off the roof – menstruating; sexually incapacitated; fall in the furrow – ejaculate
5. fall in love; his/her eye fell upon me; fall for – captivated or deceived by
6. to die; "The Fallen"; fell in battle; fall asleep (in Jesus); fall off the perch (Monty Python's dead parrot sketch); fall off the log
7. fall – arrested; sentenced to prison; fall money – bail; fall guy; fall in the shit
8. fall on your sword – admit responsibility
9. fall from favour – misfortune; fall foul of; fall out; fall on evil times; fall down on – fail, come to grief
10. fall apart – break down; collapse emotionally; fall apart at the seams
11. fall off the wagon – drunk; break temperance pledge
12. fall about – collapse with laughter
13. fall on your feet – get lucky
14. fall in – collapse; take place in line or squad; go to bed; arrive; fall up
15. fall out – consequences; nuclear radiation; to faint; surprise; consumed by laughter
16. fall downstairs – get a haircut
17. fall off the back of a lorry – stolen goods

Jump into the unknown.

W
 e
  e
   e
    e
     e
      e
       e
        e
         e
          e
           e
            e
             e
              e
               e
                e
                 e
                  e
                   e
                    e
                     e
                      e
                       e
                        e
                         e
                          e
                           e
                            e
                             e
                              e
                               e
                                e
                                 e
                                  e
                                   e
                                    e

*e*
*e*
*e*
*e*
*e*
*e*
*e*
*e*
*e*
*e*
*e*
*e*
*e*
*e*
*e*
*e*
*e*
*e*
*e*
*e*
*e*
*e*
*e*
*e*
*e*
*e*
*e*
*e*
*e*
*e*
*e*
*e*
*e*
*e*
*e*
*e*
*e*
*e*
*e*
*e*
*e*
*e*
*e*
*e*
*e*
*e*
*e*
*e*
*e*
*e*
*e*
*e*

e
e
e
e
e
e
e
e
e
e
e
e
e
e
e
e
e
e
e
e
e
e
e
e
e
e
e
e
e
e
e
e
e
e
e
e
e
e
e
e
e
e
e
e
e

The sheer joy. The sheer terror.

The Cartoon Consciousness by Digby P. Barnaker.
Published 1987. Relativity Press.

Chapter 2: The Evolution of the Pratfall.

The quintessence of British music-hall comedic culture, the pratfall (OED: Fall on buttocks, humiliating failure) has a long and honourable history. Appearing first in the Elizabethan theatres of London as a humorous addition to the classical fool's arsenal of entertaining devices, it developed its subtleties on the stages of the Reformation until flowering into its full subversive splendour in the Victorian era. A mechanism for the debunking of the arrogant, snobbish and pretentious, it was the first weapon, and I would argue one of the most effective, in the emerging war of the classes. Camouflaged by laughter it wrought its damage, undermining the foundations of society, corroding its very structure. Humour, often self-deprecating, used as a battering ram for change.

How different from the spectacular cartoon falls of the heroes/anti-heroes from the American cartoons of Hannah and Barbera, et al? Yet maybe not?

My thesis is that the cartoon consciousness, as I shall call it, is fundamentally revolutionary undermining societal norms subliminally. It is, I will argue, the potential culmination of a long and effective campaign by writers in the popular media to undercut the consensus.

Imagine the scene: the "Roadrunner" hurtles over a cliff, he continues his forward trajectory for seconds, the realization of his perilous situation dawns, the forces of gravity still held at bay, he attempts desperately to retrace his tracks, legs spinning furiously ...

All is ultimately useless and he plummets downwards, the exaggerated soundtrack to his misfortune (the extended whistle, the protracted weeeeeeee) never failing to raise a smile. The impact, when it comes, is cataclysmic, total destruction, at best the flattening of the body (the pancake) at worst the complete atomization of the character (the nuclear option). Devastating yes, but never fatal – the "Roadrunner's" concussed revival verging on the instantaneous. Hero and villain restored to the circle of comedic strip life, all actions ultimately futile. The characters never learn, but we do, that no progress is possible, that they are trapped. Death and regeneration are one and the same thing. Falling is used as a metaphor for the ultimate negativity of all human effort. This was a radical concept in prosperous Fifties America, with post-war optimism at its peak, yet with a Cold-War paranoia building. The cartoonists were fuelling a pessimism and cynicism that would set light to the radicalism of the forthcoming decade – the Sixties.

2,666 metres

**Home Office Guidance for Her Majesty's Official Executioner (Restricted Access) February 12th 1954.**

Annex 2.a – Table of recommended drops against body weight (includes comparison with the drops that were officially sanctioned up to April 14th 1913)

| Prisoner's body weight | Drop (1888-1913) | Modern Drop |
| --- | --- | --- |
| 14.0 stone (196 lbs.) | 8ft 0in | 5ft 5in |
| 13.5 stone (189 lbs.) | 8ft 2in | 5ft 6in |
| 13.0 stone (182 lbs.) | 8ft 4in | 5ft 8in |
| 12.5 stone (175 lbs.) | 8ft 6in | 5ft 11in |
| 12.0 stone (168 lbs.) | 8ft 8in | 6ft 1in |
| 11.5 stone (161 lbs.) | 8ft 10in | 6ft 4in |
| 11.0 stone (154 lbs.) | 9ft 0in | 6ft 6in |
| 10.5 stone (147 lbs.) | 9ft 2in | 6ft 8in |
| 10.0 stone (140 lbs.) | 9ft 4in | 7ft 1in |
| 9.5 stone (133 lbs.) | 9ft 6in | 7ft 5in |
| 9.0 stone (126 lbs.) | 9ft 8in | 7ft 7in |
| 8.5 stone (119 lbs.) | 9ft 10in | 7ft 9in |
| 8.0 stone (112 lbs.) | 10ft 0in | 8ft 0in |

Note: executioner discretion is allowed for prisoners weighing greater than 14.0 stone (196 lbs.) Drops of less than four feet are not permitted.

The air had qualities unknown to earthbound mortals, a presence much greater than a simple combination of physical and chemical parameters – temperature, humidity, pressure, molecular composition. X could sense it, his body finely tuned after falling over a thousand metres, seeping in, tingling. A sensation so intensely uplifting that for a moment he believed he was cradled securely, cocooned, metamorphosing from the physical to the gaseous.

The hot moist air hit X like a hammer as he passed the armed security guards and pushed open the exit doors from the airport concourse and stepped outside, a blow across the face that caused him to wince. Blinded by the needle-like glare, his head spun as he staggered across the ragged concrete, tripping over a raised kerb as he desperately searched sodden trouser pockets for his Ray-Bans. Disconcerted he dodged the crowd waiting for passengers and the touts soliciting for business and ventured out on to the exposed roadway, the tarmac, soft and tacky beneath his feet, producing an unpleasant sinking sensation as he walked, the soles of his shoes making slight impressions, leaving a trail of ghost footprints behind him. The atmosphere was malevolent – X had heard it described as sauna-like, but that failed to do justice to its nature – instead of warmly enveloping the body the humidity bore down, the air sitting weightily on the shoulders, like an overladen backpack, full droplets of sweat beading on his exposed face and running into smarting eyes, streaming over the chaffed skin of his neck, dribbling across his chest, ponding in the small of the back and groin. A body melting.

Movement was hampered by the viscosity of the medium, pulling at limbs, sapping the will and crushing enthusiasm. Embalmed by a tropical cocktail – vital channels swamped, cloying vapours filling the lungs, constricting the airway, stifling his breathing – X sucked in air. Coughing and wheezing after a few tiring steps, he halted, savouring the tang of decomposition, intermingled with petrol fumes and the fine dust rising from the red earth, that was the aroma of the city. Blinking through aching bloodshot eyes he looked up taking in the beauty of the pink aura that circled the huge fireball of a sun hanging lethargically in the hazel sky above his head.

X had been warned about the debilitating heat, but had not believed it, much as he had been told that passenger's bags often go missing at Murtala Muhammed airport and so his had. Annoyed, he urgently needed to find his Lagos contact, who was supposed to have met him in the arrivals lounge half an hour ago.

"Where the fuck is he?"

A tall man, dressed in a loose-fitting blue shirt patterned with elaborate black swirls, his beaming face heavily pock-marked, appeared at his side.

"Taxi, hotel, women?"

X shook his head.

"Anything you like?"

"Look mate, I'm waiting for someone."

He could feel the sweat running in rivulets down his back, his spine tingling.

"Beautiful women, will do anything you like. Hashish? Just tell me. I can be your guide. Go anywhere. Get you what you want."

Another younger man approached, a long string of gaudy worry beads dangling from his hand, but was waved angrily away.

"Not good man. His girls dirty. He charge a lot of dollars. Me, I'm cheap."

"Go away will you, I'm expected."

As a distraction X pulled a Red Sox baseball cap from the back pocket of his jeans and slipped it on.

"My car, over there."

The driver pointed towards an old, rusting red Chevrolet, the dented taxi sign hanging lopsidedly from the roof.

"Air conditioned…"

"No thanks."

"Where are your bags?"

"Good question, mate."

X was beginning to feel faint, the close physical proximity of the man – the radiant body heat, hands fleetingly touching, and moist, warm, spicy breath – added to his sense of oppressive discomfort and he turned away.

"Let me fetch them for you."

"I said no man and I mean it."

A car horn blared and X felt the warm metal bulk of the vehicle brush past him.

"Fuck me. You bastard. You almost hit me."

The words were croaked and barely audible, his parched throat failing to articulate his anger. He glared as the black Mercedes S-class sedan drew up outside the main doors and two heavily built men in dark suits got out and rushed into the terminal building. A warm breeze offered no relief.

"Be careful, boss."

The man was grinning.

"Lagos drivers no good. Many accidents. You need a guide who knows the city working for you."

He spat out a torrent of spittle that spattered onto the parched ground, coalescing rapidly into large dusty globules.

"You need me boss."

Exasperated, X began to walk back towards the shaded airport entrance, then had a thought.

"Do you know Elechi Odulawe?"

The man stopped and stared at him without expression.

"Elechi Odulawe, or something like that?"

He nodded his head and stepped back.

"Big man boss, big man."

He waved his hands dismissively and turned away from X, strolling nonchalantly back to the group of drivers, sitting beneath a rust-pocked corrugated iron shelter, who had been closely watching their conversation and were now all smiling broadly. Relieved X reeled back into the relative cool of the arrivals lounge, his shirt and trousers soaked.

The drop laid senses bare rendering them susceptible to refinement: fingers spread – existence dissolving under the pressure of his touch; eyes open – sights unseen blurring a vision of the world; ears attuned – hearing the constant rush of the atmospheric ocean; mouth agape – tasting the overbearing sweetness of ripe fruit, full-bodied on the cusp of bursting with decay; nose receptive – smelling the chemical putrefaction of the air swirling with pollutants man-made and natural, inescapable at any height. He was familiar with them all – the touch, sight, sound, taste and smell of falling.

The automatic doors had barely closed behind him when he was accosted by a plump man in flowing embroidered robes of white, gold and red, a matching brimless cap sitting low on his head.

"Sir, are you looking for someone?"

"Leave me alone will you, for Christ's sake."

His irritation was intense. The drafts of warm air from the rickety overhead fans barely impinged on his overheating body and he was distracted by the need to find something to drink and to sit down.

"I've just about had it up to …"

He swallowed his words as he noticed his name scrawled in black felt-tip on a piece of torn cardboard the man was holding up to him.

"Mr. Odulawe?"

There was a moment of incomprehension, then the man smiled broadly.

"Odulawe, you say it Odulawe."

"Odulawe, right."

"That is good."

X looked at him expectantly, noticing for the first time how artfully he cultivated an air of obsequious indifference. Engaging without committing. Flitting eyes, never settling.

"Ah no, I'm not Odulawe."

X could feel the throbbing in his temples and a disconcerting tic in his left eye and suddenly overwhelmed with fatigue, he desperately needed to rest. His first trip to Nigeria was already mired in frustration – his luggage and contact missing, officialdom chaotic and grasping, the unhelpful, milling mass of taxi drivers and hawkers outside and the unforgiving climate – and he had only been in the country for a couple of hours.

"Who are you then?"

The calmness in his voice, masked his growing irritation. Losing control was unfamiliar to him, an alien state.

"Shehu Aluko," he extended his hand, gold rings on three of his fingers, "I work for Mr. Odulawe. He sends his apologies. He is tied up on another job for the chief."

The relief was intense, a powerful surge of heady optimism, disproportionate to the event.

"At last," X grasped the warm pudgy hand with enthusiasm, "pleased to meet you."

"I'm sorry we are late, but Lagos go-slow, what can we do?"

He shrugged expansively, his portly body galvanizing into a theatrical gesture of hopeless futility. His expression exuded disappointment.

"This is life! Is it not so?"

He flung his arms wide and grinned.

"But we are here now. Welcome to my country, welcome!"

He slapped his charge playfully on the back.

"I trust everything is good with you? That you had a fine journey?"

The man's exuberance was displeasing and X pulled away.

"I've lost my bloody bags, some bastards' nicked them, I'm sure."

His contempt poured out in a torrent of frothing words.

"I can't believe the fucking police or customs or whatever they are, they wanted money to help me get my own fucking bags back."

"Please, please. It is important that you stay calm."

Mr. Aluko was agitated.

"Dollars, that's what they wanted, and nothing small either. One of them asked for $20."

"Please. I understand."

"Dollars, not even pounds, they wouldn't do for fuck sake. What sort of country is this?"

"Please. It does no good to get angry with these people."

Aluko's voice was raised, attracting attention in the bustling hall.

"Please be calm."

"Dollars and I've only just bloody got here."

"Please, please I'm sorry we will sort this out, please."

He grasped both of X's hands.

"We will make it up to you, this not a good welcome to my country, for such an honoured guest."

Beneath this onslaught of apologetic concern X's anger subsided rapidly into mild embarrassment. Aluko waved at the two men in dark suits, who had been standing, watching some distance away and they approached rapidly. A few words in Yoruba and they nodded.

"Follow me please, we will get your bags and then we can have some much-needed refreshments."

Aluko took X by the arm – he was relieved, all responsibility had been lifted from him – and they headed back into the customs area. It was quieter now, the rush of passengers from the Heathrow plane had passed through, only a few stragglers remained, one arguing with uniformed officers, another sitting dejectedly beside a damaged trunk, her head in her hands. The row of metal trestle-tables, previously cluttered with passenger's personal effects, were now clear, stripped of all confiscated goods. A single upturned sandal lay overlooked in the shadows, its price label clearly visible on its pristine sole. The air, barely disturbed by the desultory fans overhead, was still heavy with the bittersweet scent of teeming humanity, expensive perfumes, suntan lotions and perspiration.

"This way, please."

A nod to one of the custom officers and they were through the green canvas screen that shielded the baggage areas from the gaze of the public and entered a world of ordered chaos. Rows and rows of grey ceiling-high shelving stretched away into the gloom, luggage – suitcases of all shapes, sizes and colours, rucksacks, hold-alls, bags, canvas, plastic, and fabric – much open or damaged, was piled haphazardly on the shelves and strewn across the floor. Three airport employees in high-visibility vests seated at a table cluttered with assorted cameras, laptops, electric shavers and sunglasses – a momentary flash of recognition for X – rose lethargically to their feet as the group entered, then stiffened on noticing Aluko, acknowledging his presence with bowed heads.

"Point out your bag please."

"You're joking, aren't you."

"Please."

A barked order and all three men pointed to a scattered pile of cases heaped to their left.

"Take a look over there, please. That all came from your London flight this lunchtime."

"A right little scam they've got going here. Shaking down passengers."

Most of the bags appeared untouched, but not all and X's Hedi Slimane suitcase was badly damaged, its leather straps hacked through and its strong locks levered open. The contents had been ransacked, clothes protruded haphazardly from all sides, his favourite shirt, an orange-print Peter Jensen, a sleeve of his white Canali dress shirt and the legs of his grey Paul Smith fatigues, all creased and soiled; a pair of his Miu Miu brogues lay discarded nearby and the cosmetics from his leather wash-bag were scattered across the rough concrete floor.

"Here it is and look what the cheeky fuckers have done to it."

He turned angrily to face the culprits, who stared back impassively.

"Please, don't do anything. Leave it to us."

Aluko placed a restraining hand on X's chest.

"Please, we will fix this, please."

Another shouted order and the baggage handlers tentatively approached the pile of luggage. Show them, please."

X indicated his belongings with his foot. His bag was carefully re-packed and secured with brown tape.

"One more thing, please."

A nod from Aluko and one of his bodyguards stepped forward and grabbed the nearest worker, who visibly sagged, his expression dimming, the others slipped away to cower in the shadows. Moaning quietly and barely struggling the man was dragged down one of the aisles between the shelves. In the dim half light X watched as he was slashed across the upper thighs with a machete. His screams stifled by the firm hand of his assailant, and as he sank to his knees, blood rapidly stained his dirty khaki shorts. Words were spoken and seconds later he was released, collapsing silently to the floor.

"Accidents at work, very common here. It is very dangerous area." Aluko chuckled, "These people are so careless. Come my friend."

As they left, X snatched up his pair of Ray-Ban Predator sunglasses from the table as well as an expensive looking Nikon digital SLR camera.

"Very good. Compensation eh? That is fine."

The whole of Aluko's bulky frame shook, his long robes swaying comically as he laughed, a deep, full-throated, infectious guffaw. X couldn't help smiling. For the first time since touching down he was at ease, the nascent despair he'd felt standing alone in the oven of a Nigerian afternoon was fading. He was glad he'd agreed to come on this trip. These were obviously people you could do business with.

Shimmering in the relentless sunshine, lapping over murky submarine canyons, masking cracks in the earth of vertiginous depth, the ocean was a magic floating carpet of subtle patterns, shading greens into blues. The Westerlies rippling across the surface towards their destruction or the unforgiving rocks of the Californian coast, presented as a broad swell running in wavy lines for great distances, eventually pointedly diminishing to his birds-eye along the far-flung watery horizon. Down below thrashing and foaming in their death-throes the indomitable tides hit back rolling out to sea in fractured lines of choppy resistance mirroring the shape of the promontories, cliffs and beaches that had spawned them, only to be overwhelmed and rapidly obliterated by the relentless, onrushing Pacific currents.

The chill of the air-conditioned Mercedes was disconcerting. It was refreshing yet uncomfortable, heightening X's perception of the cloying stickiness of his body, his sopping clothing and the dusty coating clinging to his skin, that felt gritty and harsh. He shifted uneasily, his shirt and trousers adhering unpleasantly to the leather seats. His nose began to run and his head ached.

"Would you like a drink? We have a good choice. All cold."

"You must be a bloody mind-reader. I could murder a beer."

"We have Guinness, Star and Gulder?"

"Guinness, fuck me I can only drink that if it's pissing down outside and the temperatures about forty degrees lower than now. D'you have a lager?"

"Star? It is my favourite."

"So long as it's cold, I'll drink it."

The dripping bottle, its soggy pale blue and gold label hanging loose, was passed over and he gulped down the ice-cold beer greedily, conscious of the chilly liquid coursing down his throat – a snapshot memory of childhood doubling up with cramp after the first mouthfuls of freezing milk in the dingy kitchen in the basement of the terraced house in Shoreditch, his grandmother chuckling, "What do you expect, love, drinking it that fast. Slow down. Take your time."

Wiping his mouth and nose with his hand, X sat back gratefully into his seat. Through the tinted glass he could see tattered palm trees, all haphazardly leaning, with broken fronds silhouetted against the smoky sky, large ragged birds circling. The car slowed down at a military checkpoint – their chauffeur nodding at the heavily armed soldiers seated around a smoking brazier and was waved through – carefully navigated the obstacle course of oil drums and tree branches placed across the lanes of the dual-carriageway, passed under the ornate triumphal arch that marked the entrance to the international airport and pulled out from the grand uncluttered approach road into the teeming, pot-holed streets of the city. A bustling humanity, vivid in dress, varied in attitude and occupation, surrounded them, crowding in, blocking the light, slowing their progress, the cries of traders pierced the hum of the air-conditioning, the blare of rattling horns sounded loud and unrelenting. Men and women brushed past, dusty-faced hawkers tapped on the window with newspapers, peanuts, water sachets, plastic coat hangers, batteries for sale. Aluko waved them away.

"Go slow." he laughed, "Always like this. A busy market. You can buy anything you like in this area. Very good."

He looked at X seeking affirmation. X nodded.

"Better speed soon, once we get past here."

He gestured vaguely with his hand.

"Cheers!"

Their bottles chinked together.

"Welcome to Nigeria."

The sedan crept slowly forward, the throng parting reluctantly to allow it to pass. Flimsy stalls of rough-hewn planks, rope and frayed cloth fringed the highway, overabundant stacks of goods – vegetables, fruit, clothes, metal pots and pans, vibrantly-coloured plastic bowls – spilled onto the road, encroaching, directing the jostling flow. Time drifted.

A space opened up, the flicking shadows fled and a smoky light infused the car's interior, X looked out. People had dispersed and were picking their way across blood-soaked ground, stepping over puddles of black viscid liquid – flights of flies swarming – moving around heaps of folded animal skins and avoiding spattered scrawny cattle, shackled and broken, theirs heads down, blasted eyes staring, lowing pathetically. Cavernous booths, their interiors in darkness, peeled back from the road, flayed carcasses and strings of bunched entrails hung dripping in the entranceways, adjacent ramshackle counters were heaped with hunks of bleeding flesh. Shoppers milled outside shouting and gesticulating to the market women sitting behind brass scales, tarnished and worn – soiled notes and greasy packages passed back and forth. Under the shaded corrugated-iron overhangs butchers lounged in stained leather aprons covered in gore, bloodied knives tucked in their belts, cleavers in one hand, cigarettes in the other, sizing up the next beast. The shambles were shadowed by an indifferent vitality and X, sheltering behind burnished metal and tinted glass, recognized it. The car gathered speed as they left the market behind, then slowed at an intersection as a large herd of dusty black and white goats was waved forward by a masked traffic policeman standing on a metal podium in the centre of the junction. There was a blaring of horns and the animals scattered, impatient drivers edging forward.

Through gaps in the thinning crowds, X could see the clutter of low-rise mud-brick ochre buildings that lined the narrow street, scuffed and lived in, interspersed the occasional unfinished modern structure, upper storeys empty, the detritus of abandoned construction work strewn across the dusty uneven surfaces, brown rusting steel rods protruding from jagged concrete stumps like tendons in severed chicken legs. Piles of rubbish – indeterminate masses of smouldering decay and plastic – tumbled from waste ground onto broken pavements, forcing the bustle of the street out into the path of the interminable traffic. Vultures, dusty brown, balancing wings extended, scavenged the ridges and peaks of these waste ranges, often rising into the air in dispute, before settling again to their ravening task.

"Please, another beer?"

"Go on."

The cold frothing lager splashed onto his trousers, pinpricks of sensation punctuating his leaden reverie. As they crawled forward, he watched a smiling, bare-legged young girl jumping from rock to crushed oil can, haphazard stepping-stones scattered across a stagnant pool of fetid, turbid water, that lapped against another dam of garbage. The psychedelic rainbow sheen of leaked petrol glinted on the ruffling surface, her play stirring a soup of bubbling degeneration. She was not alone, X caught a fleeting glimpse of rats scurrying through the debris along the pool's edge, their presence betrayed by frenetic ripples in the water. Close behind them a destruction of scabby, emaciated feral cats, hunting agilely through the refuse dump.

The air was heavy with diesel fumes, a faint trace detectable even inside the air-conditioned car, and X found he could taste the smell, foul at the back of his throat. Gulping lager, he stared into the crusted eyes of three children, their scrunched faces pressed hard against the side window. He waved, a friendly gesture invisible behind the dark glass, and bored they stepped back, revealing dusty bellies protruding between torn, grubby T-shirts and ragged shorts. One of them, the tallest, lobbed a rock at a crippled dog, its broken back leg dragging in the dust, raw pink skin glaring through thinning brown fur, vestigial tufts hanging from its head and ears. Hurt the mongrel skulked off, yelping, the ricocheting stone plopping into the filthy water, the boys in barefooted pursuit. The car, accelerating slowly, kept pace and X saw the exhausted, terrified, hound turn on his oppressors, baring his teeth, only to be met with a fusillade of stones. As they pulled away, he watched through the rear window as the defeated animal sank slowly to the ground.

X had barely begun to savour his second bottle of Star, when the car braked hard and he lurched forward, slopping beer into his lap.

"Fuck, not again. What's happening?"

Aluko stiffened beside him. The driver hissed a warning and a pistol – the new Micro Uzi semi-automatic X noticed – was thrust into his hand.

"You'll need this my friend. Take it."

Hesitant, X sat up.

"What the fuck?"

"Armed robbers, lots of them. They are coming for us."

There was nobody to be seen through the tinted glass. Rusting names – Ikeja, Agege, Otta – on a skewed signpost, peppered with bullet holes, blocked his view. Swirling smoke obscured the rear. He was blind-sided.

"Where?"

The wheels spun and the car veered backwards, throwing X and Aluko together, their heads clashing. Stunned, the two men reeled in their seats as a high-velocity shot smashed the glass in the side-window next to X and ripped into the roof lining. A second shattered the rear window, glass shards cascading over X as he sprawled across the back seat. A woman was screaming nearby, a harrowing ululation that drowned out the shouts of their attackers. There was dust rising everywhere, clouds of it billowing in through the broken windows, breathing was difficult, and X couldn't see a thing. A burst of automatic fire from the front seat was deafening, the shock waves reverberating painfully in the enclosed space. The Mercedes sped forward, its engine racing, then turned in a skidding arc, its rear bumper hitting a rickety wooden market stall, and collapsing it, its stock of muddy yams tumbling across the boot of the car in a thunderous barrage. A slug sliced into the side door, hissing, and exited through the other, daylight punching through the neat holes.

The repetitive sound of gunfire, the yelling and shouting, the high-pitched scream of the engine, revived X to a confused consciousness. He pushed against the dead weight of Aluko's prone body stretched out across his legs and rolled him into the seat well. He grunted. Raising himself up, his hand resting in puddle of cool liquid on the seat, he stared blinking into the swirling dust storm. There were people running, mere shapes, trying to reach the car as it rocked and swerved, their driver desperately searching for an escape route. The air cleared and X could see the road ahead blocked by a crude barricade of rubber tyres and wooden planks. There was another sudden burst of gunfire from the front seat, X noticed the light glinting dully on the snub barrel of an Uzi submachine gun. He could smell spilled beer. A peripheral shadow threatened, instinctively he raised his gun and fired twice, he watched one bullet and then another explode in the centre of a man's chest, crimson staining his bright green and yellow shirt, as he spun backwards, teeth bared in a gape of agony, his rifle – a Kalashnikov AK47 – flying through the air.

The Mercedes accelerated, skidding from side to side, wheels spinning. X braced himself, head down, arms folded across the back of the forward passenger seat. The impact with the barricade was jarring – the front of the vehicle was lifted into the air and they almost came to a halt. X was thrown forward, crumpling against the seat, as splintered wood and debris clattered across the bonnet and roof and spun past the windows. His nose, crushed against the headrest, spurted blood and he swallowed hard, the harsh metallic taste infusing his mouth and throat.

In a series of faltering hops the car lurched ahead, bouncing over obscure obstacles in the road, then sped away in a cloud of dust and exhaust, the engine knocking ominously. Within seconds the pall lifted and the crowded bustle of the city engulfed them, their progress slowed. Short of air X exhaled – he realized he had been holding his breath – then coughed, inhaling deeply. He smelt petrol and spent propellant. Through the smashed back window, he could see no obvious sign of any pursuers.

"Hey mate," he wheezed, nudging the shoulder of the bodyguard with the Uzi, who turned a grin fixed on his face.

"Shouldn't we be shifting it?"

There was no response. The dry, cloying, dust was irritating his throat. He coughed.

"Putting our foot down, speeding up, you know going faster?"

"Aaaahhhhh Chief, we safe now. No need to rush."

"How are we safe? What about the police, won't they be down here any moment?"

"Chief, police no come …"

X looked puzzled.

"… no good for them, eh Chief?" he laughed, "this bad place for policeman."

A horn blared, followed by another, their driver joining in the rising cacophony.

"This is a fucking nightmare. Can't you keep it down mate," X was shouting, "I need to think."

He had shot a man. Dead. He was certain of that. He had seen wounded men fall still twitching with a spark of existence, their bodies broadcasting their agony. His attacker had fallen inertly, like a hewn log crashing to the ground in a shroud of sawdust. There had been no pre-meditation on his part, no chance to consider his actions, just pure reflex, kill or be killed, a base instinct that had saved his life.

Chemicals buzzing his brain, senses acute – blinding lances of sunlight pierced his eyes through the non-existent windows, the traffic noise painfully loud, exhaust fumes stifling his sense of smell, dominating, his heart racing, blood surging, a flood about to burst forth – he anxiously fingered his left eye soothing the nervous tormenting tic and fought his nauseating panic.

"I should never have come. Fuck me. I know nothing about this country. The jails are bound to be shit. And they'll certainly have the fucking death penalty. Christ."

The thought – life being squeezed out of his body, the rope tightening around his neck, the sickening fall, the last minute reprieve arriving too late – was so immense he could scarcely breath.

"Murder or self-defence? How would they see it, the wonderful Lagosian police? It's no sodding question."

Drops of blood coalesced at the tip of his bruised nose and spattered his white shirt, seeping slowly through the fine cotton weave, seeding a galaxy of misshapen dark stars.

"And I'm in the hands of these cowboys."

He frowned as the bodyguard turned to face him.

"You say something, Chief?"

His face was still wreathed in a smile.

"So, who were they then, those men that attacked us?"

"Bad men, Chief."

"Bloody well-armed bad men."

"Yes Chief."

Aluko groaned at his feet, his body stirring, as another thought came to him – his stunned mind capable of working only linearly, one question after another, yawning seconds between them, time for the sickening answers to come to him and for the truth to sink in.

"They were after him, the gunmen? Of course they fucking were, it was so obvious."

The Mercedes juddered, the engine backfiring – all in the car inadvertently flinching – before it crawled forward.

"Everything OK, boss," the driver spoke cheerily for the first time, "This good wagon boss."

His companion nodding enthusiastically.

"Who knew he was here? Who knew he was making this trip?"

"We make good time up ahead, boss. Not long now."

"There can't be many people? Certainly not at our end. Ramona always plays things tight. God knows about here though."

Listening to the two security men's attempts to reassure him worried X. He nudged Aluko's body with his foot.

"Lagos go-slow, Chief, big problem."

"Sorry-o, all the time, Boss."

The car stopped. Grinning children crowded round, his presence a novelty, faces pressing hard, dusty hands pushed through the broken window reaching for his hair, clutching at his clothes. Laughing they cried out, "Oyinbo, oyinbo."

He sunk back into the leather seats.

"Go away," he croaked lamely, "Leave me alone."

There was no let up. Their vehicle began to creep forward, a high-pitched whistle coming from the racing engine, and the heads began to slip away. He could see clearly, the outline of buildings against the pallid hazy sky, the silhouettes of passersby, criss-crossing, the gaudy chaos of the streets.

The tang of the sea. Open-mouthed with amazement. The taste. He was surfing the airwaves – arms extended, body arched, feet splayed – riding the pressure banks rolling across the oceans, sodden with the perfumed moisture of the Tropics, cresting the turbulence as the warm dry air of the Americas swirled up to meet it, sliding down the face of the breaking intercontinental slipstream. The wonder.

Aluko stood groggily in front of him, face bruised, but smiling, the metallic heat of the damaged Mercedes fierce on their skin, the bitter smell of diesel heavy in the air. The intense shade of the Bombax trees that overhung the driveway offered no relief from the oppressive warmth and humidity. The atmosphere was still, suffused with a heady mix of fragrances – chemical, aromatic and organic. Tall, bedraggled oil palms cast harsh shadows on the high whitewashed walls, topped with broken glass and barbed wire, that isolated the lush, verdant compound from the desiccated, dangerous world outside. Elaborate wrought-iron gates, overlaid with riveted sheets of burnished steel, glided shut, blocking out the view of the street – a wide residential avenue lined with tall dusty camwoods, all the houses closed in on themselves, shuttered and encircled, armed watchmen guarding their entryways. A heavy chain and padlock noisily secured the entrance, and everyone relaxed.

"Thank you, my friend, for what you did. Tunde has explained everything."

Aluko clasped his guest's hand with both of his and shook it enthusiastically. The shock of the attack was easing, but X was concerned, aware the reassurances of the chauffeur and bodyguard were mere formalities, subordinates deferring to the needs of their charge.

"Who were they, the men who attacked us?"

"Armed robbers, it happens all the time. Lagos is a bad place."

"You're telling me."

"We will deal with it. We have our contacts. We will track down the miscreants."

He flung his arms wide and smiled broadly.

"You are safe now. This building, the surrounding neighbourhood is Chief Idowu's home village. He is working here. It is his office. He is the big man."

"So, the attack was nothing to do with me being in Nigeria then?"

Aluko frowned. An iridescent green and yellow hummingbird, flitting fitfully between overblown orange flowers in the nearby tangled herbaceous border, momentarily hovered in front of the vivid scarlet blooms dotting X's chest, a passing interest only, before streaking away.

"Nothing to do with my visit?"

"My friend no. You mustn't think that. Believe me, your visit is hush-hush. We have told no one."

"You're saying it was just a coincidence, the attack?"

Aluko shrugged.

"What about the police?"

"No problem. Cash, dash, the police no problem. Trust me."

X, uncomprehending, stared blankly.

"The police are not interested in our little misadventure, you understand? They're interested in other bigger things."

Aluko rubbed his fingers together and grinned.

"Money, my friend, money. Come you worry too much, Chief Idowu is waiting to meet you."

He took X by the shoulder and limping slightly, guided him slowly up the driveway towards a large three-storey building, castellated, with many balconies and walkways, its pale concrete walls disfigured by blotches of black and green mildew, the ugly boxed-ends of air-conditioning units protruding from every window. Armed men loitered in the shade of the grandiose entrance, framed by the cascading, twisted, abundance of a giant creeper laden with luxurious scarlet blooms. A young girl wearing flip-flops, her tall thin body wrapped tightly in radiant red and yellow cloth, was sweeping fallen, crushed petals into small fragrant heaps as they approached. She stepped aside and bent one knee to the ground.

"Come, we will meet the Oga."

Prince Stanley Idowu rose to his feet with difficulty as they entered the vast sparsely furnished meeting room, an aide handing him an intricately carved walking stick. The tiled floor was highly polished and the pale blue walls were covered in large framed photographs of the chief and his extended family. Three large green leather sofas with ornate wooden armrests were arranged against the walls in a U-shape facing an oversized chair sitting in the middle of a ruby-red Persian rug, the abstract pattern picked out in gold. Their host moved sedately, his assistant always hovering at his back, his precise actions deliberate and considered. The Chief was corpulent, self-satisfied, and immaculately dressed in impeccably laundered traditional Yoruba robes – a flowing open-necked, long-sleeved agbada in blue and black patterned cloth interwoven with silver thread, over loose trousers in the same material, low-cut brown leather loafers with tassels, and on his head perched a matching pale blue woven Fila hat. He greeted X effusively, grasping his outstretched hand with both of his. The head of his ebony cane, a roaring lion, glinted in the harsh artificial light.

"I cannot apologize enough," he sounded breathless, his voice surprisingly high-pitched for a man of his girth, "so uncivilized to be assaulted in that violent way when it is your first visit to our beloved country. Please forgive us."

X nodded his assent, but said nothing, distracted by the Chief's pronounced facial scarring, the intricate net of fine ridges covering a full face, worn and distinguished, his tightly cropped hair greying at the temples, only his dark bloodshot eyes betraying a hint of ruthlessness.

"Please be seated. Refreshments?"

"Thanks, one of those beers I had in the car on the way here would be good."

Aluko, who had slipped away, spoke up from the doorway.

"Star, Chief."

"Very good, bring a Star for my guest and a brandy for me."

Prince Idowu clicked his fingers as he eased himself down into the padded armchair.

"How is my good friend Ramona? I haven't seen her in a while. I do hope she is well? We have been doing business for some years."

"Good thank-you. She sends her regards…"

Idowu nodded.

"… and I have a gift for you from her …"

X looked around searching for Aluko.

"… in my bag."

"That is very kind of her. But later, my friend. There is no hurry. Maybe after some food."

A young girl appeared carrying a tray with a sweating bottle of Star, a frothing part-filled tumbler of beer and a large brandy snifter. It tilted perilously as she placed it on a small wooden table pulled forward by the Chief's silent aide.

"First a toast," the foaming head furiously climbed the sides of X's glass, peaking, then decaying back, "to prosperity and a full life."

"Prosperity and a full life."

Their glasses chinked together.

"And to our new business venture."

"Our new venture."

"Long may it prosper."

X drained his glass.

"Thirsty work being ambushed."

The Chief laughed.

"More Star and bring the brandy."

His voice rang authoritatively round the room, then he leant forward and in hushed tones spoke confidentially to X.

"The incident today was most unfortunate. But you have nothing to worry about. I will talk to the Head of Police here – a good man from my village –he will deal with the hoodlums. There is no way you will be connected to what happened. There will be an investigation and your name won't even come up. Now, you must forget everything. Come, drink my friend, then we'll eat."

A fresh beer and a bottle of Hennessy cognac had appeared on the table together with a small earthenware dish filled with polished red nuts. The chief broke one and offered pieces to X.

"Kola nuts, take, they are good for dispelling stress," he nudged X's arm, "chew on it, you will like it."

The surge of bitterness from the hard kernel as he bit into it was invigorating, cleansing the palate of the dusty street grime, that even the chilled beer had been unable to swill away. The strong hint of rose in the snack's prolonged aftertaste soothed his temper. A semblance of contentment settled over X, for a moment he forgot about bloodletting and violent death and relaxed, sinking back into the vast leather sofa. He closed his eyes.

"They're ace them Kola nuts, aren't they Chief?"

The Essex accent was unmistakable. X stirred, turning his head to see a tall, thin white man with long, disordered hair stride across the room. Dressed in a vivid Hawaiian shirt, covered in bikini-clad women intertwined with palm trees, creased khaki chinos and black Converse All-Star Hi-top baseball boots, he patted the Chief informally on the back before collapsing onto the sofa beside X. Prince Idowu was grinning.

"Here is someone you should meet. Our very own medicine-man, Tony. Tony Scullion. He knows everything there is to know about computers and the internet."

"Never a truer word was spoken, Chief, never a truer word."

"He's an expert on our business as well. A really useful fellow."

Tony held out a cold clammy hand to X.

"Call me Ace, man."

They hurriedly shook hands. His face was long and angular,

with a narrow nose and prominent cheek-bones, his skin, pallid and pock-marked. There were ashen-grey bags rimming blood-shot blues eyes, a fine two-day blond stubble, and flaming red spots on his neck. At close quarters X could see that his "unkempt" flaxen hair was a contrivance, highlighted and gelled into spiky existence with a great deal of care.

"Glad to see you, man."

"Me too. So, you're the genius Ramona's told me so much about?"

"The very same. Don't you just love that chick, Ramona? Old enough to be my mum, but awesome none the less. How is she? Haven't spoken to her in a while. Kola nuts don't you dig 'em?"

He reached across and grabbed a large jagged piece of nut, popping it eagerly into his mouth. It bulged prominently against his sunken cheek.

"They're cool man. The taste grows on you, believe me and the after-buzz is wicked."

"They're good, working a treat on me. You look wasted."

"Dead fucking right man, it's the work, if you know what I mean. 24/7… Any chance of a beer, Chief?"

Idowu appeared indulgent of Ace's casual behavior and lack of decorum, meeting his request amiably, constantly smiling and gazing benignly at him.

"… and the night life. Shit the women and the rest, get my drift? A1. The Chief here," he raised his bottle, "provides me with everything my heart desires and more. You'll enjoy it in this country, man."

"Did you hear what happened this afternoon on my way from the airport?"

"Shit, yeah man. Just the vaguest, but I'm not surprised it's gang warfare out there. Happens all the time."

He laughed.

"Don't look so worried man, it'll get sorted. The Chief here is very well-connected, well-staffed if you get my drift and well-tooled up."

"Everybody's telling me the same."

"Believe it, man, and relax."

Chief Idowu beckoned to his aide and began to ease himself slowly out of his seat.

"Come friends why doesn't Ace show you around, introduce you to his toys, and then when you've seen enough, we can have food."

Ace leapt up and helped the old man to his feet.

"Good plan Chief, good plan. Man, prepare yourself to be gobsmacked!"

He looked gleefully at X, who reluctantly nodded his assent. He was tired and wanted to drink beer and unwind. Ace's exuberance was wearing.

"Ace here can tell you how it's all going. Very well I think!"

"It's cool man, very cool. Here, follow me man, let's visit the special unit. It's over here hidden away at the back of the compound."

Ace skipped across the floor and hovered in the doorway as X ambled after him.

"Security is pretty tight here."

He punched an eight-number code into a keypad on the wall and a heavy door, that X hadn't noticed before, swung silently open.

"Needs to be, if you get my drift," Ace had lowered his voice, "trust no one that's my motto."

He began to walk down a long, narrow, ill-lit passageway.

"Even the Chief?"

"Even the Chief, nice as the old boy is, you've got to remember I don't work for him, I work for Ramona. Who does he work for, eh? Doesn't take too much to work that out, does it?"

"Himself."

"Exactly my man, exactly."

At the end of the walkway he stopped outside another door and looked around.

"That being said man, watch your back and you can have a great time here. And bear in mind how lucky you are you've got Uncle Ace to show you the ropes and take good care of you."

He winked, unlocked the door and disappeared into the subdued indistinct glow of the high-tech netherworld he inhabited and flourished in. Following him, X was shaken by the strange transmutation that took place as he entered the secure rooms. The change was breathtaking, outside the harsh blood and gristle of the dusty everyday world, inside a subterranean electric universe of vast potentials, clean and clinical, the air, appreciably cooler, possessing a charged, static quality, pulsing at the very limit of audibility. X stepped out from the dingy corridor into the tinted, understated laboratory lighting of the future. Facing him a low-ceilinged white walled hall with three closed doors, a sofa and water-cooler lined the far end. He shivered.

"It's a bit Brasso in here, isn't it?"

Ace laughed and lightly punched X on the shoulder several times.

"Nothing gets past you does it, pal. The Chief makes sure the air-con works here. We have our own dedicated power supply with a back-up generator if things get iffy. Vital to the whole scene, if you know what I mean? This little lot starts getting hot and sweaty and we are fucked."

Ace's tactile familiarity annoyed X, and he pulled away, even though he was under strict instructions from Ramona to get on with him.

"He's the only bloody vital cog in the machine we've got, so see he's happy. We don't want him going native or worse being poached by some rivals, now do we? If it looks like its going tits up, let me know, pronto. He's a weird git, though. You may like him."

Ace didn't appear to notice X's disdain.

"There's one thing you can say about the Chief he gets things done if it's in his interests, which these little babies certainly are."

Ace pointed at the first of the locked doors, which was heavily strengthened with sheet steel. A notice hanging lopsidedly from one of the protruding rivets read, "Our motto: We're only too pleased to help."

"That's the server room, not much to see, but it's them little beauties which keeps our site up and running and keeps us in wedgies."

X peered through the misted security glass at the two bays of equipment, red lights blinking unceasingly.

"To tell the truth I had big problemoes getting the bastards up and running. But it's all sweet now. Nothing's gone wrong for a couple of months. Touch wood."

Before X could move Ace patted him on the head and laughed.

"Welcome to the nerve-centre of my domain. The Mothership!"

He tapped a code number into an electronic pad on the wall, waited for the telling metallic click, then pushed open the door, wedging it with his foot to allow X to squeeze past. Two large computer screens dominated the small cubbyhole – their jittering screensavers, mesmerizingly attention-grabbing and crude, showed three mongrel dogs mating with naked women as they floated through space from screen to screen, and at irregular intervals flashing cheesy grins at the user, saliva dripping from their gaping jaws.

"Sweet eh?"

"Nice."

"It took me ages to sync up the doggies so they were doing it altogether. The Chief thinks it's dead funny."

The air smelled stale. Recycled. Dirty plates and cups were strewn across the cluttered surface of the desk, and the surrounding floor. Ace cleared a space with a sweep of his arm, and pulled up a chair for X.

"It's a bloody pisser, I can't allow anybody in here, so I have to tidy up myself."

"Tough on you."

"Spot on, brother. Seen enough?"

A touch of the mouse and the dogs disassembled instantly in sizzling pixel clouds, their yelps echoing around the enclosed space, to be replaced by screeds of text, in which only the occasional word was recognizable to X: toot, blow, whizz, Audi, acid, Special K – embedded within paragraphs of incomprehensible digital script.

"What the fuck's all this?"

"This my friend," Ace was enjoying himself, "is the dog's bollocks. This is what makes me God. From here I can make anything happen. Turn people's worlds to cock, make their wanky little days, or generally fuck with them anyway I like."

He stood up bowing to the left and right, acknowledging the adulation of an imaginary capacity crowd.

"I can rule this fucking world and all the others, the King of all known Universes that's me, a Time Lord messing with people's minds."

Aware of Ramona's instructions, but unable to bear Ace's antics, X tugged at his T-shirt.

"Any more of this grandstanding bullshit and I'm going to twat you."

The young man turned and looked down questioningly at X, then dropped back into his seat.

"Fair enough. You're as close to a boss as I'm likely to get for a while, so what do you want to know?"

Relieved, X tried conciliation.

"Ace, we all know you're a fucking genius so just put me out of my misery. Tell me what I'm looking at."

"This is the code for our little life-saver of a website. Here I can stroke the vitals of the beast, making it do what I like."

"Ace, what the fuck does that mean? Come on man, the sooner we get this over, the sooner we can get back outside for a few beers and some eats. I'm fucking famished."

"Now you're talking my sort of language, man."

The screens instantly transformed into a mass of vibrant swirling colour and multi-hued lettering, the font a direct homage to the plump fluid curlicue scripts of the late-sixties "happening" posters of West Coast jam bands – the home page of "Far-macy-out".

"What a beauty."

Ace sat back admiring his handiwork.

"Come on, man. Beautiful it is, but I've seen it all before."

"All that code means I can run the site from here – update products and prices mainly, special offers that sort of stuff, but I could do far more, but she won't let me. I could redesign it, harden it up, make it more contemporary you know. Give it a bit of street cred, but Ramona says no. No toucheeee. She seems to like all this psychedelic on the road shit."

"You're telling me! Ramona's always had a soft spot for San Francisco, the Summer of Love and the Acid Tests, said if only she'd been born a few years earlier she wouldn't be wasting her time in straightsville UK, but dealing the high life in Southern California."

"Whatever! She always seemed a slightly weird bird to me."

"Weird maybe, but she knows her shit. All this hippy nostalgia stuff sells. Plugs into what she calls the "retro-cool" vibe, which seems to be a winner with our punters. It's all clever niche marketing, you know, the result of extensive research into the target client group. Hours of focus group discussions have come up with this design concept and shown it to be the most effective in attracting the customers we're looking for."

"She told you that did she?"

"Sure did. She even sat in on some of them."

"Bullshit, it's just that Ramona's an old hippy at heart, a flower child, a free spirit, a stoner."

X laughed.

"Never a truer word, mate. I can't argue with you there."

He was happier now the atmosphere had lightened, and mildly intoxicated from the strong lager settling on his empty stomach.

"Come on how does it all work? You're sitting at your laptop and you want to place an order for, let's say, a dozen E. What happens then?"

"Ah that's yet another devilishly clever bit – it's all very simple, no specialist knowledge required, even the computer illiterate can cope – first you have to have downloaded the secure browser we recommend and be OK using it."

"What's that? Why do you have to use it?"

"Basically, it ensures you remain anonymous online. All your traffic is encrypted shed-loads of times so you are free to roam far and wide. The advantages are obvious in so many areas of life, not just our own. Just use your imagination."

Ace giggled and nudged X with his elbow.

"It gets better. There are layers of protection on top of all that. The browser in question isolates any website you visit, like ours, so that third-party trackers – like the police, other organized crime syndicates – and other things like advertisements that can give you away in your search history, can't follow you. And when you have finished your business with us it wipes that said search history so nobody would ever know you'd paid a visit. In short anybody monitoring your activities on the web won't know what you've been looking at and where you've been. All they'll be able to see is that you have been doing something online using that particular browser. Which may be suspicious but is not indictable."

Leaping to his feet Ace flung his arms wide, palms upwards, seeking approval from X, with none forthcoming he sat down and continued his monologue.

"We have our own security walls as well. You log on to our site using a personal password, which unbeknown to the punter is exclusively linked to their smartphone or computer – laptop or desktop whatever – and IP address and none other, which means if he or she tries to get access from anywhere other than their registered base and/or use another phone or terminal it won't happen for them. Astute, don't you think?"

X realized that Ace seemed to require approbation at very regular intervals. It was an annoying trait that was beginning to grate, but for the moment, only too aware of his mission, he played along.

"Ace, Ace!"

"Your order comes through here from your UK ISP, it's processed digitally and encrypted and then all the details: your name, delivery address, drug of choice in this case E, amount and payment details, usually cash on delivery, as you'd imagine there's a bit of punter resistance to handing over credit card details on a site such as ours, although a few high rollers do it, are relayed back in scrambled form to the UK for distribution which is I believe your little part of the operation. In the interest of complete disclosure you should know I've been trying to get Ramona interested in using cryptocurrencies for payments using peer-to-peer networks there are so many advantages – better security, instant payments, costings all that sort of thing and it would make your end of the deal in sales a lot easier – I could go on, but so far boss lady hasn't taken the bait. Maybe you could put in a word."

"If I knew anything about them I would."

"I'll send you some links. You can bone up."

"Cheers."

"To continue my little tale of deception and deceit. The routing through Lagos, the sophisticated encryption, courtesy of yours truly, plus the very restricted access to the site makes the whole operation virtually untraceable."

"How do you mean?"

"Which bit don't you understand?"

Ace's supercilious manner was a further irritation.

"Encryption must be self-explanatory, routing it through a third world shithole like this means there's no one paying any attention to what we're doing, particularly if enough money passes into the right hands. It's all pretty much untraceable. You'd have to be a fucking clever bastard to get anywhere close and I'd see them coming."

"Yeah, yeah I get all that, it was the restricted access bit I didn't follow."

Leaning back in his chair Ace stretched his arms.

"You've used the site, haven't you?"

X nodded.

"Only at Ramona's."

"Bloody awesome innit, even if I say so myself. The whole shebang is in deep, deep cover. The site is virtually impossible to get into. It's designed, once again by your man here, so that only one search term will find it. There is no other way of getting to it. Putting in its web address, which you may have if you've visited the site once before, in the UK or anywhere else, without going through Google or wherever won't work."

X appeared perplexed.

"You know how search engines like Google work?"

Ace waited until X acknowledged that he didn't.

"In a nutshell then. They all rank the importance of sites by how many other sites link to them, so sites with thousands of links will come out top in any search request you stick in and sites with fewer links will come lower down in the search. With me so far?"

"Yep."

"Well our little website here has only one link and it's hidden away in one of them forgotten regions of the internet where connectivity with other sites is very low. The dark web as it's known. Like a lost city hidden in the jungle with only one secret pathway into it. So the site can only be found with one unique search term which we give out to our clients – I still can't get used to that term, it doesn't really tally with the old dopers I know – when they sign up."

Ace raised his open hand in anticipation of a high-five, X hesitated, then responded, the sharp clap reverberating round the small room.

"And one other brilliant feature, we can keep changing the search term, if the plod or anyone else unsavoury get on to it."

"How would you know?"

"Unnatural activity matey. I can monitor that from here. I'm able to trace all access requests to the site, and I've devised an algorithm that flags up any strange formats, locations, repetitions that type of thing."

At that he pulled up on the computer screen a matrix of constantly updating data, figures crawling along the top of the page like black insects, lines jerkily scrolling down the screen.

"There is a familiar pattern of usage which I can now recognize – same punters come online regularly – an' Ramona keeps me informed about all new hop-heads signing on."

"Valued clients to you, if you don't mind."

Ace grimaced.

"You bunch of fucking poseurs, is that what you really call them?"

X nodded.

"It's big business now."

"I can't believe it, Ramona used to be so right-on."

"Still is man, believe me."

"You would know, I guess. Anyway this means I can keep tabs on it all and if anything looks odd – if I sense the Old Bill might be sniffing around for example – I can just close the site down for a short time so that all connections are lost, and they're left sitting there wondering why their desktops are so crap, then change the search term, which gets e-mailed more or less instantaneously to all our known client base, then fire up the site again with the new code word and away we go. Takes less than ten minutes. Impressive eh?"

"I am impressed, as I said you are a fucking genius and, I'm glad to see, a quick learner."

"Oh man you're too kind. Another thing I'm thinking of proposing is that as the business expands, we change the search term and maybe even personal passwords randomly – adds another level of security and keeps everyone guessing. Banks use devices that generate specific time-limited codes for access to online accounts. Maybe we could use something like those little beauties in the future. And by the way, as you know, this is currently a relatively small-scale operation run by yours truly, but we are going to get bigger so the system is designed to be easily replicable."

X was uncertain he understood.

"It means it is easy to upsize everything. We can add extra technical modules – exactly the same as these…"

He grandly gestured towards the screens.

" …to cope with additional business traffic. Deliver the deliverables. Shift more gear in the parlance of the doped-out senior industry executive. Neat, if I say so myself."

"I said I was impressed!"

"Thank you, my man. I mustn't claim all the glory though, you boys out on the streets do your bit with your secondary checks on new addresses, wacky orders etc. and I get tipped off and can change everything."

"It all works well. I'm glad to see it in the flesh. I'm happy, you happy?"

"In the main man, Ramona keeps me sweet. Could do with a bit more leeway if you get my drift. Bit more of a say in the running of it all, a little less processing orders and fucking troubleshooting, otherwise I'm fine."

"Good, cos Ramona's happy if you're happy."

There was a hesitation.

"I'll run your ideas past her of course Ace. Do my best to spell things out."

"I'm happy."

"Sweet. Enough of this shit then, lets have a beer."

Desperate to get away X walked out of the room and hurried to the exit.

"Hold up man, I need to lock everything down."

Communing with the world as he fell, all physical ties to his immediate environment a subtle distortion of the stationary, was a profound experience. Everything the same yet changed. Precipitation no longer rained down, instead X swam through showers of glittering droplets, a body drenched – face, chest and thighs as wet as hair, back and calves – as the water cascaded down at the same speed as he did. This fleeting downpour would never spot the ground, it would be wrung out and dissipated in the unremitting gleam, unlike X who fell mouth open, drinking in life. Sunlight diffusing into rainbow shrouds of incorporeal colour. The dazzle-razzle.

Emerging from the secure area wrapped in a blanket of sticky air – the humid residue of faltering air-conditioning – blinking in the dull oppressive light of early evening, the lustrous chill of the control centre banished, X paused and looked around. Now the property appeared drab, the rooms exuding a down-at-heel aura, the paintwork scuffed, the walls stained with rising damp and mould, the furniture faded and worn. Ace joined him.

The Chief was waiting for them in the adjoining room where a small low table surrounded by three large armchairs was laid out with bowls of steaming food. It was brighter and airier than the reception room they had been sitting in earlier, a large tinted picture window opened onto the garden, flooding the space with opaque sunlight. Outside a Doberman Pinscher rolled lethargically on the parched ground, an emanation of pale dust shimmering in the air above him. In the hazy middle distance among the stunted trees that fringed the high perimeter wall, an armed guard strolled lethargically back and forth along a well-worn path.

"Please… there is water for you to wash your hands," Prince Idowu waved his arm expansively, "then make yourself comfortable, take a seat."

He clicked his fingers and two young girls appeared, one carrying plates, the other a tray of drinks.

"They will serve you, take what you like."

X nodded his appreciation as he sat down. The food looked delicious. He was ravenously hungry.

"These are all local delicacies. Nigerian cooking is the finest in the world."

One of the girls spooned meat stew onto X's plate followed by a heap of mucilaginous green vegetables, which he thought he recognized as okra, she then pushed a bowl towards him, piled high with steaming, thick, glutinous mash.

"You should try some of these, they're great."

Ace nudged a plate in X's direction.

"Looks like banana."

"It's dodo man, dodo. And not the fucking bird … it's plantain."

"And the rest?"

X gesticulated at his plate.

"Goat stew, ila, that's okra you know you get it in Indian takeaways, and that is eba made from some root. It's like our potatoes, you have it with everything."

"Drink my friend? We have plenty more beer or we have wine."

Chief Idowu hissed and one of the girls appeared carrying a bottle of "Mateus Rosé" on a tray, displayed in its raffia basket.

"Beer's fine, Chief. I'm not much of a wine man."

"Star then," he announced imperiously, banishing the servant with a wave of his hand. Ace was already eating.

"Come on man, tuck in. Use your hands. It's cool."

Reluctantly X dipped his hand into the bowl of eba, the heat was intense and he pulled them back, the pain searing the tips of his fingers. Ace and the Chief both laughed.

"You could have warned me, you bastard," he muttered through clenched teeth.

"They catch out everyone that way, man. Nothing personal. You get used to it. Try the stew, it's good."

Tentatively, X scooped up a chunk of meat dripping with sauce and popped it into his mouth and attempted to chew it. The piece – a slippery roll of goat skin – yielded to the pressure of his bite, but did not break up, maintaining its leathery resilience and inducing a gagging reflex that X fought hard to suppress. Ace looked on, amused.

"My friend, how did you find our little operation in the technical hub? Impressive isn't it?"

His mouth full, X tried to smile, while nodding assent.

"We'll be very successful and make everyone much money, don't you think?"

X nodded again, struggling against the bilious taste of his discomfort.

"We should have a toast to our mutual friendship and respect and ask God that our collaboration is a long and productive one."

Ace audibly sniggered as the Chief beckoned to the servants to hurry up with drinks.

"It has always been a pleasure doing business with my good friend, Ramona. I've met her personally several times on my visits to London. She treats me with a high regard and I've never failed to have an amicable time. A wonderful lady, I'm sure you agree."

The focus of the Chief's attention, X could only grin uncomfortably.

"At last the drinks. Hurry up," the Chief's tone was briefly severe, before mellowing, "Ah, here is Yewonde, come and greet our important visitor from London."

In the instant he stood and turned to meet the tall elegant woman, wearing traditional dress, X spat the gristle into his hand. Her expression registered a flicker of surprise before settling into an open smile of complete engagement. Enthralled, X stared into her dark clear brown eyes, his reflection sinking into their depths. She bowed her head slightly as she spoke, her voice husky and lilting.

"Pleased to welcome you, sir. You have come a long way."

As he sat down, he noticed she was barefooted, her pedicured toe-nails painted a deep crimson.

"Yewonde will look after you during your stay. She will get you anything you want. You are our honoured guest."

The bedroom door clicked shut, X tired and pleasantly light-headed, stared incredulously at the huge bed that lined one wall. Ace had murmured about "king-sized", but this was of imperial proportions, the carved headboard – a menagerie of lions, leopards, water buffalo and antelopes writhing in a death struggle frozen in mahogany-hued splendour – reflecting in its rolling outline the coming together of three double beds into one giant "love arena." Ace had not been wrong about that.

Yewonde was suddenly an ethereal presence at his side – they had not touched, yet he could sense the heat radiating from the curving contours of her body and smell her perfume, tasting the rich floral fragrance at the back of his throat. Carefully unwrapping her elaborate headscarf, she placed the colourful cloth on the bed, then bending her head slightly, she flicked the tip of her tongue into his ear. Her warm, moist breath caressed his cheeks and neck, his alert frame immediately heedful and receptive. She whispered, "I like making love without the air-conditioning on…", the calculated pause stimulating, "… do you?"

X nodded and reached out to embrace her – he had never before been with anyone taller than he was – but she pushed him gently away and walked over to the air-conditioning unit in the window, reached up and switched it off. Its omnipresence instantly marked by its absence, a heavy silence replacing the comforting companionship of its perpetual rattling hum. A narrow band of dark skin had been tantalizingly exposed at Yewonde's waistline, as her loose necked long-sleeved blouse lifted as she stretched on tip-toe, then it had vanished as she settled back, her close-fitting clothes unruffled, her elegant composure undisturbed. X watched entranced. She turned. His skin was tingling as the temperature started to climb, a hint of prickling moisture already in the air.

X, in thrall to a free falling sensibility, was rarely willing to use the word "beautiful' to describe anything beyond the aerial wonders that he had been privileged to see, humankind always comparing unfavourably, but Yewonde was deserving of the term. Tall, thin and statuesque, dressed in sleek striking robes, that endowed every shift of her body with a seductive gravity, her black hair woven into a tight mass of entwined plaits piled elaborately on the top of her head, she was an ineffable presence, her attraction irresistible.

Yewonde's irradiant smile transfixed X, swathing him in desire. Powerless he gazed back at the round full face that was tilted towards his, devouring every detail. The high unlined forehead, her floating liquid eyes, alive and expressive, skin of glowing luxurious velvet. A shimmering beauty, she brimmed over with a passion for the present, an observation he found invigorating, dispelling in that instant his innate sense of weariness with the act of love.

There was nothing for him to do. Reaching down she raised the hem of her blouse and eased loose a corner of her ankle-length, cloth wrapper that had been carefully folded then tucked around her narrow waist and handed it to X.

"Pull on that please ... gently."

The softly-spoken command was impossible to disobey. Yewonde began to slowly rotate like a child's toy top, moving unsteadily away from him across the room as her long skirt unwound. She spun in a large circle, moving back towards him, as folds of material spiralled to the floor. His excitement kindled memories of a distant Christmas morning unwrapping presents, and passionately wondering, barely able to contain himself, what was hidden inside?

He closed his eyes in anticipation, prolonging the exquisite enjoyment for as long as he could bear. As the fabric fell limp in his hand he peeked through hooded eyelids. Yewonde was bare from the hips down, long perfectly shaped legs slightly apart, she was opening her blouse, fine fingers caressing and entwining the buttons as she deliberately worked each one loose. He noticed she was not wearing any jewellery, that her nails were filed short and finely manicured, varnished a shade that matched the desert sands of the Sahara, observed from 30,000 feet on his flight from London, and there was a pale scar running across the knuckles of her left hand. His craving for detail was insatiable.

The blouse draped open, revealing the smooth partial ellipses of her breasts, their faint mirrored silhouettes overshadowing the stark barred imprint of her ribs, which in turn accentuated the gentle curve of her taut stomach, the only discordant detail the slight protuberance of her navel – a subtle, inflammatory, imperfection. X knelt before her and suffused in a sweet fragrant fug, kissed the salty nub, then buried his face in her pubic hair invisible in the sculpted shadows of her lower torso, but pleasantly abrasive to his lips and probing tongue. The embroidered hem of her blouse brushed deliciously across the scruff of his neck, as he burrowed deeper, downy nape aroused.

"Now it's your turn," Yewonde whispered, pushing him away with a light pressure on his shoulders. X sat back on his heels, beads of perspiration stippling his body. Towering above him Yewonde indulgently let the blouse slip first from one shoulder then the other, before allowing it fall to the floor. She stepped back naked and stood before him smiling.

"You must take your things off, yes?"

"Yes."

The definition of her tall, thin body was muscular yet voluptuous, angles rounded, the details blurred, her skin tones shaded across a dark-hued spectrum that deceived the eye with shifting colour, obscuring her true form.

He undressed slowly, never glancing aside as he discarded his clothes. Nude he sat cross-legged, waiting to be told what to do, content for the moment to seek gratification only with his eyes, relishing the abnegation of responsibility.

The spell held until Yewonde moved.

"Come with me" she beckoned, backing over towards the huge bed. He obeyed, staggering as he reached out for her. Avoiding his grasping hands, she turned away and bent forward over a corner of the mattress, both feet placed firmly on the ground, her legs rigid.

X felt he had never been so attracted to a woman and entered her forcefully, a wish satisfied, the physical yearning easing. The flow of her body, rising and falling to a charged rhythm, roused X further and he clung to her.

Every sliding, slithering movement lubricated by the moisture leaking from their pores, bodies sopping, sodden hair falling lankly across his dripping forehead, his kneading hands slipping across her clammy back as her skin glinted in the rippling motion.

The metallic ring of X's mobile phone was shocking and it stilled their lovemaking, a frozen tableau of lust, that rapidly thawed in the heat of their passion. Yewonde moved first, arching her back and pressing hard against X's taut thighs. Sensing his immobility, she murmured indistinctly, her voice muffled by the bed cover.

"Leave it, it will go away."

The phone was in the pocket of his shirt, which was discarded on the floor, just, he discovered to his relief, within reach of an outstretched foot. He had no inclination to break off and lose contact, there was no way he could stop. Yet the shrill insistent ringing – the cartoon-like quality of the sound and the image it conjured up of an old-fashioned telephone handset rattling and bouncing in its Bakelite cradle had seemed an amusing affectation to X when, stoned, he had set the ringtone – was tinged with menace. Only one person could be calling him here and he had no choice but to answer. Intensely irritated he fumbled for the phone.

"Ramona."

He hoped he sounded business-like and not too breathless.

"Ahhh, I wanted it to be a surprise," her laugh was chillingly close, she could have been standing behind him, "What an amazing line! That old wanker Frankie told me it was always crap getting through to Lagos, just shows what he knows. How's it going? Bloody hot I expect?"

"In more ways than one."

"What do you mean?"

Yewonde, who had been motionless, listening, began to move her body, picking up the rhythm from where they had left off. Surprised X coughed, masking his inadvertent gasp of pleasure.

"Sorry, it's dusty here, gets everywhere," he coughed again, "We had some trouble on the way in from the airport, but the Chief here seems to have it all covered."

"What sort of trouble?"

Her tone had hardened, her manner suddenly business-like and suspicious. The purple sheen of Yewonde's moist skin, distracted X as he stared down at her full buttocks pressing into his groin.

"Ambushed," was the only word he could manage and covered his mouth with his hand. There was a loud declamatory "fuck" at the other end of the line, then the sound of Ramona calling out to someone in the room. A conversation began but X was oblivious to what was being said as he reared backwards and ejaculated in grim silence – like the guilty night-time solo performances of his adolescence – his breath held, moans swallowed, body spasm suppressed, his straining chest aching.

"That sounds fucking serious? Who let slip you were coming?"

Ramona's voice was commanding.

"Hold on Ramona, it's not clear if it was anything to do with me being here. Could be just coincidence."

"Coincidence, bollocks! You know I don't believe in them. In my experience you ignore a coincidence and it comes back soon enough to bite you in the arse."

Yewonde pulled away, slipping from beneath him. The springs creaked.

"Happens a lot here, apparently. Armed robberies."

He rolled onto the bed. The coverlet felt cool on his back.

"I'm sure. This one'll need sorting though. We can't let it go."

"I know, I'll talk to the Chief in the morning."

The air-conditioning juddered noisily into action.

"I'll make some inquiries this end. How's Ace?"

"He's full of himself. A right arrogant bastard. Just spent over an hour showing me his sodding computers. He seems to be across it all though. Knows his stuff."

"Sounds like you're having a ball."

Yewonde glided silently into the bathroom, the yellow cast of the electric light reflecting on her bare, glistering, body. X felt a renewed twinge of desire.

"I am. It's like the fucking Wild West, Ramona, the fucking Wild West."

Extract from:
# The World Health Organization Annual Report 2001

Of the five million people killed globally due to injuries in 2000, approximately 1.2 million people died of road traffic incidents, 815,000 from suicide and 283,000 from falls. In addition to the considerable number of deaths, millions more are wounded or suffer other non-fatal health consequences due to injuries.

| Type of Injury | Deaths due to Injuries |
| --- | --- |
| Road traffic incidents | 1,260,000 |
| Suicide | 815,000 |
| Interpersonal violence | 520,000 |
| Drowning | 450,000 |
| Poisoning | 315,000 |
| War and conflict | 310,000 |
| Falls | 283,000 |
| Burns | 238,000 |

In the United States in 1994 29,938 people committed suicide:

| Method | Death Count |
| --- | --- |
| Firearms and explosives | 18,773 |
| Hanging | 4,073 |
| Drugs | 3,022 |
| Gases (mainly carbon monoxide) | 2,026 |
| Jumping | 719 |
| Cuts and stabs | 515 |
| Bag asphyxia | 422 |
| Drowning | 383 |

**Source: US Dept of Statistics, 2001**

2,160 metres

# Password

Enter

# Phar-out-macy = sex

this is bat country

### and drugs

OBJECTS IN MIRROR ARE CLOSER THAN THEY APPEAR

### and rock 'n roll

home   soft   hard   perscription   links   e-mail

home    soft    hard    prescription    links    e-mail

# Soft Shit!!!!

| Drug: | On the street: | Price: | Quantity: | Total: (Select £ or $) | |
|---|---|---|---|---|---|
| Cannabis – Hashish | Hash; puff; blow; blast | £13/$20 per 1/8 oz | | | Add to stash |
| Cannabis – Marijuana | Weed; grass; dope; draw | £25/$45 per 1/8 oz | | | Add to stash |
| Dope specials | Lebanese red | £28/$55 per 1/8 oz | | | Add to stash |
| | Highland black | £32/$55 per 1/8 oz | | | Add to stash |
| | Glastonbury green | £40/$75 per 1/8 oz | | | Add to stash |
| | Laotian tea | £43/$85 per 1/8 oz | | | Add to stash |
| Psilocybin | Magic mushrooms | £15/$30 per oz | | | Add to stash |
| Amphet-amines | Speed; whizz; base | £10/$18 per gram | | | Add to stash |
| Inhalents | Snuff | £12/$25 per oz | | | Add to stash |

home   soft   hard   prescription   links   e-mail

# Hard Shit!!!!

| Drug: | On the street: | Price: | Quantity: | Total: (Select £ or $) | |
|---|---|---|---|---|---|
| Cocaine | Blow; toot; coke | £40/$75 per gram | | | Add to stash |
| Freebase cocaine | Crack; rocks | £18/$35 per rock | | | Add to stash |
| Blue mystic/ 2C-T-7 | T7; 7up; Tripstacy | £9/$15 per tab (70mg) | | | Add to stash |
| Ecstasy | E; aldi; adam; brownie | £6/$10 per tab | | | Add to stash |
| Heroin | Smack; horse; junk; shit | £45/$82 per gram | | | Add to stash |
| LSD | Acid; tabs; trips | £3.25/$6 per dot | | | Add to stash |
| LSD – special offer | | £125/$230 a bottle | | | Add to stash |
| Ketamine | Special K | £22/$40 per gram | | | Add to stash |
| PCP | Sernyl; Angel dust | £15/$32 per gram | | | Add to stash |

home   soft   hard   prescription   links   e-mail

## PRESCRIPTION SHIT!!!!

| Drug: | On the street: | Price: | Quantity: | Total: (Select £ or $) | |
|---|---|---|---|---|---|
| Benzodiazephines | Diazepam; Valium | £1/$2 per 10mg | | | Acd to stash |
| | Temazepam | £1.50/$2 per 10mg | | | Add to stash |
| | Mogadon | £1/$2.10 per 10mg | | | Add to stash |
| Prozac | Spikers; prozies | £2/$3.50 per 10mg | | | Add to stash |
| Vicodin | New LSD | £1.25/$2 per 15mg | | | Add to stash |
| Percodan | Acid; tabs; trips | £1/$2 per 10mg | | | Add to stash |
| Rohypnol | | £1/$2.35 per 10mg | | | Add to stash |
| Quaaludes | Luuds | £2/$4 per 15mg | | | Add to stash |
| Amyl nitrate | Poppers | £3/$6 per 15ml | | | Add to stash |

Sometimes when he was sky-diving he would open his chute early, not out of any apprehension that his equipment would fail, but because he wanted to prolong his pleasure. Enjoy once again that brief transitional state between hurtling earthward and flying.

The jolt.

Stopping dead. For an infinitesimal time – quantifiable as the space between chemical spikes trafficking through the pleasure centre of the brain – he hangs at a fixed point above the surface of the planet. Suspended. Stationary. His relationship with the moon, the sun, with distant stars mapped out for him in a defiant rebuttal of all the physical laws that power the universe. A reassertion of human authority, of man's superiority over nature. Gravity held no terror.

The beat was insistent – baf,baf,baf,baf – beguiling, winning, and loud – BAF, BAF, BAF, faster than his racing heartbeat – BAF, BAF, BAF. Worming its way into his brain, insinuating its repetitive message into the interstices between communication and motor neurons, suppressing the need to speak, galvanizing the urge to move.

He was unable to resist the incessant sounds – Baf, Baf, Baf – shorting out the electrical charges firing dysfunctionally between the synapses of his cerebrum, an organ luxuriating in a bath of methylenedioxyamphetamine. Reactions flared sensuously. Feelings burst to the fore in a rush of euphoria-inducing awareness. Baf, Baf, Baf. He was helpless before the surge of serotonin, swept away in the chemical flash-flood.

He moved energetically, his body in sympathetic harmony with the pulsing drive of the dance music, limbs flexing, snapping out in directionless frenzy with each random sub-beat. Sweating profusely, his voice hoarse from parroting the electrically generated beat-box automatons, X croaked out his desires. He knew he was wonderful, irresistible, unstoppable. He knew everyone was listening.

There was a presence, a figure close by, moving sympathetically. The two of them had been motoring together for a while. He knew they both felt the same way.

The noise.

The beguiling harmonic rhythms teased the rapture cortex, enticing him into wanting more, stoking a ravenous appetite for ever greater gratification. His euphoria heightening a yearning for physical contact, for sexual release.

Baf, Baf, Baf.

> The relief at the
>     jolt

when the parachute opens is profound. Everyone, even the most experienced divers, cannot dispel the visceral fear that it won't happen, cannot avoid facing the fact that this could be the last few seconds of their existence on earth. The procedure, never routine, is pregnant with anticipatory peril. The tension of tugging on the ripcord, taking up the initial slack, then meeting resistance, followed by the whisper of fabric, often barely audible over the rush of air. There is always the nervous upward glance, then the trace of a smile as the chute unfurls, a scrappy shaded patch marring the seamless blue fabric of the sky. Wings again. Life saved.

Two bodies moving, performing great acts together, covering vast distances, yet going nowhere, observed by no one, seen by everyone. Expending energy in hallucinatory unison, taking part in the ritual intercourse of the dance floor, passionate yet physically chaste. Their actions synchronous, their timing perfect, the pitch of their bodies finely tuned. Every need suppressed, except their lust for water and for love. A plastic bottle filled with sparkling water shared between them, tepid liquid poured over and into overheating bodies, saliva mixing. No words spoken. This was a silent seduction amid the persistent cacophony of the extreme beats.

Dancing close together, when it came the rub of hands on his hips was stunning, a wave of sensation breaking over the defences that shored up the cerebral world of enjoyment against contamination by the commonplace. It was a momentary dousing, an earthing, making a connection to the frenetic bustle of the party, bringing him down, before he flew once more.

The touch was deliciously determined now, guiding him forcefully through the bouncing crowd. Everywhere there were faces, molten shapes, many barely recognizable, smiling blurs in the fuzzy multi-tinted lights, flashing and strobing, through the streaming wisps of smoke, that wrapped themselves around his head, stroking his cheeks, neck and chest, and plucking anxiously at his hair. His blurred vision sporadically pierced by revealing fragments of long-sighted clarity – the detail of the graffiti scratched into the abraded brickwork of one of the arched tunnels of this Victorian basement, the gothic wording on the T-shirt of the DJ perched in his glassed-in booth high above the mêlée – was disconcerting. Assailed by a vivid blitz of colour as the tempo of the music was stepped up, X buckled at the knees, sensing the faint, uncomfortable churn of nausea as he blacked-out, welcoming the enveloping darkness.

– he was not alone. He could see nothing, but could hear panting. A wheezing, unhealthy sounding burr, that was drawing closer. He felt no alarm just an intense annoyance that the creature wouldn't clear its throat. Then he saw the faint grey outline of a huge winged reptile slithering towards him, the only visible detail the green bloodshot eyes observing him. The fixated stare of the hunter, drilling into its prey. The rustle of wings, like crumpled parchment, the chorus line to the regular ticking of its vital force. In and out. A nudge from its horny nose, part-playful, part-investigatory and X gave in, sinking to his knees, head bowed. Jaws grasped his body, lifting him from the ground, he could see his legs hanging down, dripping with the beast's saliva, he could feel sharp painful punctures around his mid-riff. The smell of its warm breath sweet, yet stringent, of scent laced with spirits. His face was wet, his skin prickling at the chemical irritation –

The pulse of the party was reviving, he could feel the beat in his marrow, a base vibration summoning him back.

– with a powerful surge of energy the creature spread its wings and lunged forward, dropping like a stone, wind rushing –

The heaving mass of party-goers supported him, helpful hands steadying his slumped body, multifarious odours bringing him round, acute and powerful, a perfumed garden of sweat-stressed cosmetic infusions, moisturisers, body sprays, deodorants.

jolt. The falling star plucked from view, the suddenly shooting skyward, an Videos of X sky-diving capture instantaneous pinprick, punching a hole in the membrane, effecting inestimable change. A dramatic image of gut-wrenching deceleration, the power of gravity defied.

The touch eased him relentlessly forward. He was better. He could see and think fuzzily. He was feeling wonderful, gliding, all concerns lifted from his mind. The dance his heartbeat, the driving rhythm his life-blood, forcing the boiling drugs round his body. He loved everything. He loved everyone. The entwined couple, pressed hard against the wall, tongues probing each other's mouth, his hand inside her blouse, caressing a breast, her thigh forced between his legs. The smiling, leather-clad woman, in a short skirt, who had collided with him, as she backed away from someone, smaller than her and prettier. They had been shouting at each other, but he was not listening. They were not angry with him, because they loved him. Everyone loved him. He was an exotic bloom pollinating the world with desire.

> jolt

The

changed relationships, altered everything. Nothing was ever the same again.

Falling was free-form, insubstantial, shapeless. Your molecular structure has altered, the vibration of atoms subtly changed, you are not the same person you were seconds earlier, you are not the same person you soon will be. You will look different, a marginal dislocation of the norm, but enough for your appearance to deceive. A disconcerting loss of recognition common among visitors to the gallery of free falling images who are fazed by the dislocation of faces and the moulding of plastic bodies into distorted shapes, unimaginable on the ground. Chameleon-like your clothes refashion, both shade and form, at once revealing, hugging the body, highlighting every muscular ridge and contour then camouflaging the detail, billowing, inchoate, flaccid, blown by the wind.

Flying was the reimposition of order, the reassertion of humanity's authority, the resumption of normal physical inter-relations, familiar to all earthbound creatures. Yet again the character of equipment and clothes alter as tension returns. Relationships are taut, straps tighten, straining, hauling at your body, manipulating it to fit the exigencies of the moment, exerting pressure. Rough treatment that often bruises – purply-red contusions adorning all points of friction – shoulders, armpits, waist and groin – painful brands acknowledging gravity's ultimate dominion.

It was quieter now, less busy. The hubbub of the party was distant, the beat persistent but fainter. There were fewer stimuli to distract him, less to detract from the glorious feeling of well-being, more time for introspection, to sink inwards, to relish the sublime. X wanted to dance, but the guiding touch, firm on his waist, grounded him and kept him moving. The subterranean passage seemed long and twisting. It was dingy, the occasional light bulb encased behind its protective metal grille casting only pallid beams of light on to the glossy brickwork of the tunnel ceiling.

The end came unexpectedly, catching him unawares, stopping them dead. The transition was abrupt, moving one second, stationary the next. The mental adjustment necessary, reigning in a racing mind, disconcerting, only a premonition of what was about to happen eased him to a halt.

The passageway had been blocked up at some point in the past, the crude brickwork never finished off or painted, extruded mortar overhanging, casting patchy shadows. X came to a stop in one dark gloomy corner of this alcove, gently positioned by the touch. Against his spine the bass rumble of the beat resonated through the ancient walls, undermining the foundations of any resistance. A juggernaut of sensation, shaking the body, tuning onto his wavelength, colonizing his mind. Blissful oblivion.

– he could feel the beast swooping, banking out of its dive, the queasiness in the pit of his stomach returned, he found he was short of breath. Eyes wide open or eyes squeezed shut he saw the same thing, a swirling kaleidoscope of vivid colours, burning brightly, as they plunged over the crater's edge. The heat, white-hot, blackened his skin, peeling it back crisply from his face, searing the weeping flesh, burning it from the bone, his carbonized skull turning to dust. The beast, unaffected, continued to plummet, X's headless carcass limp in his jaws –

The touch eased him back. Hands fumbled at his waist, unbuckling his belt, hesitantly undoing each fly-button of his Levi 501's.

– wings flapping furiously, they bottomed out of the dive, the plumes of flame igniting his clothing, the man-made fibres crackling and sputtering like cheap indoor fireworks, peeling back and falling away. He was naked, the pale skin of his limbs and torso beginning to blister –

There was an opening up, he could feel it, a rummaging in his jeans, then cool fingers fished out his limp penis from his underwear.

The touch was energizing, the tongue gratifying, the gaping, liquid mouth a whirlpool, sucking him under.

– he was burning up, disintegrating. Soon he would cease to exist. He would have escaped from the beast. Foiled his flying demons –

He struggled for breath, clawing fingers entangled in curly hair, grasping for meaning while in the clutches of destructive pleasure. His jeans bunched around his ankles.

He had never loved more passionately.

The jolt
                   was taking control of your destiny, was saving your life, was throwing yourself a lifeline, was plucking yourself from certain death, was taking flight or was it, maybe, taking fright?

Released, X bobbed to the surface. Breathing deeply, drawing in air. The stresses of the moment subsiding, he relaxed, a sense of equanimity cloaking him in a protective shroud.

– he was rising from the flames, riding a phoenix reconstituted. Reborn in a violent eruption of molten lava and rock. A trajectory of escape, arcing through the air like a rocket, leaving the creature engulfed by the inferno way below. From this height the volcano's crater, seemed a perfect circle. He was on his way out of this world –

Yells from the dance floor drew him back, he could hear them clearly, the clapping and cheering, the beat momentarily stilled.

"Ramona's part. For those Yanks."

He was thirsty. He could see shadows.

"God, I'm blitzed."

– dark roiling shadows, more like clouds, billowing upwards from the smoking cone. Belching sulphureous fumes that were enveloping him. A clinging noxious mist that stung his eyes and burned the back of his throat. The air was too hot to breathe. Suffocating –

Then the touch dragged him under, turning him round to

face the dank wall, his cheek pressed against the chill bricks, his hands sliding across the greasy condensation-stained surface as he struggled to find his balance. He felt uneasy. Uncomprehending. All senses jarring: he couldn't see clearly, every object was out of focus; the decaying paintwork smelt musty; the taste of mulch seeped into his consciousness, his mouth awash with stale saliva; hot breath in his ear, a frisson of sexual attraction, panting, a tongue licking his lobe, plowing the canal. A fleeting intimacy, a body adjacent, accommodating, accepting of all imperfections, then it was gone.

X wanted to dance, the beat had kicked back in, he could feel her embrace through the wall. Spitting fire into his belly, goading and cajoling, she was a partner of infinite fidelity. He wouldn't let her down.

Hands were at his waist pulling roughly at his briefs. He was exposed. A figure drew close and he could feel the aroused penis, pressed against his buttocks, probing. Confusion at the unexpected, melding with the non-linear logic of his drugged sensibility, induced a physical collapse – X sank to the ground, dragging his erstwhile lover down on top of him, his feet slithering across the gritty uneven floor as he struggled to escape – followed by a violent lashing out, as in an instant, he realized that he had been getting it off with a man.

Disorientated, he kicked wildly, his fists striking indiscriminately, hitting the ground, the walls, himself. One flailing leg tripped his unknown assailant as he tried to get away and he crashed to the ground alongside X.

"Fuck me," he grunted, the Bronx accent unmistakable.

Instinctively, X grabbed the American's dishevelled clothing and in a narcotic haze pummelled his prone body.

"Enough already, fuck you, enough."

The threat was clear as the sobering rush of adrenaline enabled X's faculties.

"Fucking stop."

He could see now, the blood on the battered features, the mop of curly black hair, the wild eyes. Tightening his grip on the man's shirt, X pulled himself up onto his elbows, and with a gargantuan effort reared back his head before flinging it forward, his forehead smashing into the gaping face rocking in front of him. Dazed, drained of energy he fell forward onto the ground.

The dumb roar of agony reverberated in the narrow confines of the tunnel, drowning out the party music. X listened but could barely register the pain, nor its significance. His wounded adversary, hands clutching his broken nose, scrambled to his feet, blood dripping through his fingers, kicked X twice in the stomach then hobbled away.

The impacts were registered outside the body, the jarring external to his core, the wayward sensations circling before consolidating in the gut. The nausea was intense, a bilious soup welling in his throat, threatening to spill over. He registered his determination to follow and the need to wreak retribution, but he was incapable of getting up. Confused he struggled to disentangle his legs from the clothes bundled tightly around his ankles.

X was aware he was not meant to be there, thousands of metres above the ground passing through natural layers alien to humankind. Moving across foreign territory. Inhaling air and absorbing chemical compounds antithetical to life. The protective blanket of the atmosphere threadbare, less comforting. It was an airy world of restless motion, of ever-changing pressure gradients and moisture levels, of slipstreams and thermals, of flows diverted, natural progressions reversed. Eternal flux. The narrative no longer straightforward, up and down, above and below, all purely relative. Were there any consequences of being there? Of being somewhere you were not supposed to be? Of trespassing? Were they life-altering or immaterial? X knew the answer to these questions. He was fucked.

Partially dressed, X crawled around in the narrow, deserted tunnel, searching for his keys in the gloom. He realized he had lost them, he understood it was important to find them, but between these anchors of certainty, his mind drifted aimlessly from the ecstasy of the high to the paranoia of the encroaching hangover. His impaired mental capacity unable to still the choppiness of his thoughts, stirred as they were by the indignity of the deception. Blindly he patted the grimy concrete with outstretched hands, cursing, his erratic vision – at one moment perfect, the next hazy and blind to real colour – inducing overheating and a disturbing queasiness.

X crouched, all movement thwarted – a static object in a swirling universe of blurred shades – his discomfort the focus of attention. The concentration required was sobering. Instinctively resisting the symptoms of his affliction, X battled with the inevitable. Breathing deeply, clutching his stomach, rationally dissipating the pain, while demanding the suppression of the chemically induced spasms stimulating muscular contractions the length of his abdomen. The futility of these efforts appealed to him and he held on for as long as he could. Having eaten nothing in twenty-four hours and having sweated out the liquids he had consumed, he threw up drily, straining trunk muscles and violently expelling a foul-smelling fan of viscous bile that spattered across the floor, spotting his jeans and coating his key-ring, which he could now clearly see lying just out of his reach.

"Sod."

He retched again, empty, wrenching sensitive abdominal muscles, gagging on air. He then lunged for his keys, flicking them out of the pooled vomit with his forefinger. He gingerly picked them up and wiped them with his hand. He sat back, leaning against the wall. His growing sense of equanimity was sobering and concentrated his thoughts on revenge.

Pulling the ripcord too early was spurned by many free fallers, unable to see beyond the trepidation it seemed to imply. Rule breakers by instinct – there was a safe, sensible, recommended height to unfurl your chute – they often failed to appreciate you could flaunt the regulations equally by being cautious and pulling high. With his eyes on the distant horizon, X was one of those people who, when it suited him, didn't care about appearances, he sometimes just wanted to take his time and enjoy the view. Channel the "rush" into a new aesthetic. Appreciate the beauty. But not today. Today he was going to the limit.

Ramona gazed at X inquiringly as she approached him. He was leaning unsteadily against a tall bar stool and staring vacantly into the crowd. The lights were strobing. The music was loud, driving and uncompromising, drowning out all voices. Dancers seethed.

"God, what happened to you?" she mouthed.

X read her lips and shrugged.

"A spot of bother, that's all."

Ramona frowned.

"Nothing to worry about."

She gestured at the bruise on his face and at his filthy jeans and soiled T-shirt. He touched her on the arm and smiled.

"It's nothing."

He enunciated the words clearly but silently. Ramona leaned over to him and shouted in his ear.

"Your flies are undone."

He smiled wanly.

"I don't want any bloody trouble, while the Yanks are here. You understand?"

X nodded, squeezing her shoulder affectionately.

"We have to do business with them. No fucking around."

X nodded again.

"Talk of the devil."

A tall man with a handsome lined face, thinning swept-back, blond hair and dressed entirely in black – Merino wool sweater, open at the neck, Polo jeans and highly polished finely-tooled cowboy boots – came up to Ramona. Together they moved over to the bar, X following.

"Great party, hon."

"Thank you, Joe."

He grasped her round the waist and kissed her on both cheeks.

"I just love it over here in London."

"Good to have you, Joe."

He laughed.

"Who's this?"

"Ah you haven't met. This is one of my key people."

X shook hands.

"What the fuck happened to you?"

He stared amusedly at X.

"A spot of rough sex."

Joe indicated with a hand to his ear that he couldn't hear. Ramona who had caught what X had said, scowled. X waved his hands.

"Good to meet you, Joe."

He then tried to slip away into the crowd bouncing around them, but was restrained by Joe's hand on his arm.

"There's someone I want you to meet. My main guy."

X had a headache. He needed to escape, to take something strong and obliterating.

"Here he is ... Billy. Over here."

He beckoned to a thick-set young man, with curly black hair and a beaten face, nose broken and caked with dried blood, who loomed out of the rainbow-tinted, semi-darkness of the dance floor.

"Jesus Billy, what the fuck?"

Billy was about to speak, when he noticed X and said nothing, his expression flattening, draining of sentiment. X understood immediately, he sensed their mutual history, even though he had no memory of the damaged countenance, no recall of the stooping frame, the clenched fists, the malignity in the hooded eyes. The two men knew each other, but gave no outward sign of recognition. Joe glanced back and forth between them, before finally comprehending their mutual injuries.

"You two. Sweet Jesus."

Ramona bridled beside X, a look of angry consternation clouding her expression.

"What the fuck's been going on? You know anything about this Ramona?"

"No, Joe, I don't," her acid voice, stripped the veneer of indignation from X's anger, leaving him silent and swaying slightly from side to side.

"Billy?"

"A slight misunderstanding, Joe. Nothing to worry about, man."

He hugged his older, taller companion.

"Come on let's not spoil the party."

Joe paused, then shrugging, acquiesced.

"We came from the big Apple to party, do a little business, and party some more. So, let's party."

Ramona smiled and nodded. A knot of stress lines creased her brow, failing to ease with the apparent ebbing of tension. Her complexion was pallid.

"I'll be right with you, Joe. Get yourself and Billy another drink."

She grabbed X roughly by the arm and pulled him away. Her two guests, enveloped in a spectral mist of exploding colour, watched from the centre of the bustling bar.

"For fuck's sake, what did I just say?"

"It was that little shit."

"Christ, you fucking do my head in sometimes. This is business, big business. We can't afford to fuck around, picking fights with the boss-man's best boy. For Christ's sake. Don't you know who they are?"

X nodded.

"They're bollock-gripping serious types. They could cut us off at the fucking knees, as soon as look at us. Shit, I don't believe this."

Ramona seethed, her mouth grimly set, as she fought her anger.

"They could also make us a pile of money," the words were expressed through clenched teeth, the steel in her message unmistakable, "So get a fucking grip. Go and make it up to the little monkey."

X grimaced.

"That's a fucking order."

He was feeling strange. Ramona's face slipped in and out of focus. His mind was racing, random thoughts and images crowded in, jostling for his attention, pigments flaring, pictures merging, voices burbling. He belched, the chemical residue, sharp on his palate washing up on his tongue, the flotsam of a stormy ride.

"Ramona I can't," his voice was weary, "he's a real prick."

"Fuck me, I can't take much more of this."

He staggered.

"Honest, Ramona," her name slurred, barely audible, "It's impossible."

"You're off your tits, aren't you?" her voice noticeably more sympathetic, "Fucking hell I'll have to do it myself, go and schmooze these bastards."

He loved deeply, his affections indiscriminate, he attempted to kiss Ramona, but was pushed away.

"They're fucking watching for Christ's sake."

The two American drug-dealers moved onto the dance floor, their view partially obscured by the seething crowd of partygoers, but Billy's malevolent gaze was fixed on Ramona and X.

"You're a total dick sometimes. You've got to clean up. You can't keep doing this to me."

He craved clean air, to breathe deeply, to suck the sweetness into his lungs, let the oxygen rekindle the flames of his anger. He had unfinished business and there was still plenty of time left to make amends. He had to find Benny. Where was his man? He was never far away, the well-paid fall guy. He would give you more or less whatever you wanted, whenever you wanted it, no questions asked. It was almost as good as if you were carrying it in your own wallet, but with none of the risks. Benny was one of the un-taxable perks of the job. The only stipulation Ramona laid down was that whatever he provided you with was for oral or nasal intake only, while you were on the job anyway.

"Benny, Benny, oh Benny."

X scanned the room for the bulky figure, wrapped up in the green fishtail parka he never took off, cool, aloof and unruffled even in the most sweltering atmosphere. He could see very little clearly, his world was a series of technicolored cut-outs, bobbing across his line of sight like the flexible characters in a Chinese paper theatre, wavering caricatures of people he partially recognized and vaguely knew. They came and went, each one assembling and disassembling in a stream of disjointed clarity, until he spotted Benny's unmistakable profile hunched in a corner near the bank of speakers by the DJ's booth – broad shoulders, thick-set neck partially obscured by a ruffle of faux cinnamon fur and large shaven head with pronounced sticking out ears – wreathed, as always, in the smoke from a large joint. He was there, then he was gone. He had to follow, yet Ramona still held him in her orbit, she said nothing, but had not moved. Always decisive, a natural leader, for the moment she appeared uncertain. This was disconcerting, but there was no time to worry as the compulsion was growing. He needed to get away, to replenish, gather his strength. Ramona was sucking the life from him. Didn't she realize he was no use to her like this.

"You're in real trouble, you fucking hophead!"

Her reprimand the release he'd been waiting for.

"You can tell me what happened when you're back with us, you little shit."

Nodding he moved away, hugging the walls, until he felt her give him up. Navigating by touch, his fingers following the rippling mortar grooves in the brickwork, he stumbled slowly round the sweating basement, an obstacle course of ecstatic, whirling dancers, scantily-clad women gyrating, entwined couples writhing and comatose bodies spread-eagled across the floor, hindering his progress. His name was shouted in greeting as he groped his way forward, but he ignored the overture, focusing instead on getting to

Benny. This fixation was pressing in on him – he had no choice to make, he could not function alone. He had to be rescued.

He was almost there. Benny had his back to him and was talking to a shaven-headed man, who looked familiar just like everybody else he'd met that evening, wearing black Doc Marten boots, Sta-Prest flat-fronted slacks with red braces, a Ben Sherman check shirt and a dark Crombie three-quarter length coat, their bodies leaning in close so they could hear each other. They were laughing. He reached out to touch Benny on the shoulder and lost his footing, his shoes slipping on the greasy concrete. He fell against a woman, who shouted at him and veered away, letting him crash heavily to the floor. Disorientated he felt nothing as he slithered helplessly on the treacherous surface, gazing up in wonder at the strobe lights flickering across the arched brick ceiling, people moving in slow motion, the din of the party raucous and out of sync. Stretching out, he relaxed captivated by the illusion of sensory oblivion. He saw inquiring faces above, then felt a scorching pain in his hip. He winced, sobering, crying out. Nobody heard, the insistent music drowning out his anguished appeal, the beat of the gathering pounding the foundations beneath his back, the stomping slap of the dancers' feet marking time. Limbs in the air, flailing helplessly, X found himself channelling the torment of the upturned beetle he'd seen that lunchtime on his way to the Island Queen for a pint, struggling in its protracted death throes on the pavement in front of him. He believed he was dying too, like that doomed insect, and that it would take forever. Benny turned, he smiled. Benny looked down, mouthing words. Benny extended a hand.

"You twat."

Hauled to his feet, head spinning, dizzy, X staggered, leaning on Benny for support.

"Thanks mate, my mind was somewhere fucking else I can tell you."

"You twat."

"Stop fucking saying that."

"You twat."

"Fuck off."

The throbbing in his side peaked then subsided, he bent double.

"You're twatted."

"Dead fucking right," he hissed, "I need something to pick me up," he winced, "fucking fast."

"Lucky for you I was still here."

"You're always fucking here."

"Twat."

"Twat."

Benny reached into one of the fur-rimmed side pockets of his parka and pulled out a small re-sealable plastic bag filled with white tablets. Carefully peeling open the fastener he tipped out several pills and passed two of them to X.

"They'll straighten you out; twat."

He then swallowed the rest that he had in his hand and took a swig from a bottle of water, before passing it over to X.

"You're a fucking mess. Have you seen the state of you?"

X drained the bottle and tossed it away. He felt better already.

"Fuck off you twat."

Benny raised his eyebrows, took a long draw from the joint he had secreted behind his ear, then dismissing X with a wave of his hand, returned to his conversation. X teetered on the cusp, psychologically reassured by his recent dose of uppers, but still discomforted by the chemical imbalances from earlier. He retreated to the shadows, where he lurked, seeking refuge from the maelstrom. Beat by beat his strength returned, the persistent rhythm inveigling its way into his consciousness, galvanizing him to action. Without any hesitation he leapt back on to the dance floor, resolved to beat Billy senseless and take his chances with Ramona. He dipped, he sashayed, he pogo-ed, his actions exuberant, his moves emphatic. Edging ever closer to his target.

The music and light show abruptly stopped, there was an audible "ahhhhhh" from the stunned party-goers, and the overhead fluorescent strip lights – harsh, ugly and temporarily blinding – flickered on. Deflated, he stopped dancing, a numbing frustration blanketing a thwarted mind. The beat pulsed impotently in the muscle fibres of his charged limbs as he wound down – an electrical imprint of a phantom rhythm, a relic of a bygone vibe. There was shouting, glazed, sweat-stained revelers stood around momentarily perplexed, unsure what was happening. X shielded his eyes against the painful glare then saw the blue police uniforms fanning out from the club entrance and moving resolutely through the parting crowd. No one could leave. He slipped to one side and merged with a huddle of people, yelling abuse. He joined in. The chilling banality of his profanities a balm for seething thoughts of revenge. He was too stoned to think tactically, too hopped up to remain silent.

"Fucking plod."

A girl next to him laughed. Encouraged he continued.

"Fucking bastards in blue. Piss off you fucking …"

He looked round seeking her approbation and noticed that as she giggled, she stared blindly through opaque pink-rimmed sockets, her eyes having rolled back into her head, to reveal only blood-flecked whites. The corners of her mouth were slick with foam. She was semi-conscious.

"Fucking hell."

X intended to say something reassuring, had formed the words in his milling brain, but was incapable of articulating them. He watched as she sunk slowly to the floor, clinging desperately to the clothes of those around her, stretching cloth, her nails snagging fabric. Her friends were oblivious to her plight as they chaotically engaged with the police onslaught.

There was a resoluteness to the crowd as it surged back and forth, dumb, doggedly compliant, yet resisting, proud beasts driven into the narrow, fenced alleyway leading to the abattoir's killing floor. Everywhere an eagerness to break loose and escape, coupled with a wild-eyed acceptance of their fate. There was a corralling, a drawing together, people converging on the exit were forced back, X was happy to be swept along in the crush, glad not to be singled out. The violent thumps and bumps of a microphone being roughly handled silenced the shouts and yells and stilled the motion. The crackle of static heralded an announcement and all eyes turned to the raised DJ's glass control box at the far end of the dance floor. A distorted booming voice adrift in a wash of feedback flooded the room with noise, incomprehensibly echoing round the low-ceilinged basement. There was laughter, jeering and disdainful catcalls. The pushing and shoving resumed.

"Attention …"

The subsequent statement was drowned out by a piercing electronic wail that had people clutching their ears. Then the sound of dead air, of space, of emptiness, of nothing, a blessed silence. There was an amplified tapping, merging into a heavy breath of resignation, before intelligible words issued forth.

"Attention. This is a Metropolitan Police operation. Will you all please stay calm and co-operate. This shouldn't take long and then you can be on your way."

There was an audible click.

"This is fucking great. What time is it?"

X had no idea. He registered he had lost his Rolex Air-King watch – a genuine one that had been expensive even for him. He shrugged. The police were already manhandling people into line and conducting cursory interviews. Repressing a strong urge to express himself physically, he could sense pressure building behind his eyes as his indignation grew, there was a ringing in his ears and he felt flushed and was sweating, nerve endings on fire. His right leg twitched incessantly. The police officer in charge, a young woman, pale skin, wan, tired dull blue eyes, streaked blonde hair tied back in a bunch with an elastic band, dressed in a dark trouser suit and wearing a black ski jacket, moved rapidly along the row of partygoers occasionally asking for identification then passing on. She was looking for someone in particular. X, normally cool under pressure, was nervous, uncertain of his chemically charged mood and how he would react. He was aware his behaviour was suspicious, but could not stop shaking.

"Name?"

She barely looked at him, just a sideways glance, he was not the one she was after.

"Do you know Ramona McAllister?"

X shook his head.

"You sure? This is meant to be her party."

Her voice remained even, bored, there was still no interest in him. X shook his head again, afraid if he spoke his tone might betray him.

"Are you cold? You seem to be shivering."

"Going down with something."

A flash of suspicion.

"Sergeant, search him."

"Hold on, don't you need a warrant?"

Her expression flamed disdain.

"Empty your pockets."

It was easier for X to control the shaking when occupied. He felt very hot.

"You don't carry much around with you, do you?"

"Always travel light, officer."

"No car keys?"

"Cabbing it, officer."

"Glad to hear it."

The uniformed policeman shook his head.

"Give your address to the Sergeant and you can go."

"Cheers, officer."

X could barely see. He could sense the walls were melting, seeping into the ground to reveal red fields beyond crawling with fabulous creatures. Sightless beasts that had scented him and were beginning to slither in his direction. He knew he didn't have much time. Then he saw them, fiery silhouettes against the ruby sun, his flying demons, swooping down with talons outstretched … to rescue him or …

"Move on, you can go," the voice of authority grounded him and he stepped aside.

"This way, you twat."

"Benny?"

"Who else. You lucky fucker. In your state they should have taken you in."

"Can you get me out of here?"

The beasts were closing in, X began to fear for his sanity.

"Can do. You seen the plod've taken in Ramona and those two Yanks."

"I can't see a fucking thing, man. I can barely fucking exist."

**Transcript of the cellphone message left by Emilia Sanchez on her mother's (Floriana Sanchez) answer machine at 09.51- 09.53 EST, 9/11/2001. (Unpublished annex to the 9/11 Commission Report – Final report of the National Commission on Terrorist Attacks upon the United States)**

Message opens.
"Mama, mama It's Emilia."
(sobbing)
"I'm trapped at work (words indistinct) explosion. The buildings on fire."
"I can't get out. The stairs are on fire ... I can hardly breath."
(words indistinct) smell of gas and the smoke."
"I've always hated working this high mama, you know I'm scared of heights." (shouting – male voice)
"Mama help me."
(crash)
(scream)
"Some guy has just smashed the window. I can breathe."
(Fuck – indistinct male voice)
(coughing)
"It's sucking all the smoke this way... it's worse."
(coughing)
"I can hear the flames ... it's so hot."
"The smoke is so black it's hurting my eyes. I can't see anything."
(coughing and indistinct shouting)
"Mama, I want to come home."
"It's hot, it's burning my skin."
(Another voice cuts in – thought to be Philip Bosworth, Ms Sanchez's co-worker) "Emilia, this way."
"No. Oh my God ... I'm on the edge."

(gasp)
"I'm looking down. I feel sick."
(retching)
"I can hardly talk, Mama. My mouth is so dry."
(coughing)
"Mama... Mama.'
"It's so hot. I'm burning."
"My eyes hurt."
(coughing)
"The smell is horrible."
(sobbing)
"I don't want to. I don't want to (words indistinct)"
"Mama, tell Papa and (sobbing) and Raul ... (words indistinct)"
"It hurts."
(shouting)
"I can't bear it. I feel ill."
"I'm scared."
(coughing)
(crash – possibly office partition collapsing)
"Mama."
(coughing)
(male voice thought to be Philip Bosworth)
"Emilia, where are you?"
(sobbing)
"Over here."
"Mama, I'm ill (words indistinct) can't feel. It's hard to breathe. There's no air." "(words indistinct) right by the window. Smoke everywhere."
(male voice thought to be Philip Bosworth)
"(words indistinct) can do it together. I don't want to burn."
(coughing)
"It's a long way down."

(male voice thought to be Philip Bosworth)
"Hold my hand."
"Mama I love you."
(sobbing)
(sound of an object – possibly a cellphone – hitting a hard surface)
(screams)
Message ends.

**Emilia worked as an account executive for Hazlitt Brothers on the 89th floor of the South Tower of the World Trade Center. The tower collapsed at 09.59 EST, 6 minutes after the message was recorded. Emilia Sanchez and Philip Bosworth's bodies were never recovered.**

1,574 metres

Extracts from "The Interpretation of Dreams" by Sigmund Freud

Chapter 6. The Dream-Work

Section E. Representation in Dreams by Symbols: Some Further Typical Dreams

"To the second group of typical dreams belong those in which one is flying or hovering, falling, swimming, etc. What do these dreams signify? Here we cannot generalize. They mean, as we shall learn, something different in each case; only, the sensory material which they contain always comes from the same source.

We must conclude from the information obtained in psycho-analysis that these dreams also repeat impressions of our childhood – that is, that they refer to the games involving movement which have such an extraordinary attraction for children. Where is the uncle who has never made a child fly by running with it across the room, with outstretched arms, or has never played at falling with it by rocking it on his knee and then suddenly straightening his leg, or by lifting it above his head and suddenly pretending to withdraw his supporting hand? At such moments children shout with joy and insatiably demand a repetition of the performance, especially if a little fright and dizziness are involved in it. In after years they repeat their sensations in dreams, but in dreams they omit the hands that held them, so that now they are free to float or fall. We know that all small children have a fondness for such games as rocking and see-sawing; and when they see gymnastic performances at the circus their recollection of such games is refreshed. In some boys the hysterical attack consists simply in the reproduction of such performances, which they accomplish with great dexterity. Not infrequently sexual sensations are excited by these games of movement, innocent though they are in themselves. To express the matter in a few words: it is these romping games of childhood which are being repeated in dreams of flying, falling, vertigo, and the like, but the pleasurable sensations are now transformed into anxiety. But, as every mother knows, the romping of children often enough ends in quarrelling and tears."

"Dr. Paul Federn (Vienna) has propounded the fascinating theory that a great many flying dreams are erection dreams, since the remarkable phenomenon of erection, which constantly occupies the human phantasy, cannot fail to be impressive as an apparent suspension of the laws of gravity (cf. the winged phalli of the ancients)."

"Dreams of falling are more frequently characterized by anxiety. Their interpretation, when they occur in women, offers no difficulty, because they nearly always accept the symbolic meaning of falling, which is a circumlocution for giving way to an erotic temptation. We have not yet exhausted the infantile sources of the dream of falling; nearly all children have fallen occasionally, and then been picked up and fondled; if they fell out of bed at night, they were picked up by the nurse and taken into her bed."

His knees were very close to hers, they were not quite touching, but almost. He could sense them, there was a discernible tension. Their bodies had fleetingly collided earlier as, rushing in the busy London street, they had both tried to squeeze into the back of the black cab at the same time. She registered her dismay at his lack of civility by taking the comfortable rear leather seat, throwing her raincoat and briefcase onto the space beside her and sitting back, a folder of legal documents open on her lap. X had been forced to perch on the pull-down seat opposite her, holding onto the handle above the door for balance. Irked by his crass behaviour he took comfort from where he was positioned. He had a perfect view and the two of them were so cramped there was no way his companion could cross her legs and spoil it. The sensation of their brief connection lingered, a tingling of the nerve endings in his legs, which X found oddly invigorating. He hoped they would come together again as the cab negotiated the potholed roads, throwing their bodies from side to side, keeping time with the erratic motion.

Amanda was a former flatmate of Ramona's from their student days at Leeds University, where they had both studied for a law degree. As a qualified solicitor she had helped her friend out with a number of legal problems over the years, the current one already being described as potentially one of the most serious. X always wondered how much Amanda knew about what went on in their line of work, but Ramona was always very tight-lipped whenever he raised the subject. His interest was not simply one of concern for the business, but also one of personal ambition, for he lusted after Amanda, beguiled by fantasies of strong intelligent women powerfully dressed in dark pin-striped designer suits, as she was today, with a tailored white blouse just visible at the neck, short skirt and expensive Christian Louboutin high-heeled leather shoes, tooled to a vicious point. She also matched perfectly X's image of the classically attractive female lawyer with her studious air of intensity, her black iron Dita Telion glasses, blonde hair tied back severely from her face, and clothes that seemed ill-suited to her trim athletic figure and shapely legs, yet adorned them perfectly. Ramona had been only too aware of his interest and had warned him off.

"Out of your league, mate. You should stick to the old bits of rough you usually go for, like me."

X smiled at the memory. If there was one thing you could say about Ramona, she was very protective of the people she knew, keeping the demarcation lines clearly drawn between social and professional, school and university, stoned and straight. He had had a relationship with her for a number of years, on occasions intimate and intense, and yet he had not met socially any of her friends or family, bar her sister, Ali, and that had been a long time ago. Their affair remained a discrete one, known only to close colleagues and a few business clients.

Absorbed in her papers, glasses perched on the end of her nose, Amanda had said very little, and did not appear to notice X's fascination with her body. He took advantage of her distraction, sitting on the edge of his seat staring intently into the hidden region bounded by her taut skirt and silken calves, musing about how to breach that gap and occupy the territory beyond, his innate sense of optimism relegating any concerns he had about Ramona's plight to a position well below his enjoyment of the here and now. It was always difficult for him thinking in the abstract, when the present was so enticing.

The cab veered suddenly, the driver cursing under his breath and wildly sounding his horn. Amanda swayed back and forth and her legs parted, as she scrabbled to hold her documents together and prevent them sliding onto the floor. X, his reverie interrupted, lurched violently to one side swinging from the handle to keep his balance, but his gaze remained fixed, registering a fleeting image – the bright sheen of smooth skin, the delicious curve of thigh, a glimpse of white underwear visible through sheer light-tan tights.

"What was that?"

Amanda's tone was soft yet quickened by a sharp bite of irritation that hinted at her professional expectation to be always told the facts succinctly and truthfully. The moment had passed, she was aware, and her interest in the incident was only fleeting, but once composed with her deportment again refined, she gazed inquiringly at the taxi driver expecting a response.

"Bloody woman, just walked out in front of the cab. Daydreaming or summat."

"How long till we get where we're going? I haven't got all day."

"Who knows love in this traffic."

The driver noted her displeasure in his rearview mirror and added hastily.

"Around twenty-five to thirty minutes, I should think. Best guess. They keep digging up these roads, it's diabolical. The surface is terrible, I dunno, so many potholes."

Amanda had returned to her reading, no longer listening. X relaxed, he had half an hour of sexual introspection ahead of him, before facing the depressing prospect of visiting Ramona in Holloway Prison.

Free falling filled his dreams. Awake he could surmount the yawning emptiness of the drop, the suck of the earth draining the essence from his body, the vacuum of support that was the free fall, but asleep he was its prisoner, formless and plummeting. Always dropping, never touching down, always avoiding a hard landing, the ultimate impact. He believed, had since childhood, that if you hit the ground in a dream then you wouldn't be waking up, that you had died. That at that very moment your subconscious and conscious selves would collide with an impact so devastating as to be instantly terminal. The shards of your shattered ego impossible to put back together again. It was the one irrefutable fact in his life he never ceased believing in. It was the truth. He trusted in it and was never afraid. He was expecting to die soon. He was not immortal, yet he felt close to the Gods.

"Those bastards treated me like shit. It was as if I was the bloody criminal, not an innocent member of the public visiting a good friend in prison."

Amanda told him curtly to "cool it", as they walked down the dimly lit grey-painted corridor away from the checkpoint where two female prison officers had insisted on him undergoing an intimate body search before he could continue with the visit. Belligerent, he had almost refused to go on, before being reminded by Amanda that Ramona had asked for him, she added emphasis to the word, to be present.

"I strongly object to this treatment, my client is only on remand. That does not warrant such treatment of her visitors."

X appreciated her efforts, even though he knew it was only for effect.

"He is a known associate of McAllister, we are under instructions to be particularly thorough."

"Fine, go ahead."

Disappointed that she had not made more of a fuss, X was ushered into an adjoining room and undressed behind a screen. His clothing was searched, while he was cursorily inspected by a glum male officer wearing white plastic gloves.

"They're bastards. That was all just to get up my nose."

"Please keep your voice down. You give the impression of thinking this is all a game. Believe me it is not."

Her tone was quiet but firm, each word clearly enunciated, as if she was addressing a recalcitrant child.

"She thinks I'm an idiot. I've blown it now."

His recurrent dreams were all similar, in structure, if not detail. He would be flying, a joyful sense of abandon and freedom prevailing, then something unspecified would go wrong and he would be overwhelmed with anxiety. He would then fall. Head first. Somersaulting down. Accelerating. There would be clear views of the sky – the blinding sun, wisps of cloud, vapour trails – then of the earth, getting ever closer. He would be able to see the white caps of the breaking waves, the top of the tree canopy, animals – cows and sheep – grazing in the fields, cars and buses motoring along highways, a lone cyclist in bright yellow Lycra mending a puncture, people gaily dressed walking resolutely here and there. The clarity was astonishing. The silence was profound. It was nearly over. He would wake up soon.

For the first time he saw Ramona as a middle-aged woman. She was ten years his senior, that had been part of the attraction, but she had never looked or acted like it before. Sitting hunched under the harsh lights in the prison interview room, dressed in ripped blue jeans and a Patti Smith "People have the Power" T-shirt, that he remembered from her flat, without make-up, hair slightly disheveled as if tied back and brushed without the help of a mirror, it was clear she had visibly aged. It had only been three weeks since he had last seen her at the party, but the stress of her arrest and imprisonment had taken its toll. The drawn face was that of the forty-year old woman she was, the strain of her ordeal ingrained in the lines scoring her forehead and framing her watery eyes. Her skin was blanched and waxy, its complexion poor, a rash flaring from the corners of her mouth, lips cracked, every few seconds her tongue would flick out tentatively to moisten the rough edges and, crowning her decline, the greying roots of her hair were visible. To X her famed resilience, a quality that he had admired so much, seemed to have drained away, leaving a shell. He was worried.

Ramona looked up when they entered and smiled wanly, her hands entwined on the bare table in front of her. As they pulled up chairs and sat down, she nervously clicked her nails. The prison guard left the room, slamming the door. Amanda leant across and touched her gently on the shoulder. Ramona nodded and held out her hand. She seemed to have slowed down, every weary movement deliberate, as if the effort involved was enormous and the reward negligible.

"Thanks for coming," her voice was quiet yet unexpectedly firm, "we need to talk."

Her eyes moved pointedly from Amanda to X and then up to the door behind them.

With his dreams the devil was in the detail. The minutiae of the disaster that befell him – a chute splitting at the seams as the stitching comes apart or the fabric just disintegrating, the stuff perished and useless, lines fraying in front of his eyes then snapping, harness buckles warping, twisting and opening, separating him from his pack, the ripcord coming away in his hands, turbulence, his airplane breaking up, vanishing from the radar, disappearing into the ether or worst case being shot down, the missile locking on, the arc of its trajectory keenly traced, the explosion's rip – had a profound affect on his mood on waking. In everyday life a man of immense practicality, anticipating every possible eventuality, weighing his options carefully before taking action to ensure that whatever did or didn't happen the outcome was optimized for the maximum possible personal advantage. He lived his life asking, "what could possibly go wrong?" and then acting on his answers. But in the world of dreams he was helpless, a mere follower of fate and he found it debilitating. There was no pleasure to be had in the relentless buffeting of unpredictable events.

"We haven't much time and I don't know if they'll be listening in on this."

"I'd be surprised if they'd do that."

Amanda peered over the top of her glasses as she spoke, fixing Ramona with a compassionate stare. Her tone was assured yet X could tell she was concerned. Her unlined brow was furrowed at the bridge of her nose, her lips firmly set.

"It would be risky, not to say illegal," she hesitated, before deciding to continue, "they seem to have a strong case against you already."

Ramona started, her listless body slumping further into her chair.

"But we can deal with it, I'm confident we can counter what they've got."

Positive words, but X sensed her lack of conviction and he watched Ramona closely to see if she was reading her friend in the same way, but she appeared reassured. Her need for encouragement appearing for the moment to override her normal scepticism.

"Good, good…" her voice faded to nothing as she reflected on the serious drug dealing and conspiracy charges she faced.

"Where are they getting it all from, Amanda? They appear to know a hell of a lot about me and my business. Who's grassing me up?"

She looked at X, an appeal for help in her eyes. He shrugged.

"No whispers, Ramona, nothing at all. But we're looking. And we've shut everything down, as you asked, then going through it all with a fine toothcomb. Anything dodgy will stand out. We'll find the bastard."

"I'm pushing for full disclosure. The prosecution will have to let me know what they have and who their witnesses are sooner or later. We'll get a clearer picture then." She paused. "Mind you they'll probably have cut a deal with the person or persons you're looking for. But still."

Ramona was momentarily nonplussed, shrugging her shoulders, before catching herself and continuing, her tone even.

"Check out the Americans. Are they still here in London?"

"Dunno Ramona. Haven't seen or heard from them since the party."

"The police must have spoken to them?"

"They took both of them in at the same time you were arrested, so they must have been interviewed, yes."

"How much do they know about your end of the business?"

Ramona wrung her hands, the action obsessive and distracting.

"A fuck of a lot," her voice had dropped to a whisper and she leant forward conspiratorially, "I was trying to get them interested in our operation. I had a view to collaborating with them. It would have been a major expansion for us. It could have been very advantageous for both parties. They seemed interested. They asked a lot of questions. I thought they were kosher."

"We don't know it's them, do we? Realistically, what would they have to gain by landing you in it? We need to know more before we can draw that conclusion, until then …"

"It feels right, it bloody well feels right. It has to be them. Fuck."

"We don't know, Ramona."

She was not dissuaded.

"Did you find Ray? He made the introductions."

"No, he's out of the country. I went round to his gaff but none of his lot would speak to me."

"Don't tell me he's in the States?"

"No idea, they wouldn't tell me anything."

Ramona frowned.

"They wouldn't even say when he was coming back."

"Fuck, the bastard has stitched me up as well. I know it."

The old Ramona sat opposite them again, inexorable logic leading to conclusions that stoked her fury, an emotion possessing restorative powers.

"God knows what they're going to try and pull next, we've got to be prepared."

She stood and paced back and forth, hands fisted. X noticed she had lost weight, the belt of her ill-fitting jeans was tightly buckled, crumpling the loose denim waistband into a series of ridges, that rested on protruding hips. He had always admired her Seventies fixation with body-hugging flared Levi's and it dismayed him to see her so diminished. He wanted to hold her.

"Ramona calm down. This doesn't do any good. Come on take a seat." Amanda glanced at her watch.

"We have a lot to get through."

He dreamt often and vividly. No amount of sedation could black out the night-time theatrics in his head or hinder his ability to perfectly recall the dramas for days afterwards. The narratives clogged his waking hours with base sentiments, that were debilitating if not challenged and rapidly expunged. He tried but often failed. One dream recurred more frequently than all the others.

The sun was bright and it was a balmy day. A gentle breeze ruffled his hair and lifted the sweat pleasantly from his bare skin, cooling and refreshing his labouring body. An athlete in his prime, he liked the physical exertion, circling ever higher, keeping company with the falcons and the hawks, besting the kings of the air in their own domain. He was flying high above an azure sea dotted with rocky islands, the efforts of mere men visible as feeble scratches on the surface of this immaculate scene, minor blemishes on a masterpiece of creation. This was his paradise on earth, soon he would conquer heaven as well. He flexed his muscles and beat his vast wings, soaring upwards effortlessly.

The heat was intensifying as the atmosphere thinned, the flaring sun burning his face and branding the marks of leather straps onto exposed skin. The air was rarefied, it was harder to breath, his chest was heaving with the effort. He felt light-headed, yet joyous, he could see over the edge of the world. He was looking a smiling God in the eye.

It was silent at this lofty altitude, except for the measured rush of his heavy breathing. Nature was stilled, acquiescing in his ascendancy, while the sounds of humanity were obliterated by distance. He was alone, the birds of prey far below. A solitary speck on the face of the sun casting an immense shadow across the known world. Immortality beckoned, for no man had reached these heights before.

His wings curved away from him in perfect crescents – the work of divinely inspired craftsmen – flexing in the updraft, lifting him higher, cradling him against danger. Eyes scanning with satisfaction from wing-tip to wing-tip, admiring the symmetry and beauty of the construction. He marvelled that something so delicate could enable him to perform such superhuman feats. It was a contraption made by human hands, yet it helped him to transcend all earthbound constraints and escape the limitations of the mortal. He was a man in love with himself, a man enraptured by a machine. He was immaculate.

Ramona sat down and X caught the faint whiff of perspiration, a desperate aroma that for an instant masked the musty institutional staleness of the cells. This was a tang X knew would stay with him on his skin, clinging to his clothes long after he had left the confines of the prison. He was feeling sorry for Ramona for the first time in their long acquaintance, an unwelcome sensation.

Seated she answered Amanda's questions, but was distracted, hands constantly in motion, legs shaking, the rubber soles of her soiled lace-less plimsolls tapping relentlessly on the concrete floor. Every so often she would interrupt the flow of the discussion to bark out a series of non sequitur instructions to X. They had an internal logic, when taken together, but to Amanda and X they seemed random and a disturbing sign that Ramona seemed unwilling to face up to the seriousness of her legal predicament and was instead focusing on the far from urgent, but for her more satisfying, issue of getting her own back, on exacting acts of revenge.

"Ramona, I don't think you should do anything precipitate. You must not be reckless at this sensitive time. It will only make things worse."

"No, no we've got to sort out Ray. He's the fucking key to this, I know he is."

"Ramona."

She looked at X and he knew from her expression that there was no arguing with her.

"You know what to do. I'm relying on you."

"Ramona, please. You can't be talking like this in front of me. I can't have any knowledge of what you plan to do, you know that. So, stop now."

Amanda closed the file on the table in front of her. Ramona nodded and gave her, her full attention. Minutes later she suddenly blurted out.

"Track down the Americans."

"Ramona, I've warned you."

"Go over there, to New York if necessary, but be careful."

She turned again to face Amanda, smiling grimly.

He was well prepared for the inevitable, knew it was coming, every dream was the same after all, yet was still horrified when it happened. A flickering shadow glimpsed out of the corner of his eye, announced his imminent downfall. Anything marring the sleek surface and perfect lines of his flying machine was a disquieting experience, but this blemish took his breath away. A golden eagle's feather, one of the thousands making up the body of the wings, was lifting and ruffling in the cross winds. He could hear the whispering burr of its futile resistance to the air current – a faint portent of his rushing oblivion – as it fleetingly stood proud against the flow, before twisting free and spiralling into the abyss. It was followed by another, then another. Each feather leaving behind a small well of molten wax, whose liquid sheen glinted in the fierce rays of the sun. His beautiful wings were breaking up in a sparkling diamond shower of fluttering auric light.

A guard tapped gently on the door and entered the room.

"Do you need any more time?"

Amanda shook her head. After an hour of questioning Ramona was exhausted.

"No, thank you."

They stood to leave. There was no chance for intimate physical contact and they shook hands formally across the table. Ramona sank back into her chair, deflated, her eyes dead, their departure a reminder of her dire situation.

"Can't you get me out of here?"
"Sorry, I've tried."
"I'm only on remand."
"I know, but …"

"Fuck me, not that Icarus shit again. Such a cliché."
As he fell, he wondered what it meant?

An extract from "Artistic Gems: The World's Ten Most Influential Paintings" – Dr. Arnold Merchant, Emeritus Professor of Art History, the University of Aberystwyth. Published in the Journal of Contemporary Art Inquiries, Faculty of Arts, the Universities of Wales. October – December 2013.

6. The "Wow" factor in art appreciation.

"F..k me!" is sometimes the only way to size it up. Crude, earthy, but a perfect summation of your life at that particular point. It marks a moment when you realize that things are never going to be the same again. It could be a work of art that overturns the way you look at the world, altering your perception of what is real, this happened to me when I visited the Musées Royaux des Beaux-Arts de Belgique in Brussels and first saw the next painting in our masterpiece top 10 – number 6 – by Flemish master Pieter Breughel the Elder, or it might be a great symphony taking you to places you never knew existed before or it could be the portent of a change for the worse, of impending disaster. Whatever the cause those simple words grasp the enormity of what has taken place. Overusage can never diminish their impact, witness your own surprise when you saw them on the page of such a learned journal as this.

In summary they fit the bill.

The picture is small – 112 centimetres by 73.5 – its power emanating from its imagery rather than its size. It was painted in or around the year, 1558, for the salon not the gallery and requires effort to appreciate its meaning. We do not know who commissioned it or why they chose this particular subject.

The scene is bucolic, a summer's day on the coast. The sun is shining, drenching land and water with light. We can see clear to the horizon – emblematic of both the terror and potential of the unknown, uncharted future – and sense the curvature of the earth. The artist has made fine use of perspective to gently draw us in. Two ships are plying the calm waters of the bay – one returning after a long voyage, navigating between the treacherous rocks that dot the coastline, heading for the safety of the port, the other, sails unfurling dramatically (you can hear the crack of the canvas), heading out to sea. The criss-crossing of these agents of commerce drawing our eye to the centre of the painting, where a dark castellated rock catches our attention. We are not alone as onlookers, a shepherd, who is tending his flock on the cliff's edge has joined us staring wistfully, as we are, at the same harsh image of doom – so different in detail and colouration from the rest of the painting – an audience in contemplation of some imminent disaster. We fear initially for the sailors, but nature on this day appears benign, and they seem to be in no danger. But who knows, we must wait.

One man appears unconcerned – the central visual character of the painting, firmly placed in the foreground, – a farmer and his horse ploughing a field, head down, following his own ragged furrow, oblivious to the latent drama unfolding out to sea. He would appear to the casual observer to be the subject of the painting, making him part of an interesting portrayal of agricultural labour in a sixteenth century rural landscape, but not the protagonist in one of the great masterpieces of western representational art.

It is this contradiction between the apparent superficial mundanity of the scene and the potentiality of the unfolding mystery presented by the organization of the figurative forms in the middle and far distance, which underwrites the tension that points to the picture's greatness. There must be more.

Breughel's title appears incomprehensible at first – The Fall of Icarus – he was an ancient Greek royal and early aviator wasn't he and not a medieval tiller of the soil? A tragic example of hubris fulfilled – a classic Greek epic. Breughel must be bringing the myth up to date and using it to emphasize its relevance to contemporary society, but how?

Scanning the sky yields no clues. There are no soaring birdmen to be seen, no tumbling figures plummeting to earth in a cloud of feathers (everyone – his audience through the ages – knows Icarus's fate). Great works of art, by definition, grab your attention and the artist has done that very effectively. The mystery is profound.

Finally, after a period of intense scrutiny, all is revealed. Hidden in the lower right corner of the painting is Icarus, caught in the moment before he disappears forever below the waves, his flailing legs all that are visible. The splash is insignificant. No one has noticed, in fact Breughel, as we have discussed, has us all looking the other way. Herein lies his genius.

This brilliance has not gone unnoticed over the years. The British-American poet, W. H. Auden, in "Musée des Beaux Arts," a poem inspired by this painting exploits the exquisite visual imagery transforming it into a written/aural picture about the facility of the Old Masters to appreciate that human suffering is an intimately personal tragedy that the rest of mankind can blithely ignore. The splash, the forsaken cry, may be heard by everyone around the World, but they are of no ultimate consequence.

This painting presages the fall of kings, the overthrow of dynasties. It punctures the inflated egos of tyrants, and emphatically expresses the indifferent emotions of the small man – the ploughman labouring in the field, the shepherd tending his flock, the sailors setting their sails – perfectly. In doing so he also loosens the oppressive centuries-long hold of Greek tragedy on the mindset of European societies and affirms the essence of revolution in thought and process. To the rulers of the Netherlands in the sixteenth century it states nobody cares, nobody gives a f..k. Pieter Breughel's master canvas is a miniature gem of the northern Renaissance that discretely screams this fact to the world.

1,014 metres

**Clicking for global domination – how to make your site the most popular on the web. An outlaw's guide to bombing and hijacking your way to success!**

**Online Correspondent, Hector "the hacker" Reeves. Webwise special supplement. Interconnected World – June 2002. A "Keep the Web Free" publication.**

It's a no-brainer – more is better. It's as true on the web as it is everywhere else. More money, more fun, more food (only joking I've lost weight, honest!), more visitors, more friends – it's a virtuous circle.

So how do you do it on the web? How do you get those punters clicking your way? How do you trick the search engines into giving your site the high-ranking it deserves? It's the eternal battle between good and evil – us, the masters of the web, wanting people to visit us, them, the search engine straights, wanting to give people the pages they want rather than the ones we want them to see. Drastic measures are called for. This guide is not for the faint-hearted – if you have any scruples at all read no further, this is strictly for all you bush-whackers out there. This is hardcore.

Step 1. Publish an awesome site, full of content that rocks. Good start, but it's not enough, if people can't/don't find it. So proceed to:

Step 2. Learn some/all of the tricks of the trade. There are a good few, believe me, that will give your site the boost it needs. Here are my particular favourites in no particular order:

**Page Hijacking:** this involves copying a popular page and submitting it from your own site. Search engines will credit your site and point people at it. They get something unexpected and you get those extra vital clicks. With luck some of them will be interested and return.

**Fooling the "crawler":** search engines regularly trawl the web with crawler programmes to find out what is on all the pages. You can help them think your site is more popular than it actually is, by putting lots of irrelevant but popular words on your page. This list can be as long as you like, because you will mask them by making them the same colour as the background, so that nobody can see them except the crawler.

**Copying meta-tags:** the crawler also looks at web page "meta-tags", which summarize what the page is about and are invisible. You can "use" popular pages meta-tags on your site so that any search for them will turn up your site as well.

**Making bridge pages:** some search engines, such as Google, rank pages on a particular subject by the number of other pages that link to them. In their eyes the more links to a site the more likely it is to be useful. You can take advantage of this by creating pages (hundreds if you have the time and inclination) that have key words that suggest they are all about your particular subject. You then make them all slightly different so that the search engine thinks they are all unique, but they **all** point to your site.

You can **cloak** these bridge pages so that people never actually see them, they just get bounced directly to your site.

**Google bombs:** using the above bridge tactic you can "bomb" Google to improve the ranking of your site so that it appears at the top of the results for a particular search phrase. Set up pages (it's been estimated as few as thirty will be enough with certain phrases) that all host a link to your site and describe it in the same way then as far as Google is concerned the page they refer to (yours) is likely to be a good one. Make sure your link is kept on the front of each page and Google will rank it higher as a result.

Step 3. Put some/all of the above into practice. Success is guaranteed, but be careful. It's lawless out there. Watch out for the Sheriff and you won't go wrong.

Happy Trails.

Breathing hard, bathed in sweat, X ran, the repetitive slap of his trainers on the never-ending PVC belt of the treadmill whirring beneath his feet, audible over the sound of David Bowie's "China Girl" booming from two Bose 891 speakers mounted on the wall above his head. The video screen on the running machine flickered with the images of two naked bodies entwined on a beach, briefly distracting him. He had been staring at Annie, he thought that was her name, working out beside him on a rowing machine, her body tensing and relaxing with mesmeric regularity. Her taut abdomen barely strained as she leant forward, then back, hauling on the stunted oars, her pectorals pliant, skin glistening with perspiration, her dark black hair swept back from her narrow, angular face and tied tightly in a bunch with a bright red band. She was panting heavily and gruffly counting strokes between gritted teeth. A smile seemed imprinted on her delicate features, barely fading even though her mouth was locked in a rictus of exertion. The evening before in "The Dockyard", he had been attracted by her resemblance to the younger Ramona, now seeing her naked in the hazy sunlight of a late November morning, the similarity was even more striking.

He had no explanation for his current obsession with Ramona, beyond the fact that for the seven weeks she had been locked up in Holloway he had been living in her flat, drinking his way through her stock of spirits and fine champagne, driving her vintage Jag and exercising on her gym equipment. He was now beginning to miss her, but he still drew immense satisfaction from looking at Annie's body, casting his mind back and visualizing Ramona, his long-term lover – X always had difficulty describing the exact status of their relationship: partner seemed too presumptuous, girlfriend too cute, employer too banal, only lover seemed to sum it up – as she was when they had first met. Lean, semi-emaciated, skin stretched over the clearly-defined cage of her ribs, her youthful body tanned, except for a pale narrow line around her groin, her pubic area shaved, small breasts that had grown larger over the years, but still retained their long erect nipples protruding from dark pronounced aureoles.

Demanding, devouring, Annie reminded him of Ramona; the violence of their intimacy, bruising yet sensual, the physical exertion exhilarating, their hungers only satisfied in the half-light of a gloomy dawn. Beguilingly hung-over, wallowing in the befuddlement of a semi-drugged consciousness, his two lovers' bodies merged with his in an erotically tinged hallucination of yearning, one of a growing sequence of sentimental flashbacks, recently often lachrymose, to the era of his youth. For X was feeling his age, he had had to work hard the previous night to keep up with Annie, her stamina outdid his, the ongoing demands she made had been exhausting. To earn some respite, he had finally been forced to fake an orgasm, juddering to a sodden breathless halt, before rolling guiltily to one side. It was the first time he had acted out a climax and it had been surprisingly easy, yet he worried she had noticed. Lying rigid beside her listening to her breathing, he charted her somnolent passage into deep sleep with growing relief. Acutely aware of having failed in some way, he lay awake as the room lightened around him, but could not be put his finger on anything more specific than his simple deceit.

"It was a one-off, down to all this fucking stress. Ramona, holed up in her cell, had no idea what he was going through holding the fort while she was away."

The demands of running the operation had if anything increased with her being incommunicado – a fact that was disconcertingly widely known among her business cohorts – rivals were constantly trying to take advantage of her absence, probing the strength of the organization, stress testing the resilience of her staff. Raw capitalist competition at its most ruthless, he understood that, but X was finding his competences stretched to the limit.

Annie said nothing when she awoke and appeared as friendly as ever, goading him on to the exercise machines with a coquettish charm he found irresistible. That was unlike Ramona, who barely touched the gym equipment despite cluttering up her apartment with it, viewing repetitive exercise as a last resort she had not yet reached.

"You'll only get me on those things when my thighs are rubbing together and my tits are down to my waist."

She had blurted out this emphatic statement on the one stoned occasion he had suggested some exercise.

"Sex, drugs and rock 'n' roll keep my weight down. That and picking at junk food."

Her laugh was infectious and they had wrestled each other on to the bed, their grappling growing increasingly rough as Ramona's exuberance grew. X had cracked his head on an empty bottle of Moët & Chandon Impérial, lying discarded in the tangle of the duvet, and began to bleed profusely.

"That'll teach you to call me fat, you bastard."

He had hated her then for the first time in the ten years he had known her. He liked women with an appetite for excess – drink, drugs, sex, and even violence – and Ramona was the hungriest one he had ever met, but as he lay dazed on blood-soaked sheets, head aching, he realized he had a limit, which she had just crossed. There had been a hardness in her eyes that he had not seen before, a hint of sadism. If he believed in anything, and he'd long debated that, knowing all talk of criminal codes to be a load of bollocks, it was that his actions, however wild and dangerous, never gratuitously harmed anyone. He never inflicted unnecessary pain. She had been a kindred spirit, or so he had thought. From that moment on he had no longer been faithful to her, they had continued to work, party and sleep together, but at every opportunity he had sought out the company of other women. Most markedly different in looks and character from Ramona, there had been, he found, a great release in sinking into the warm embrace of buxom long-haired blondes, curly-headed brunettes, voluminous red-heads, cushioned by inconsequential chatter and mindless hedonism, all a great distance from his charged relationship with the beautiful, angular, sinewy, edgy, Ramona, intellectually committed as she was to a manic, headlong confrontation with life. In her company he had never been sober or bored and it was exhilarating battling against the world, yet it was draining. Other women were a retreat, free falling a release. He jumped to escape.

Annie was the first woman he had deliberately slept with who looked and behaved like Ramona, not a perfect likeness – she didn't drink for one thing, which made her the only adult he'd ever met who didn't. She just consumed drugs – speed and ecstasy – at an insatiable rate, which made her a close enough match. There had been others exhibiting facets of Ramona's appearance or character but he had noticed the similarities only later, on reflection. With Annie he had actually imagined he was with Ramona, making love to her, it had been a night of firsts. Watching her now out of the corner of his eye he realized her body was a thing of beauty and that he loved her. He took a sip of champagne.

"What are you smiling at?"

Annie's voice was slurred as she rested on her oars gulping in air, her chest heaving.

"You've been looking at me for ages, you voyeur."

"You look great. You do this regularly?"

"Most days."

She sat astride the rowing-machine and stretched her arms.

"The gym?"

"Sometimes or I go running in Victoria Park."

"You lift weights?"

"What you saying?" she laughed, "I look butch?"

"No, you just look very buff."

X switched off the treadmill and jogged slowly to a halt, then with relish drained his glass.

"You want some?"

He lifted the bottle.

"No, ta. I told you I never touch the stuff."

She hauled herself to her feet.

"Can you pass me that towel, I'm dripping?"

He grabbed two from the rack beside his machine and flung one at Annie.

"Ta."

She draped it over her shoulders, letting the ends dangle down across her chest covering her breasts, then stepped up and on tiptoe kissed him on the lips. The hair at the back of her neck hung in damp rat-tails and he touched them tenderly, the moisture greasing his fingertips, he then dropped his hands to rest them on her buttocks, her skin slippery and warm. He could feel the dank heat radiating from her, smell the vestigial traces of her scent. Her tongue slipped into his mouth and for a moment he felt a tremor of arousal, tinged with reluctance, yet his tongue parried hers, their embrace tightened, then to his relief she stepped back.

"I need a shower, you coming?"

He nodded, thinking, "I need a drink."

"I'll be with you in a sec, I'll just get another bottle."

Through lidded eyes he admired her figure as she skipped across the room to the bathroom, her narrow hips and the pronounced gap at the top of her thin legs. It was one of the few objective criteria by which he judged a woman and he mused with satisfaction that Annie scored very highly. His mobile phone rang, the ringtone distant and muffled.

"Oh God, where the fuck is it?"

The air was startlingly clear at this height, the detail microscopically precise. Often this close to the ocean you would dive into a bank of mist, the salt haze fusing nature's patterns into an indistinct mass of rippling water, merged wave forms and blurred edges, your body absorbed. Today X could see below the heaving limpid surface of the swell to a kaleidoscopic fusion of lights refracted through the layered depths. Shimmering organo-chemical effusions of green and blue incorporeal hues. Partial liquid rainbows arcing in all dimensions. An obscure, seething world of colour. Shadows of infinite size, density and shape passing above, below and through.

X rummaged through the scattered detritus of the previous evening – clothes, champagne bottles, Rizlas, cosmetics, oils, assorted drugs in plastic bags, glasses, used condoms, Zippo lighter ("that's where the bastard was"), CDs, broken cigarettes – as his mobile sounded relentlessly, then stopped.

"Shit."

Exasperated he turned and headed for the fridge. The phone rang again, almost at his feet, it was lying hidden beneath Annie's creased black dress, which he picked up and threw aside before answering.

"Yep?"

"It's Danny, have you looked at the site recently?"

"Morning to you too. You're fucking joking aren't you, it's only 11.30 on a Sunday. I haven't even had breakfast yet."

"Well you need to take a butcher's, mate."

"What, you're taking the piss aren't you?"

He could hear the distant sound of rushing water, Annie singing.

"No seriously it's fucking weird."

"That's your job to sort things, why you fucking with me on my day off?"

"You know me I wouldn't jerk you around for nothing, honest mate."

"Fuck Danny," he needed a drink, "what is it?"

"Well it's not there."

"What the fuck do you mean it's not there?"

"Just that. It's not there."

"I don't need this Danny. You're starting to get on my tits."

X opened the fridge and stood for a moment luxuriating in the engulfing wave of chilled air, then took out a bottle of champagne.

"No listen, all you get when you log on is porn – very nice don't get me wrong – but not what you're bloody expecting or needing if you're strung out and in search of your latest fix."

"Porn?"

"Yeah, 'Hairy Twat,' or summat like that."

Clamping the phone between his head and left shoulder, he began to open the champagne bottle, ripping off the foil wrapper and carefully unscrewing the wire fastener.

"What?"

"Yeah birds in all their fuzzy glory, none of this shaved shit. Much more natural if you ask me."

"For fuck sake Danny, I can imagine what a hairy twat is. You've just logged in to the wrong site, you wanker."

"No, I've checked it over and over and the same thing happens every time."

Enveloped in clouds of steam, Annie dripping wet, hair plastered to her head, peered round the door of the bathroom, and beckoned to X.

"Are you coming?"

"In a mo. I'm just sorting something."

"Who was that?"

"None of your fucking business. Now, where were we?"

"It's true, you check it out."

"I will. It'll be some glitch in your computer, you fuckhead. Or you doing something stupid."

The cork exploded from the bottle, arced across the room and ricocheted off a framed Peter Blake limited edition print of "The First Real Target" hanging on the wall, cracking the glass, foaming champagne spilled over his hands and dripped onto his bare feet.

"Shit, I'll call you back."

"Cheers."

"Fuck off."

X swigged thirstily from the bottle, bubbles spritzing his nose and chin.

"That Danny is a wanker."

Muttering to himself he picked up his flute, filled it to the brim and stepping carefully over a pair of shoes, straightened the damaged picture, then went into the bathroom. Annie was silhouetted against the steamed-up glass cubicle, her body golden and diffuse, mottled with lather. Exhuberently washing she slipped in and out of focus, a shimmering icon of desirable intangibility. The air around her filled with the transient gush of cascading torrents of water. Clouds of steam billowed upwards, rolling in waves across the tiled ceiling before sinking to the floor in a diffuse scented fug. X was enchanted by her but felt detached. He breathed in deeply, the astringent atmosphere clearing his head. The mirror was misted and he stared into it, his face obscured, its outline barely discernible, and yearned for anonymity.

"I've had enough of this bollocks. I really have. The sooner Ramona is out of the nick, won't be soon enough for me. Fuck!"

He started as the shower door slid back, releasing a bank of warm, humid vapour that engulfed the room, lifting the humidity and temperature.

"There you are," she smiled, "problems?"

"Oh nothing, just the usual work shit."

He shrugged and wiped the sweat from his forehead.

"What is it you do?"

She rubbed her eyes with the back of her hand.

"Bit of this and bit of that, not very interesting really."

"I heard you were a drug dealer?"

"Who told you that?"

"Someone at the Roxy. They told me you were the man to see."

X didn't answer, just turned and stared into the mirror.

"You're not angry, are you? I'm sorry if I've got it wrong."

"No, they could be right."

"So, it's true?"

Her eyes widened and she stood in the shower doorway, mouth slightly open, looking many years younger than he remembered. X smiled.

"What do you think, am I the man?"

"You are definitely. Come on."

She held out her hand. They embraced under the stream of

hot pounding water, the beating on his skin bracing, her caresses reinvigorating. His weariness dissipated and they made love, Annie standing on tip-toe, her back pressed against the streaming tiles; X, thigh muscles aching, teeth gritted, labouring to dispel his disappointment of the previous night. Flushed from the shower onto the bathroom floor by the cooling water they finally climaxed together on the sodden bath mat. Shivering they rolled apart, the chill driving them in search of warm towels. Vindicated, X dried himself, in breathless, dripping silence. Then he heard his phone ringing again.

"It's me, Danny. Have you checked it out?"

"I thought you were sorting it?"

"I've tried man, but no one here knows what's going on. All we know is that it just ain't working as it should. In fact, it ain't working at all."

"Fuck me Danny I'm busy."

"I know man …"

"Really busy."

"I know man, but this don't seem right to me. I've seen nothing like this before, I can tell you."

"You're still getting porn?"

"Yep, same old stags."

"Bollocks."

"I'm sorry man. You need to know. Ramona …"

"Don't go on about her, she's not here is she."

"No, exactly mate."

From behind Annie grasped X's buttocks.

"Shit."

"What?"

Danny sounded angry, no longer contrite.

"Not you Danny."

He impatiently waved Annie away.

"Sorry!"

Her tone was sarcastic. She bent down to pick up her bra.

"Look mate I know you've got a bird in there, but you need to take a look. If it's nothing, it won't take long an' you'll be back on the job in no time."

"Fuck. I'll get on it."

"You'll give me a bell?"

"Yep."

"Cheers."

"You better be right about this, you cunt."

"I hope it's fuck-all, I really do."

At such a height with the detail so precise, the contours clear, the landing zone identified and clearly demarcated, he had often imagined the impact, as most free fallers he knew did, some out of morbid curiosity, others, like him, out of some warped nod in the direction of responsible behaviour, which was unlike themselves in everything else they did. The logic being know the dangers and be better prepared. It appealed to X to have an area of his life that followed such different rules, ones he could imagine his mother subscribing too, yet applied to such a mind-blowing activity. As an aid to his better understanding of what could happen, he had even borrowed medical directories from the local library and pored over the anatomical drawings of the human body, factoring in the descriptions of impact injuries and their effects on different organs, bones and muscle groups. Anodyne and vapid study until he turned to the photographs of crush and crash victims, which made up one of the annexes of the weighty encyclopedia, the images firing his imagination, conjuring up twisted bodies, broken and unidentifiable, lying in pools of blood. There were no answers in the gore, just a flood of questions. Did your soul, your sense of being, fall as fast as your body? Did they both hit the ground at the same time or was there a lag as you caught up with the yourself? A chink of time through which you could survey the past and future, a moment when, your life almost over, you could evaluate what you had done and see the way ahead? Would you have the presence of mind to take full advantage of this opening or would you misjudge the opportunity? Could this peep-hole remain open for eternity? Maybe body and soul never linked up again and your essence just floated above the smashed, bleeding hulk of your carcass forever? Suspended in a state of serenity or in agony? Never religious in the formal sense X found it hard to accept a crunching end, believing that was too brutal, too final. He imagined the impact to be brilliant, an explosion of psychedelic swirling lights, the rich spectrum of life's experiences funneled through the body's dying senses. A belief in a brief life after death? What did you feel, if anything, when you hit the ground? Did it hurt? Were you conscious for any period? How quickly did you die? The moment of extinction fascinated him – when did it happen? Was it the cracking of the skull? The eruption of the contents of the cranium? The splattering of your brain across the hard ground seeding islands of matter marooned in coalescing, coagulating lakes of life's liquids? The rupturing of the body cavity, muscles tearing, limbs breaking, bones splintering, organs bursting? Or was it a sensory overload of the pain centre of the brain? When did that ill-defined organ succumb to the tidal wave of sensation? How agonizing did it have to be? Were you terrified or resigned, the certainty of death reassuring? If terrified was that because of a genuine horror at the imminent end of your existence, the inevitability of the smash, the expectation of excruciating pain, or all three? Was one worse than the others? Why would you, given all these unknowns, choose to jump from a high place as a way to commit suicide? X had never understood how people could do it. The idea was too horrible to contemplate.

A friend, Troy "Laughing-boy" Samuels, who he'd known since secondary school, had recently unexpectedly jumped off the top of a three-storey car-park, brimming over with vodka, VitaminK, and a mistaken understanding of the fickleness of height. This destructive act had left X depressed for weeks. If Troy had confided in him, which would have been unlikely as they only ever talked about football and women, he would have told him, "thirty feet is not fucking high enough, mate. You'll most likely break your back and end up in a wheelchair, not in a coffin. The drop may look a long way but there's no guarantee it'll kill you. You need to go much higher to be certain, but you can't do that can you, you wanker, as you've no head for heights. Remember what happened when you came sky-diving with me, you bottled it, couldn't leave the plane. You were never the same with me again, Thinking showing fear would mean I had less respect for you, you stupid sod. You had no fucking idea, but a fear of heights is the one thing I do respect. One other thing I should mention is the higher up you go the further you have to come down, which means you have an age to regret your decision to jump. Not pleasant, all that time to think. My advice is use a shot-gun, it's the only guaranteed way to do the job. Blow your brains out in a micro-second. Bang, all gone."

They would have laughed, as they always did, and changed the subject. X confident in the fact that Troy disliked guns as much as he hated heights. He was one of the few sensible bastards he knew. The conversation never happened though, much as X wished it had, and the "stupid fucker" killed himself falling exactly thirty-one feet from the top of Terminal 1's short-term car-park in the sterile wasteland of Heathrow airport.

"The ugliest place I could think of," he wrote in his farewell note that he sellotaped to the steering wheel of his BMW together with his car and flat keys, "no one I know will find me here."

His broken body was discovered in a patch of desiccated long grass by a nine-year-old boy, playing hide and seek with his father while they waited for his mother's delayed flight to arrive from New York, just seconds after "Laughing-boy" breathed his last, having taken over half an hour to bleed to death.

There were so many questions, more than he had ever asked in the whole of his thirty-year life.

Naked, X sat in front of his laptop and switched it on.

"Danny's a tosser. He's probably still pissed," he murmured.

"What?"

Annie was lying on the black leather sofa, tugging on her pantyhose.

"He'll have been partying all night, not pulled, come home, had a few more drinks, logged on for a wank, then forgotten what he was doing and called me."

Annie laughed.

"He's a friend of yours?"

"Work colleague and not for much fucking longer if he goes on like this."

"Why'd he call you on a Sunday?"

"God knows…" He moved uncomfortably in his chair, then stretched, "'cause he's so fucking predictable, that's why. Always cocking everything up. He's a cunt."

"Sounds like a lovely bloke. I'm hungry. How about breakfast?"

"Help yourself. There's bacon and eggs in the kitchen."

"You want anything?"

"Coffee'd be nice, ta."

"Can't you leave that until tomorrow? It is the weekend."

"Na. I'd better check it out. Just in case the wanker's right."

"Check what?"

"Oh, a little website we look after."

"Cool."

Double-checking each instruction from a hand-written crib-sheet he kept folded in his wallet, X logged on. The broadband connection was unusually slow and he waited exasperatedly for each stage to complete. The first two passed off normally, then on the third, to his intense irritation, the lurid banner for the "All Natural Hookers" website unfurled across the screen, prefacing the appearance of a series of graphic close-up images of dark pubic hair-rimmed vaginas, luxuriant pudenda, dense hairy buttocks, bushy armpits and the invitation to "Enter here for thousands more natural women, just as you like 'em. You must be over 18." As X moved the cursor across the screen a small moving icon appeared in the top right-hand corner of a couple copulating, the man thrusting rapidly and repetitively.

"Shit."

Returning to his home page X repeated the log in procedure and reached the same site.

"Fuck."

He tried again with the same result.

"Fuck it."

Annie handed him a steaming mug of coffee.

"Bad news?"

"Yeah."

"I wasn't sure if you took milk and sugar, so I added both. Just a spoonful mind."

X shook his head.

"No sugar."

"Don't know much about you, do I?"

She returned to the kitchen.

"Bacon sarnie OK?"

"Nothing for me. I've got fucking calls to make."

With shaking hands, he fumbled for his mobile. The number rang through to voicemail.

"Shit."

"If it's Danny you want to talk to leave a message, if he's not who you want, fuck off."

The recording forced, wooden and unamusing.

"Danny call me immed…"

"It's me."

"Where the fuck have you been?"

"For Christ's sake! Keep your hair on. I was taking a leak."

"Sorry mate this is doing my head in. Looks like you were right. The site is buggered. Fuck it."

"What you going to do?"

"Fuck knows. I don't understand how any of it works technically. I'll have to call Ace, see if he can throw some light on what's going on."

"Who's he?"

"You remember that dude I told you about, out in Lagos. A total tit but he knows his shit."

"Oh yeah."

"A right computer nerd. He's fucking mad, I wouldn't trust him with most things except when it comes to his area of expertise."

"Yeah?"

"Buying and selling stuff on the internet. He designed our site for fuck's sake."

"Sounds like you should give him a bell. In the meantime, what about the punters? They're going to be hacked off about this."

"Don't fucking talk to me about it."

"We'll lose a fucking bomb."

"You always were a fucking genius."

"Ramona's not going …"

"Don't keep bringing her up. It's starting to really piss me off. She's not here, is she? If she was, I wouldn't be doing all this fucking worrying would I?"

"Cool it man. No fucking offence."

"Look OK you're going to have to help me here."

"Uhh yeah."

"We've got mobile numbers for some of our regulars, haven't we?"

"Some but we haven't used them since the site got going. A lot of 'em will have changed or were just burners in the first place."

"Yeah, but we've got to do something."

"Most don't like giving out their numbers."

"I know, but you got any better ideas?"

"No, what do I tell them?"

"Any old bullshit. You know temporary problems with site, we'll soon be up and running that sort of thing. Offer them a sweetener if they get arsey."

"Like what?"

"Use your fucking imagination. Discount, longer line of credit, whatever keeps 'em sweet. Freebies may be, that sort of thing. Not too many though."

"OK."

"Do this Danny boy and you'll be a hero. Get some of the lads to help you. I'll call Ace and get to the fucking bottom of this load of wank."

Diving head then feet first, turning onto his back, flipping somersaults, corkscrewing downwards – movement in three-dimensions – an infinity of amazing deeds beyond the imagining of prosaic earth-bound mortals. Aerial gymnastics of the spectacular, X had done it all, yet he would swear time altered too while falling – stopping (floating still, limbs outstretched, going nowhere), reversing (growing younger as you drop, landing before jumping), disappearing (seconds falling away, missing in space) – he was a traveler in four dimensions. He was a stoner.

X knew it was serious, as soon as Ace answered the phone.
"Yo, man."
"It's me."
"What a fucking screw-up man."
He felt nauseous.
"You've seen it then?"
"Wow, seen it man, I've been trying to suss out the problem for hours."
His voice was distant, the line quality poor.
"You've no idea what's going on?"
"Yeah man I know what's happened, it's how that's bugging me."
"Can't you fix it?"
X's emotional equilibrium hung on the next answer.
"Difficult without starting over. What I don't know is how they got at it. I was pretty sure it was tamper-proof. You know I thought I'd shored up the fucker pretty damn well."
X felt incredibly nervous as this new information hit him.
"It was deliberate?"
"Deliberate sure, but more than that it was malicious mate, fucking malicious."

"Shit, I thought …'

He couldn't think.

"I know man so did I. This blows me out."

X paced the room. Annie was singing along to the radio in the kitchen.

"What's the fuck's happened."

"We've been page-jacked, that's fucking what."

"Christ Ace, what does that mean?"

"Dead simple in effect, more complicated in execution."

"Cut the bollocks and tell me."

"Stay cool man."

"I'll stay cool when you tell me something I can fucking understand."

His head throbbed and there was a sharp pain on his left side.

"Well put simply, some clever bastard has linked our site to this hairy cunt cornucopia."

"So …"

"So that every time you try to log on to our site you get an eyeful, not the fucking fix you're seeking."

"Christ."

There was a fierce static on the line, then it died.

"Ace? … for fuck sake."

He flung the phone onto the sofa.

"Shit, fuck, bollocks."

Annie called out.

"Are you OK?"

"Fucking ace, baby, fucking ace."

The phone rang.

"Shit line anyway …"

"Is this true for everyone logging on?"

"Yep, every sod with a chemical craving anywhere in the whole wide world who logs on looking for us."

"Fuck. So no one is getting through to our site?"

"Nope."

"No one can place any orders?"

"Nope."

"Christ. This'll put us out of business."

"Yep."

"How long has it been like this?"

"I only noticed it this morning. Probably happened overnight."

"Can you sort it and fucking quickly?"

"The answer's yes and no."

"Ace, you wanker."

X was finding breathing difficult. It was very hot, even though he was naked.

"I can fix it, but it will take time."

"How long?"

"Well, I'll have to take the site down, unpick the code then republish."

"How fucking long?"

"Most of today at least, maybe longer."

"Shit."

"And there's nothing to stop them doing it again, until I discover how they are hacking in."

"Fuck."

"Tracing who's doing this and where they are doing it from is going to be very tricky. To be honest, it'll be difficult to get at those responsible even after the current problem is sorted and it may never be possible."

"Great. Any good news?"

"Nope."

X was sweating profusely and short of breath.

"Then you'd better start work on the current problem."

He coughed.

"Already started mate. But it gets worse."

"Worse? You're bullshitting me?"

"No."

"For fuck's sake, Ace. What could be worse?"

"It looks like we've been Google-bombed as well."

Ace's superior tone of condescending jollity was grating – X wanted to hurt him, grind the mobile into his face and smash his head against the wall. He dropped the phone and clenched and unclenched his fists and stared in desperation out of the window at the River Thames three storeys below, glittering in the limpid mid-day sunshine. A rusty barge piled high with black rubbish bags – many split open, displaying their rotting innards – motored by, wreathed by a vast flock of swooping, screaming gulls. Prow low in the water, surging bow waves almost overtopping the gunwales as they sinuously coursed the length of the vessel before ebbing away into the wake's foaming churn. The captain was leaning on the guardrail of the bridge, smoking. He called out and gestured to someone, hidden from view on the quay directly below the apartment window where X was standing. Resigned he picked up his mobile – he could hear the whisper of Ace's voice – and returned to the conversation.

"Tell me what the fuck a Google-bomb is."

"I just was."

"I didn't hear you, the line dropped out."

"Fucking hell. This job does my head in sometimes…"

There was a pause.

"… As I was saying a friend discovered we'd been bombed by accident, so we're lucky to know about it. These bastards who are targeting us are fucking fiendish."

"Tell me."

"No need to fucking shout."

"I'm not fucking shouting."

"OK, ok. In simple terms it means that if you type in the words "Met Police" into Google…"

"Yeah, yeah."

"Then our site comes up in the top three results."

"You're fucking joking?"

"No, I've tried it hundreds of times. If you want to get in touch with the fuzz then you get the chance to buy some drugs as well. Sweet."

"Shit."

"Dead clever not only can't our regulars buy anything off us, but the whole world will soon know all about us."

"How for fuck sake?"

"The speed these links spread round the net, there will be no stopping it. If my friend knows then you can bet your fucking Maserati, shed loads of other fuckers will. Not least the plod."

"God."

"Brilliant, they must have a hell of a lot of clever sods working for them to have created the pile of blogs needed to pull this one off. It must be hacker central where they are. I probably know a lot of them truth be told."

Ace sounded impressed as he breathed out heavily.

"Fuck brilliant. Someone's having a serious pop at us. Can you sort it?"

Jumbled thoughts and images, an angry Ramona to the fore, crowded in on X as he succumbed to a paralysis of his mental and motor functions with the passivity of someone, unlike him, unfamiliar with the onset of panic.

"It'll take time."

"Don't say that you shithead. We haven't got time. It needed to have been sorted yesterday."

X could barely speak. His hands were shaking. He wasn't sure he was following what Ace was saying as it was difficult to hear him over the static.

"I'll do what I can, but it will take time. There's nothing I can fucking do about that. It'll take as long as it takes."

There were other voices on the line, heavily accented, talking animatedly, drowning out Ace. A conversation about football. The interruption was disconcerting, Ace was X's connection to a universe of understanding, a reassurance that there was a way forward, an escape from this trap they were ensnared in and which X couldn't even comprehend the dimensions of, he was a lifeline, losing contact with him would be a disaster.

"Ace, can you hear me?"

The voices stopped momentarily, then picked up again.

"Fuck off will you, get off the line," X screamed, "Some of us have important shit to talk about."

Silence.

"Impressive. It never works for me. Shouting my mouth off usually gets me an earful of abuse."

"Ace?"

"The voice of authority."

"Fuck off."

"Look I'll try and sort this, but at your end you need to be thinking damage limitation, if you know what I mean. Best case there'll be a whole bunch of pissed off punters who'll need sweetening, worst case it takes me longer than I think, the fuzz are all over us and everybody's fucked off elsewhere. There are other sites you know, providing similar services."

"You don't have to tell me about the fucking competition."

"Not to mention the Chief here, he won't be mightily impressed …"

"Don't tell him then, you wanker."

"I won't have to, he takes a very keen interest. Proactive type, if you get my drift? You need a plan of action mate. I know Ramona's a touchy subject but shouldn't you be thinking …"

"Yeah, yeah I'll tell her."

X felt sick.

"She'll find out soon enough, even in the slammer."

"Don't I fucking know it."

"So, do it man sooner rather than later, if you want my advice."

"I do want your advice but not on dealing with our friend. What I want is for you to advise me on fixing this mess."

"Don't you want to know how they're doing it? Aren't you curious about how they're shagging the site?"

"Enough's enough Ace, it would fucking mean nothing to me. You've already told me more shit than I can take in."

Unnerved by the sudden attack from an unseen enemy, outside

the ambit of his experience, and unable to influence events, X found himself devoid of ideas, incapable of formulating a strategy. Not for the first time in recent weeks he found himself hard against the limits of his capabilities and in grave danger of stumbling beyond them. He needed a steer on who was responsible, ideally an individual he could target and physically pursue and he desperately hoped Ace would provide him with a name.

"Who's doing this?"

"As I told you it's difficult to say."

"Can't you find out?"

"Maybe, maybe never. You should have an idea though."

"How come?"

"Well it's got to be some fucker trying to muscle in on our territory and put us out of business. There can only be so many people who know about our little operation and have the resources to pull a stunt like this. They will have needed plenty of dosh and someone with know-how, someone like me."

"Yeah funny."

"Nerds rock."

"Yeah, yeah."

"Not necessarily from old Blighty either."

"What?"

"Well it's a global market ain't it."

"Have you any ideas? I can't fucking think at the moment."

"Nice of you to ask."

"Ace, you are a tit sometimes."

"Granted, but it's difficult, my guess would be either Russia or the States."

"Russia?"

"Yep, would make sense. They've got the money and the know-how and they've certainly got the capability. But then so do the Americans. It's a..."

"Fucking hell."

"What?"

"I've just had a thought."

Relief at enlightenment was tainted for X by the menace of a threat made manifest.

"Who?"

"Some fuckers from over the pond who Ramona was cosying up to."

"Could be."

"Ramona asked me to fly over to New York and see them when I last saw her inside."

"She knew this was going to happen, fuck me. It's uncanny, I always said she was a clairvoyant."

"No, that was about something else."

"You going?"

"I need to do something solid. I can't just sit around. All this virtual shit is doing my head in."

# Extracts from
# *The Man Who Fell To Earth,*
## by Esther Addley and Rory McCarthy.
## The Guardian 18/07/01.

The police didn't know how long the body had been there, but it was clear the man was dead. Tucked under a tree, just inside the railings of Homebase car park, the prone figure was spotted by one of the store's staff as she arrived just before 7am. She assumed he was a drunk who had tumbled over the railings and fallen asleep while staggering home along Manor Road. It was only as she edged over for a closer look that she noticed that his limbs were grotesquely misshapen, and the pool of lumpy liquid in which he was lying was not vomit, but the man's spilt brains.

The area was hastily screened off and police launched an immediate murder investigation. But it soon emerged that a witness had seen the dead man a few minutes before his body was found. A workman at nearby Heathrow airport had glanced upwards to see him plummeting from the sky like a stone, his black jeans and T-shirt picked out against the washed blue early morning sky.

A month after he died the police have finally managed to piece together the skeletal details of Mohammed Ayaz's long journey from a remote village in north west Pakistan to his final sorry end in the car park of a DIY superstore in Richmond, west London.

… he crossed into Bahrain and climbed on board the flight to London. Getting into the wheel bay of a Boeing 777 is not easy. It involves climbing 14 feet up one of the aircraft's 12 enormous wheels, then finding somewhere to crouch or cling as the aircraft takes off.

... the undercarriage compartment has no oxygen, no heating and no pressure, and there is certainly no way out.

By the time the plane reached British airspace, he was almost certainly long dead. Shortly after 6am, somewhere between 12 and 20 miles from Heathrow, the plane locked on to its approach path and began to descend over Barnes in South West London. Between 2,000 and 3,000 feet, the captain opened the under-carriage and lowered the wheels; the young man was tipped out into the early morning sky.

Across the road from Homebase, a few yards to the left, is an enormous Sainsbury's supermarket, completed a year ago on the site of a derelict gasworks. It was here, in October 1996 that 19-year-old Vijay Saini's own journey ended. He had stowed away in a jet from Delhi in the same way that Ayaz did, and fell out at almost exactly the same spot. In August 1998 a couple drinking in the nearby Malborough pub saw another body tumble from a plane. There were reports of a fourth body being discovered while the Sainsbury's complex was being built.

"The undercarriage is always lowered at the same point, that is why they are falling at the same place," says John Stewart, of the airport noise pollution lobby group Hacan Clear Skies. "But it's an almost uncanny coincidence – these people fly right across the world in this way from different places, and they all end up in a car park in Richmond. If there are any more bodies to fall, that's where they will fall."

# 344 metres

# FILM FUN MAGAZINE – APRIL 2002
## Hand of God or Just Bloody Lucky?

Entertainment Editor, Cindy Baxter, hangs out with maverick German director, Werner Herzog, and shoots the breeze about his latest documentary.

What's your greatest nightmare??? Just imagine it. I bet it doesn't match up to Werner's bad dreams.

"Believe me I've had a lot of sleepless nights working on this film."

His accent still charmingly German despite years living in exotic locations around the world.

"It's not one of my usual epics about man's visions failing in an agony of doomed excess. You've only got to have seen "Fitzcarraldo" to know what I mean."

He sighed and went silent for a moment – so unlike him – this doc really does seem to have affected him badly.

"No, this time it's just plain horror and it's all true."

So, what's it about? A blood fest with a gang of teenagers holed up in some decrepit old shack while a crazed serial killer, froths and fizzes in the circling gloom, gathering up implements of mutilation? Couldn't be further from the truth – Zombies, malign spirits disturbed after centuries of graveyard limbo – no.

Vampires, you cry. Wrong again. So, what's left? Let Werner set the scene.

"The plane you're travelling in – sipping your martini, enjoying the view, dreaming of the guys you're going to pick up on the beach in Cancun or wherever – suddenly explodes in mid-air, without warning, 30,000 feet up."

Again, a pause, he swallows hard.

"Horrible eh?"

I can but agree.

"There is Marta, the heroine of this story, strapped in her seat, plane falling apart around her – the blue glare of a cloudless sky suddenly surrounds her. The sun is shining brightly, yet it is freezing cold – a deep bitter cold that she has never felt before."

He takes a sip from his whisky sour.

"There is no oxygen of course, not at that height. She gasps for breath. No sound. She starts to fall, debris all around at first, but as she spins towards earth she is soon alone. Cindy can you imagine the terror?"

I shake my head as there is nothing I can say.

"Sandwiched between expanses of blue and green, falling."

I must have looked puzzled and he explained.

"It happened over the Amazon, there was nothing but jungle below. Dense steaming jungle. Marta says she was screaming but could hear nothing. She passed out of course eventually. And smashed into the trees at nearly two hundred kilometres an hour."

A pause.

"You gather she survived."

I nod, not really believing it.

"One nightmare was over, but another was about to begin." Another dramatic sip of his whisky. Werner knows how to tell a story.

"She was kilometres from anywhere in primal rain forest, hot and humid, the air full of biting insects, spiders and snakes crawling everywhere... the sound of large animals moving in the undergrowth, the cries of strange beasts ... predators."

For a brief moment I thought that was it. The famous director looked as if he was about to leave. I'd read about his eccentricities and was not going to let him get away with leaving me hanging in suspense.

"What happened next? Did she disappear? Was she eaten alive?"

His look of surprise was something to see.

"She limped out of there. Three days it took. She found a stream and followed it until she reached a village as simple, or as complicated, as that."

"How badly was she hurt?"

"Barely a scratch. Bitten to pieces of course. Starving and thirsty ... amazing."

The big question remained unanswered until he stood to depart. I gestured my incomprehension.

"The hand of God, maybe?"

He could see I was not convinced.

"Somehow the seat protected her. When we retraced her tracks back through the tangled jungle for the film and finally found where she had touched down (I swear those were his words) the seat was intact at the bottom of a four metre deep hole! Seatbelt unbuckled, just as she had left it."

Weird or what? "Hand of God" is Marta's tale and it is out now and genuinely frightening. Catch it if you can.

Sipping his whisky, the taste bitter in his throat, the chill of the ice numbing his tongue, X stared down through fine gossamer clouds at the tan expanse of the southern California desert far below. A random sprinkling of green squares interconnected by straight black lines the only breaks in the chromatic monotony. Dozing fitfully, fatigue and intoxication lulling him, he mused on the delights of America to come, the drugs, the women, the skydiving and suppressed his irritation at this enforced detour across the continent. Flying into New York as arranged, he had been met at JFK airport by two taciturn men dressed in black suits and escorted across the city in a white stretch limousine to La Guardia airport and put on a small Learjet 45 XR for a flight to San Diego. There had been no explanation for the change of plan, just a terse apology.

"Enjoy. Joe says he's sorry, but he'll make it worth your while."

The only passenger on a well-provisioned plane, X indulged himself. Several lines of cocaine smoothed the edge off his incipient anxiety, Wild Turkey 101 on the rocks lifted his depression, a hefty joint overstuffed with Stardawg eased him gently onto a plateau of wan euphoria, where his recollections of Ramona's recent fury – his employer and sometime lover had not reacted well to the news about the hijacking of the website – were less vivid and more manageable.

Knowledge of her precipitate ejection from the online pharmaceutical business had transformed Ramona's seething yet tractable resentment at her continuing incarceration into a destructive rage of verbal and physical violence. Lounging in an ample beige leather seat, high about the continental United States, he reflected objectively – something he'd been unable to do facing her in an interview room in Holloway Prison – on this assault, which had been personal and wounding. Viewing it from the perspective of their long and often turbulent relationship, he concluded that the rift between them was close to irreparable. Losing her "fucking rag" was a key weapon in the armoury of a gang boss and Ramona used it sparingly. She had never before spoken in such vicious terms to X, always leavening any criticism in the past with humour and sexual innuendo. He had struggled to defend himself, unable to break into the torrent of abuse and constrained from reacting strongly by the presence of Amanda, Ramona's lawyer, and a burly female prison guard. Inhibitions which in normal circumstances Ramona would have also paid obeisance to but on this occasion chose to ignore.

"You're a fucking dickhead, an arsehole, prick. Leave you alone for five fucking minutes and you've cocked it up. I can't fucking believe it."

She stood, hair awry, her hands fisting the table top.

"Sit down McAllister," the guard's voice firm, yet anxious, "sit down."

"Everybody said it was a bad idea, even you Amanda, letting your cunt rule your head. You're fucking weak, I've always known that. I should never have put you in charge. I can't believe I trusted you, fuck!"

She stared angrily at X, saliva spattering her pale lips.

"A wanker, that's what you are. Hands bloody off anything to do with work, just all over your other fucking women. You think I didn't know about them, you little shit."

She paused, then lunged across the table, slapping X on the arm. The guard punched the red alarm button on the wall, a distant bell could be heard ringing, then the sound of running feet.

"I'll fucking kill you, you little shitbag."

She spat and began to scrabble over the table, hands clawing at the air.

"Ramona stop this." Amanda pushed back her chair and stood up, "please calm down, no good will come of this."

Three guards burst in, barging X out of the way and forcibly grabbed Ramona, restraining her and shoving her back onto her seat.

"Calm down McALister, calm down."

"You fucker," Ramona's eyes were fixed on X, "you little fucker."

"Shut it McAllister. I mean it."

The guards twisted Ramona's arms driving her body forward

onto the tabletop, compressing her chest and forcing her to catch her breath. Finally quiescent, she was dragged to her feet and hauled backwards out of the interview room.

"You tosser, you fucking little tosser."

She kicked out with her legs, screaming at the top of her voice.

"We warned you McAllister."

The door banged shut. Muffled cries could be heard, fading to an echoing silence. Outside in the prison car park Amanda's tone was icy.

"That went well."

She had paused and glanced up at the overcast sky.

"You'd better deal with this and quickly or else I think you two and the business could be over. Call me when you've had your face to face with the Brooklyn lot. And be tactful in the meeting, remember you don't hold that many cards. I've heard Joe Barnoldini, in particular, can be difficult."

She handed X a business card and unsmiling climbed into her red Mercedes 219 SLT and drove off leaving him standing at the kerb.

A flawless five-pointed star falling from the heavens. Sparking a florescent trail across the arc of the sky. Illuminating the earth's surface below. Magnificent in its rarity. Perfect to make a heartfelt wish upon.

Dense banks of tobacco and marijuana smoke wafted around the aircraft cabin obscuring detail, erasing the substance of his surroundings. He emptied his glass and poured himself another bourbon. The sun shone brightly through the window as the Learjet banked and began to descend, the blue ocean flaring briefly through the glare, before burning out into sandy ubiquity. X shielded his eyes.

The meltdown of a relationship was never without cost in his experience, the only uncertainty was the size of the final reckoning. He had lived through a number of break-ups, getting over all of them eventually with the toll they had exacted devaluing through time, yet the consequences of this clash with Ramona had lingered, assuming an importance and commanding a price far in excess of anything he'd expected to have to pay – an undermining of confidence in his own ability to live with himself. It was not the threats of violence she had made, he knew she was capable of committing acts of savagery but didn't believe that being under duress she had meant what she said, or the threats to his livelihood, he could always find other work, but the threat to their friendship, the foreclosure of any possibility of a close relationship, a potential with which he'd lived for years, that was painful. He had told her once, in a moment of drunken passion, that he loved her, and she had laughingly broken their rhythm to say, "No you fucking don't, you're incapable of feeling. That's what I like about you."

Flying high in the hazy Californian sky X was no longer certain this was the compliment he had always taken it to be. He had feelings, he was experiencing loss, a yearning for things as they used to be. This was the closest to love that he'd ever got. What had it meant to her? He inhaled deeply, holding the smoke in his lungs, seeking an answer. Breathing out he realized he had no idea.

She had said once "you're a good lay," and he had been pleased, basking for the briefest moment in the flattering glow of her unaccustomed praise. So, was that all their time together amounted to, a decade of quality sex? As the Learjet touched down, he decided that was enough for him. He raised his glass in a silent toast. Sort this mess out and move on.

A human being transcended. Not jagged metal hardware, detritus from some obscure space programme, plunging to a fiery death in the earth's atmosphere, but a star-man. The stuff of dreams.

It was hot as he stepped from the plane, the heat radiating off the cracked, oil and rubber streaked concrete in hammer waves, striking his body, bludgeoning the sweat from his exposed skin. For a moment he could see nothing, a white glow searing his retinas, then shadows pierced the brightness, voices and the sound of a vehicle drawing up, the powerful motor idling. The smell of fresh exhaust cutting through, dousing the aroma of spent aircraft fuel. Fumbling in his shirt-pocket for his Ray-ban Predator sun-glasses, he tripped on the top step and almost fell.

"Whoa, take it easy man," the drawl relaxed, expansive, and close by. His bag was plucked from his hand.

"Thanks."

"This way dude."

A touch on the arm guided him down the airstairs, the stark clack of the man's studded boot heels on the metal steps intrusive. Vision clearing, he could see the hazy silhouettes of distant hills through the shimmering smog, dusty thermals swirling upwards from the floor of the parched valley, lifting the black smudges of circling raptors. The airstrip was deserted except for a small light aircraft parked several hundred metres away. There was a road on the other side of a chain link fence that ran the length of the runway, but there was no traffic. X could see a rusty, window-less car abandoned in the sage-brush close to the highway, its trunk open.

"Where are we man?"

"Outside San Diego, San Jacinto."

"Why are we here?"

"Just obeying orders, man. Don't ask me."

"It's the back of fucking beyond. I was supposed to meet Joe in New York."

The man dressed in a black Stetson, embroidered grey-studded shirt, blue jeans and elaborately tooled red and white cowboy boots, grunted and pushed him towards the black top of the range Lincoln Navigator Sports Utility Vehicle. The rear doors were open.

"This is a bloody shitter, much as I love California."

He raised his hand, the gesture dismissive.

"Get in."

The interior was dingy with black leather seats and fittings, the tinted windows blocking out much of the sunlight. The air was icy. It took a moment for X's eyes to adjust to the semi-darkness.

There were two men in the front seats and another in the back, the cowboy threw X's bag into the luggage area, slammed the door shut and got in, sandwiching him in the middle of the back seat. It was cramped.

"Is no one going to introduce themselves?"

X was irritated, the air-conditioning chilled his skin, but had yet to impinge at his core, he felt careworn and confined. On the cusp of intoxication, in need of refreshment and before elation evaporated into the dull ache of sobriety, he sensed an affront to his esteem. He was, after all, a senior representative of a British affiliate of their business.

"There'll be time for that later."

He was sure they wouldn't have treated Ramona in this way.

"Where's Joe?"

The SUV moved off the runway and bumped slowly over the rough scrub in the direction of the light aircraft, which X recognized as a Beechcraft King Air 90. The Learjet taxied away, the roar of its engines audible over the working of the car's air-conditioning. They halted and waited in silence as the jet turned at the end of the runway and without a pause accelerated past them, engines screaming, then rose sharply into the air and banked away into the haze. X watched the diminishing glow of the after-burners through pained eyes, a headache nascent.

"Can we get going?"

"Sure, man."

X balked at the cowboy's supercilious tone, but said nothing. He scorned the man's kitsch, nineties Californian drug dealer-style behaviour and relished the clichéd thought that these punks were just hired muscle and not worth bothering about. Amused, he resolved to say something when the deals were done. Bottom-line, Joe should be making more effort. As they tried to move off the wheels of the Navigator, caught in a rut, spun violently, spraying a golden cloud of dust and desiccated grass stalks high into the air.

"Whoa."

The driver spoke for the first time

"What this off-road shit is a tougher mother than you is used to, city boy?"

They all laughed, even X.

"Fuck off, all of youse. If you want to fucking drive."

"Na, na you're Joe's driver."

The Navigator lurched up onto the smooth macadamized surface of the runway and turned slowly towards to the King Air, which X noticed had taxied into the centre of the runway and appeared to have its engines running – he could make out the blur of the propeller and the grey translucence of the exhaust voiding from the side cowling.

"Hey, watch out, that fucker looks like its about to take off."

They laughed again, a disconcerting chorus of conspiratorial masculinity, that for the first time raised a doubt in X's mind.

"For fuck."

He jostled in his seat attempting to make more space, he was conscious of the heat of their pressing thighs radiating into his.

"Where are we going?"

There was no answer, their stolid silence, encroached on by the growing rush of the approaching 235 horsepower aero-engine. They drew up alongside the plane.

"Not another bloody flight? This is getting stupid. I've been travelling for a full fucking day already to get here."

The cowboy flicked open a cell-phone, called up a number, and waited while it connected.

"Boss ..."

"Is that Joe? Let me speak to him."

X lunged for the phone, but his arm was grabbed by the other man in the back seat, who shook his head firmly.

"Fuck me, Joe."

"Yeah boss we've got him at the plane. All go?"

The cowboy nodded as he listened, then snapped the cell-phone shut.

"Joe says hi. He hopes you have a nice day."

The greeting a signal for change. A turning point. An instant when mental processes slow down, synapses firing lethargically, while the world bursts with activity, four doors opening in unison, bodies exiting, left alone on the back seat, then arms drawing him into the void. Stepping out into the glare flare, feet barely touching down.

A moment of wry reflection – the finely-tuned choreography of capital punishment, the speeded-up actions of prison officers, efficiently executed – cell door bursts open, a squad of four rush in, prisoner's hands gripped by the two guards who, until moments before, were his partners in a game of pontoon, table overturned, deck falls to the floor, all cards land face-down, bar one – the five of spades – arms yanked behind and bound, wooden cupboard wheeled aside to reveal the gallows, through an open archway, rope dangling, a rank hood drawn over, dragged five steps forward, head placed in noose, knot tightened at the side of the neck, step back, trap door released, the drop, barely ten seconds to end a life.

Where was he? What was he thinking? – did X have the presence of mind to mull on this, he barely had the time?

"My bag," he grunted as he crossed the burning space between the SUV and the plane. The response a surprise that confirmed what he already knew.

"You won't be needing that, fuckhead."

The inexorable logic of events was underscored by the sight of Billy smiling down at him through the streaked cockpit window. X flinched and made to duck away, but in that instant, grasping hands restrained him and lifted him into the plane.

A fist opens at his centre. The speedball of terror hits, spiking through every tissue, sinew and membrane of his body. His being stretched gossamer thin, too delicate to affect the course of his life, yet a thing of beauty, a fragile blossom in the azure sky, momentarily obliterating the void and filling the vault of heaven with its splendour.

# METAMORPHOSES

By Publius Ovidius Naso, known as Ovid.
(Translated by Sir Samuel Garth, John Dryden, et al.)

## BOOK THE EIGHTH

## THE STORY OF DAEDALUS AND ICARUS

In tedious exile now too long detain'd,
Daedalus languish'd for his native land:
The sea foreclos'd his flight; yet thus he said:
Tho' Earth and water in subjection laid,
O cruel Minos, thy dominion be,
We'll go thro' air; for sure the air is free.
Then to new arts his cunning thought applies,
And to improve the work of Nature tries.
A row of quils in gradual order plac'd,
Rise by degrees in length from first to last;
As on a cliff th' ascending thicket grows,
Or, different reeds the rural pipe compose.
Along the middle runs a twine of flax,
The bottom stems are joyn'd by pliant wax.
Thus, well compact, a hollow bending brings
The fine composure into real wings.
His boy, young Icarus, that near him stood,
Unthinking of his fate, with smiles pursu'd
The floating feathers, which the moving air
Bore loosely from the ground, and wasted here and there.
Or with the wax impertinently play'd,
And with his childish tricks the great design delay'd.
The final master-stroke at last impos'd,
And now, the neat machine compleatly clos'd;
Fitting his pinions on, a flight he tries,

And hung self-ballanc'd in the beaten skies.
Then thus instructs his child: My boy, take care
To wing your course along the middle air;
If low, the surges wet your flagging plumes;
If high, the sun the melting wax consumes:
Steer between both: nor to the northern skies,
Nor south Orion turn your giddy eyes;
But follow me: let me before you lay
Rules for the flight and mark the pathless way.
Then teaching, with a fond concern, his son,
He took the untry'd wings, and fix'd 'em on;
But fix'd with trembling hands; and as he speaks,
The tears roul gently down his aged cheeks.
Then kiss'd, and in his arms embrac'd him fast,
But knew not this embrace must be the last.
And mounting upward, as he wings his flight,
Back on his charge he turns his aking sight;
As parent birds, when first their callow care
Leave the high nest to tempt the liquid air.
Then chears him on, and oft, with fatal art,
Reminds the stripling to perform his part.
These, as the angler at the silent brook,
Or mountain-shepherd leaning on his crook,
Or gaping plowman, from the vale descries,
They stare, and view 'em with religious eyes,
And strait conclude 'em Gods; since none, but they,
Thro' their own azure skies cou'd find a way.
When now the boy, whose childish thoughts aspire
To loftier aims, and make him ramble high'r,
Grown wild, and wanton, more embolden'd flies
Far from his guide, and soars among the skies.
The soft'ning wax, that felt a nearer sun,
Dissolv'd apace and soon began to run.
The youth in vain his melting pinions shakes,

His feathers gone, no longer air he takes:
Oh! Father, father, as he strove to cry,
Down to the sea he tumbled from on high,
And found his Fate; yet still subsists by fame,
Among those waters that retain his name.

1 metre

## ST JAMES' BIBLE

How art thou fallen from heaven, O Lucifer, son of the morning! how are thou cut down to the ground, which didst weaken the nations!

For thou hast said in thine heart, I will ascend into heaven, I will exalt my throne above the stars of God: I will sit also upon the mount of the congregation, in the sides of the north: I will ascend above the heights of the clouds: I will be like the Most High.

Yet thou shalt be brought down to hell, to the sides of the pit.

*Book of Isiah 14:12-15*

The sea was choppy, the surface of the water disturbed, a wave massed below him, barely breaking, a curl of white sparkling foam at its crest. The bright sunlight burnishing its surface with a superficial illumination that accentuated its rising form, infusing it with streaks of blue, green and azure, and condemning its potent depths to a dim obscurity. A hall of mirrors reflecting distorted, splintered, images of himself, a cracked shadowy distillation of his parts. There was a defect in the shimmering veneer, a scratch, stealing his attention. He would never know if it was flotsam or just a mote in his streaming eyes.

X recognized Billy, the feel and sense of him, knew he was the man leering at him from the aircraft window, yet could barely recall what he looked like, the merest outline of the face, the turn of the head was all he could remember. Face to face Billy was a young, conventionally good-looking Italian-American with his full boyish face, olive skin, dark brown eyes and tight mass of curly black hair, yet his countenance, the bland death mask of the executioner, instilled terror. Leaning over the co-pilot's seat, dark glasses pushed up on top of his head, he watched impassively as X was bundled into the passenger area of the plane, where a seat had been removed to make a space just large enough for a man to lie down. X sprawled on the dusty metal floor, hitting his head painfully on a green rucksack that protruded from the well beneath one of the remaining seats, and swore loudly.

"Shut the fuck up."

Billy sounded amused, exultant in his ascendancy.

"Fuck off yourself, you wanker."

Such defiance was a hoarse acknowledgement of X's own mortality, for he knew that he was about to embark on the aerial equivalent of the death walk, with which he was familiar as much from gangster DVDs as from his own experience. The cowboy and another man climbed in behind X, trampling him as they eased themselves into their seats. The plane door slammed shut, muffling the noise of the engine. Breathing heavily, they bound X's feet then hauled him into a sitting position and strapped the heavy rucksack to his back.

"What giving me a parachute, you're too fucking kind?"

It was difficult to speak, his mouth and throat dry, but he felt a desperate need to communicate.

"Yeah, yeah a parachute," the cowboy paused, "made of bricks."

There was laughter, X lashed out ineffectually with his fists. Blows rained down and he cowered in pain. With great effort he cried out, his cracked voice high-pitched and tremulous.

"This isn't about the fact I wouldn't let you fuck me, is it?"

All movement in the cockpit ceased, someone coughed.

"What did you fucking say?"

"I wouldn't let Billy boy there fuck me at a party when he was over in London the other day and he's pissed."

"You little prick."

Enraged Billy leant over the seat back and violently lashed out at X hitting him across the side of the head.

"You're a fucking liar."

He glanced at the cowboy for confirmation.

"Sure Billy, whatever you say."

"You've no fucking idea, you cockney bastard. We should have done you then and there, but that Ramona bitch stopped us."

"It's known as being faithful, you shit…"

He could sense the welling of blood in the back of his throat and taste the warm metallic trickle on his tongue.

"…Something you lot know nothing about."

"Oh yeah, you little fuck she's not so loyal now is she? Changed her mind, ain't she. Typical of a woman."

It took a second for Billy's barb to strike home. The enormity of the betrayal sinking in as he painfully shifted his position on the floor. Ramona's act, if true, was devastating. Sold out by his lover was a classic twist he had not considered, yet it was a tragedy he could believe he had a part in. His response was automatic.

"You liar."

Billy laughed and poked at X with his hands.

"Didn't know that did you, your sweet little Ramona fucked you over to save her own skin and her two-bit business."

"She wouldn't do that…"

His belief in her culpability growing in strength each time he denied her involvement.

"…She's a fucking friend."

The affirmative feeding the negative in a self-destructive spiral of meaning that consumed X, leaving him drained of all feeling.

"She's … I've known her for …"

He knew it was true.

"I've had enough of this shit, gag the fucker and tie him up good."

A red bandana was pulled tight across his mouth, parting his lips and fixing them in an inane grimace. With his nose blocked by bloody dust-compacted mucus, he had difficulty breathing, sucking in gulps of air through the sides of his mouth.

"Shut the fuck up with your wheezing."

He was roughly turned over on to this front, his face pressed against ribbed metal paneling and his hands bound behind his back.

"Let's go," Billy's pleasure evident in his voice.

Diving head first into a blur. A fine, moisture heavy, salt laden spray, misting eyes, blinding against all but shadows. Enveloping X in a sodden blanket, smothering him against the chill of the nether-atmosphere, drawing him in, filling bursting lungs with saline fug, drowning him.

The floor vibrated as the engine powered up, then the aircraft began to move forward, the fuselage swaying from side to side as it gathered speed. The sun shone directly through the window onto X for an instant, stoking his discomfort. He felt sick, random snuff thoughts sparking in a blank terror-wiped mind – ruby puddles of blood flooding across parquet flooring, the sickening snap of bones breaking, green-white skin stretched balloon-tight across the paunch of a bloated corpse, the tap-tap ricochet of a bullet, skull-trapped – all images and sounds that belonged to him. Anything but think of the drop.

The King Air lifted off and climbed steeply. The static crackle of a radio masking a distant voice. Rolling the plane banked to the west, heading out into the Pacific. X had pains in his chest, the exertion of breathing in the prickly heat placing a heavy physical burden on a frame flayed by nervous stress. The strain was exacting its toll, he could sense a diminution in his powers, a fraying of resolve. There was suddenly music, loud and raucous, blaring from speakers, one of them close to his head. He recognized the song and was briefly distracted, searching his memory for inspiration. It came to him – "Sweet Child O' Mine" by Guns N' Roses from Appetite for Destruction – and the relief spawned the bleakest depression he could have imagined – everything was hopeless, knowledge was futile, his short life empty of value. He was going to die for nothing. The humanity of the song made him physically sick, his body retching uncontrollably, dredging bourbon-infused bile from the depths of his stomach, despoiling his senses. There was a burning sensation in his throat, mouth and nose. He sneezed violently, mucus flying, clearing his nasal passages.

"Shut it, man."

A boot heel grinding in his back.

"That's fucking disgusting."

He could breathe. Cool air surging into deprived lungs, oxygen-rich yet tainted. There was a stink enveloping him, an animal fustiness, seeping into his being. He could smell and taste it. His fear was real, he could discern its chemical composition and pick out the individual molecules that constitute the essence of terror. He began to shake, extremities – legs and arms – first, then the tremors coursed the length of his torso. His body was out of control and he no longer had the mental resilience to enforce his will. He urinated involuntarily, a dark stain discolouring his beige Hedi Slimane trousers, the smell pervading the cabin.

"Oh God, get a whiff of that, he's pissed himself."

"Fuck me, let some air in, I'm gagging."

The roaring rush as the hatchway slid open was terrifying, the temperature dropped, sunlight flashed and X sensed he was being sucked out, drawn inexorably into the void. He closed his eyes in panic, the very bulk of the plane feeling inconsequential and insecure, the empty space beneath the only tangible reality. The volume of the music was turned up.

"I like this one."

Billy's tone was enthused, an ugly counterpoint to X's dissolving personality, who's only remaining link to the rational world was the driving guitar chords and high-pitched wail of Axl Rose singing "You're Crazy."

Lying trussed on the dusty floor, conscious of his life as a finite entity, its length rapidly diminishing, he reduced existence to a kernel of hope that sprouted, withered and died every few seconds, dragging out the time he had left.

Ramona was always there, an indistinct presence, for it was impossible for X to articulate an act of murder into the form of an object of his adoration and respect. It would not tally for him and he shaded her out, not quite erasing her, but blurring the details.

The music was suddenly switched off and in the natural roar and clatter of the aircraft he knew it was nearly over for him. He yelped pathetically and attempted to curl up into a ball, but it was impossible and he lay exposed, eyes closed and head buried in his chest, hoping that he couldn't be seen.

Billy's voice was matter-of-fact now, calmer, his Brooklyn accent pronounced as he shouted above the noise of the engine.

"They always said you were good at this shit."

He nodded at the cowboy seated behind X's slouched figure.

"Now's your chance to prove you can fly, you little prick."

Grabbing hands heavy on his back, hauling him to his feet, stooped, the pack cutting into his shoulders, dragging him down, knees buckling. Sopping gag removed, hands and feet untied, then the relentless pressure forcing him towards the open hatchway. The eddying air buffeting his body, tearing at his loose clothing, dispersing the tears filling his eyes, the fine mist dampening the faces of his assailants, who disgusted, shook their heads helplessly, their hands occupied.

Incapacitated by dread, X was speechless, his lips pinched, all communication non-verbal. His panic expressed through wild eyes that stared unblinking at Billy.

Dragging his feet was the only token of the struggle raging in X's befuddled brain. Huge surges of pure adrenalin battled the soporific elements of alcohol and marijuana in a volatile stew that induced a fearful inertia. X's was an inexorable progress that his deadweight barely impeded, he was gripped by the passivity of the waking dead, wrapped in the false calm of the resigned victim. Condemned and accepting, he understood resistance was to no avail.

The bright sunlight was dazzling giving a deceptively mundane solidity to the yawning gap opening beneath him. Head protruding from the plane, clamped, for an instant, by the differential pressures of the rushing slipstream, a sharp pain in his ears, muffling the world. His feet were hard against the lip of the hatch.

"The come-down ... fuck it!"

In the brief time he had left he couldn't hear the scream that was whipping from his gaping mouth, an agonized roar of defiance diffused into the ambient rush of the great ocean, disturbing saturated molecules, in a final act of futile verbal violence.

## The Biography of a Drug
### Professor Brian Martin

**Ecstasy.** n. & n.(sl.) **1.** Exalted state of feeling, rapture, trance; poetic frenzy [Gk ekstasis vbl n from existemi put (person) out of (his senses)]. **2.** a term for the drug known officially as methylene dioxymethamphetamine (MDMA). [syn. Adam, apples, biscuit, brownies, burgers, disco biscuits, dollar, double-m, dove, Ξ, ecky, kleenex, love drug, M25, orbit, rolling, running, snowballs, swans, tulips, whizz bomb, X]

For exclusive discounts on Matador titles,
sign up to our occasional newsletter at
troubador.co.uk/bookshop